HUMAN AMUSEMENTS

HUMAN AMUSEMENTS

WAYNE JOHNSTON

Vintage Canada
A Division of Random House of Canada Limited

VINTAGE CANADA EDITION, 2002

Copyright © 1994 1310945 Ontario Inc.

All rights reserved under International and Pan-American
Copyright Conventions. Published by Vintage Canada, a division of
Random House of Canada Limited, in 2002. Published by arrangement
with McClelland & Stewart Ltd., Toronto, Ontario, Canada. First
published in Canada by McClelland & Stewart in 1994. Distributed
by Random House of Canada Limited, Toronto.

Vintage Canada and colophon are registered trademarks of
Random House of Canada Limited.

Quotation from *Tube of Plenty: The Evolution of American Television*
by Erik Barnouw copyright © 1975, 1982 by Erik Barnouw.
Published by Oxford University Press, New York.

National Library of Canada Cataloguing in Publication Data

Johnston, Wayne, 1958–
Human amusements

ISBN 0-676-97459-7

I. Title.

PS8569.O3918H86 2002   C813'.54   C2001-903433-4
PR9199.3.J599H86 2002

www.randomhouse.ca

Text design: Daniel Cullen
Cover design: CS Richardson

Printed and bound in Canada

2 4 6 8 9 7 5 3 1

For Rose
For my brothers, Ken, Craig and Brian

I

RUMPUS ROOM

1

I have a complete collection of the early "Rumpus Room" episodes and, watching them, it's hard to believe that it's me sometimes, for I'm completely contained by that costume and I never speak. Only because I know that, before 1972, no one else ever played the part am I able to convince myself that it must be me, inside the set, inside the suit, staring out at the future from television land. Television. The Greek word *tele* means "far off," and is said to be closely akin to another Greek word, *palai*, meaning "long ago." This always seems appropriate when I think of how old I was when I first appeared on the show. For me the early days of television are the early days of everything. Television. Hindsight. Memory. Long ago and far away. When I started playing Bee Good/Bee Bad, I wondered where they had been until now. I was seven and I had a notion that long before TV had even been invented, the world of "Rumpus Room," with all its inhabitants, had been there, inaccessible, waiting for someone to tap into it. Waiting for Philo Farnsworth, the alter ego of my adolescence, though I didn't know that then.

What I remember best are not the single scenes, the big, discrete events that happened years apart, but things that happened all the time, the "bits" we kept returning to as though they were all part of some large routine that we were trying to perfect, trying to get down pat before we went our separate ways.

My parents, in that other life, were teachers. My mother taught elementary school, my father high school, but neither one of them could find a regular job so they had to settle for being substitute teachers. Mondays and Fridays, the days that teachers were most likely to call in sick, were their best days. My mother was called more often than my father, the burnout rate among elementary school teachers being greater than that among high school teachers. My mother was always worried about "The List"; that is, the department of education's list of substitute teachers. How were names chosen from the List, was there some sort of rating or ranking system for teachers, were names ever dropped from the List? If a few days went by without one or both of them being called, she would start to worry. She wondered if my father's having a beard might make any difference to how often he was called. Of course it did, my father said, claiming that, opposite his name on the List, the word "beard" appeared in brackets.

We lived on St. Clair Avenue, renting out our basement apartment. We had a succession of cellar dwellers, as my father called them, most of whom stayed only a few months before moving on, often skipping out on their last month's rent, for people who could do no better than our basement tended not to have much money. Cellar dwellers. That, I knew, was what, in baseball, they called the last-place team. The losers, though in the case of the people who lived downstairs, the loners would have been more like it, for it seemed they were always alone. That, to these people, my father was the landlord, that they were afraid of him, was something I could hardly credit. When the rent was due, they went out of their way to avoid him, often not coming home until late at night, sneaking in to their own apartment as quietly as possible, sneaking out again early in the morning.

There was a man named Doyle, on each of whose hairy forearms an anchor was tattooed, a man about forty-five who would walk around the back yard, smoking cigarettes and drinking from a bottle of beer that, between swallows, he left standing on the picnic table. I would sit out there with him while he paced the yard. He had been the driver of some sort of delivery truck, a bread truck I think it was. He often wore what might have been his uniform, a light-blue shirt, pants slightly darker blue, and still carried in his back pocket, attached to his belt by a chain, one of those conspicuous, ever-bulging wallets, though there could not have been much money in it. He was from out west, had broken up with his wife, who was from Toronto, and was forever announcing his intention to go, at some unspecified time, by some unspecified means, back home.

After Doyle, there was Mr. Colicos, who told us that he had once owned a coin shop. He had a car which he could not afford to operate, leaving it parked across the road from where we lived and going out from time to time, mostly in the afternoon, to sit behind the wheel, smoke cigarettes, watch the goings on, now and then rolling down the window to talk to someone or to shake his fist at a car that he thought was going by too fast.

One woman named Ruth, who had convinced my father she was a secretary, turned out to be a prostitute who, though not herself Portuguese, had, for some reason, an exclusively Portuguese clientele. Ruth's stay lasted three days, or nights rather. It took a while before my father realized what was going on. We woke, the first night, to an almost surreal combination of sounds: bedsprings squeaking with a mechanical, machine-like rhythm; the song "The Black Velvet Band" being played over and over at what seemed like full volume; a woman's voice droning "Oh Mario, Oh Mario," as matter-of-factly as if she were testing a microphone to see if it worked; and, finally, what might have been either a fistfight or some sort of group dance involving an indeterminate number of non-English-speaking men.

That there was no need for them to sneak around this way, that my father would never have hounded them for the rent, was something that most of them never realized. In fact, when they failed to pay it, he was more embarrassed than anything else, often making as much effort to avoid the tenant as the tenant made to avoid him, even though, as my mother reminded him, we needed the rent to meet our payments on the house. His softheartedness, she'd say, would put us in the poorhouse. "You shouldn't let people take advantage of you," she'd tell him, to which my father would reply that, if she wanted to collect the rent, she was welcome to do so. At this my mother would retreat.

Cellar dwellers. I thought for a while that every house on St. Clair had one, that it was simply the way of the world. My mother could never get used to them, was never quite able to ignore them as my father advised her to do. She often complained to my father that they were making too much noise. The gall of some people, he'd say, walking around, running water, washing dishes; why, before you knew it, they'd be talking on the telephone. To my mother, that we were unable to meet our mortgage without renting out part of the house was a shameful thing. The cellar dwellers were a constant reminder to her of what she called her disadvantaged childhood and the fate that she seemed to think we were barely keeping one step ahead of, the shame of ending up in someone's basement. "We could just as easily be them," she'd say, though this thought, rather than making her feel more sympathetic towards them, seemed to make her more resentful of their presence, as if she believed that, somehow, they might drag us down with them.

We got what my mother thought would be the perfect tenant when an old, recently widowed woman named Theresa took the apartment and signed a year-long lease, informing my father that she would stay beyond a year if all went well. She made no secret of owning a pet toucan bird, but my mother assured us that whatever noise the bird made would be a small price to pay for the advantages of having a reliable, long-term tenant. Which turned out to be the case, though it was not always easy to keep these advantages uppermost in your mind. Every now and then, François, as the bird was called, would give a kind of interrogatory squawk. "Poopwee poopweee?" François would say, his tone one of incredulity, as if he had just been told something that no one in their right mind would believe. None of us was greatly taken with François's habit of whistling cheerfully while the sun was coming up. For weeks, until we got used to it, the whole family would wake at the same time to the sound of François singing downstairs. "And now, François's Crack of Dawn," I would hear my father say, "the first of a series of symphonies in praise of Day, written in 1962 by François, The Bird of Coxwell. Note the piercing shriek with which the first movement begins, followed, as indeed, how could it not be followed, by a squawk. Shriek, squawk, for that alone he would have been remembered. But then it comes, gloriously, unexpectedly, after a long pause that has fooled many an insomniac into thinking he may get to sleep. 'Tweeeeeeeeeeeeeeee,' says François, 'tweeeeeeeeee,' and with him we say, 'Tweeeeeeeeee,' in comparison with which mere words seem so inadequate. Shriek, squawk, earsplitting whistle, the now classic opening to François's Crack of Dawn. Let's listen."

We would catch a glimpse of him, now and then, when Theresa put his cage near the window. He looked, with his oversized beak and the way his plumage arched above his eyes, like a kind of bird version of Groucho Marx. Our cat, Cooper, was fascinated by François. He would sit outside for hours, staring at him through the window, bird and cat a pane of glass apart. François would taunt Cooper by tapping his beak lightly on the glass, while Cooper would pretend not to notice, looking around as if something far more interesting, something barely out of François's line of vision were taking place nearby. Imagining what Cooper would do with François were there not a pane of glass between them gave us some comfort, as did a story my father wrote called "The defeathering of François, a feline fantasy, by Cooper," not to mention "A Cooper haiku": big beak on floor of cage/above it, feathers floating.

Theresa was a Catholic and assumed that, because we didn't go to any church, we were atheists, by no means, she assured us, the first atheists that she had met. What I heard, or saw spelled out in my mind, was "eightheists," a misconception reinforced by the fact that I had heard of the Seventh Day Adventists. She had said the word with such distaste that I imagined a kind of numerical perversion, something vaguely eight-related. When I told my father about it, he said that an eightheist was someone who denied the existence of the number eight. Even when he owned up to the joke and spelled "atheist" for me and explained to me what it meant, I couldn't quite rid myself of the notion that, in some way too sinister to be imagined, the number eight was involved.

"We're not atheists," my mother assured me. When I asked my father what religion we were, he said that we were "apocalyptic misanthropic agnostics." When I asked him what this meant, my mother gave him a look that silenced him. He would only add that we were the entire congregation of the Church of the Apocalyptic Misanthropic Agnostics, which did not have a great deal of growth potential, and which, in all likelihood, I would never see advertised on television.

My father said our bible was *Gulliver's Travels*, a book to be consulted, he said, to be thumbed through at those times when one is set upon by optimism, the horror of positive thinking, when one thing after another has gone right and one is plagued with hope and cheerfulness. It is then, at his highest point, when all seems hopeful, when it seems that nothing will ever again go wrong, that the apocalyptic misanthropic agnostic should take out his Swift and read.

This was the life that, soon, we would leave behind, though we had no inkling of it then. Sometimes, late at night, while in bed, I'd hear my mother crying and my father reminding her that we were luckier than a lot of people. "I know," my mother would say, "I know. It just seems like we'll be living here forever." When my father told her it was not that bad, she'd lose patience with him. "You don't know," she'd say. "I grew up here. When I think about living my whole life here, never getting away. . . "

They were not happy being teachers. My mother would say they both wanted to be writers, which, in a way at least, was true. My mother wrote television scripts the way that other people entered lotteries, sending them off to the networks and forgetting about them, which was just as well, for most of them were not returned. She was trying, as she put it, to "break into" children's television and, before succeeding with "Rumpus Room," suffered through a long apprenticeship.

My father's dream was that, one day, he would be able to write fiction full-time. This day, though never specified, was much talked about, much anticipated. His most often repeated phrase was "the day I quit teaching." I was often reminded that it was for this day that we were saving, for this day that my father was taking on extra work, teaching night school, and the rooms downstairs were being rented out. I thought of his teaching as something he had been saddled with against his will, something imposed upon him, required of him, for arbitrary reasons, the way that school was imposed on children. I thought my father spent his days subbing because some nebulous authority figure had decreed that it be so. It never occurred to me that it was the very existence of "us," our threesome, that made the teaching necessary, that postponed, indefinitely, the day that he would quit, that it was from a life that our existence had made necessary that our father was planning his escape, and planning it with us. "Won't that be great, Henry?" my father would say, smiling at me, whenever mention was made of his writing full-time. I would nod, smiling back at him, sharing his enthusiasm for the day that we would no longer be keeping him from doing as he pleased.

It seems hard to believe that while my mother was in one part of the house writing "Rumpus Room" scripts, my father was in another writing novels, or preparing himself to be a novelist, reading history, philosophy, psychoanalysis, physics.

At least he tried to read such things, usually running into a brick wall of incomprehensibility when it came to things written in the twentieth century. Physics, for instance. Declaring that, for a writer, a basic knowledge of it was essential, he read physics. He never got very far with it, however. He couldn't even understand classical physics, he said, most of the tenets of which had long since been rejected, so what hope did he have of understanding quantum physics? Being unable to understand classical physics was like being unable to read an obsolete map. And more lost than that, he said, you could not get.

The conundrum that, for my father, became a kind of symbol of his frustration and of the absurd paradoxes which physicists seemed so happy to accept and seemed able, with such maddening ease, to understand, was "The Problem of Schrödinger's Cat," the upshot of which was that, according to quantum physics, a cat could at the same time be both dead and alive. My father would try to follow through, step by step, the chain of reasoning that proved this apparent impossibility, poring for hours over the illustration that was supposed to make the whole thing crystal clear, an illustration showing a cat and a bottle of cyanide inside a sealed container, and an observer outside, looking in. Perhaps what bothered him most was that, even when something as mundane as a cat was involved, he still couldn't understand what was going on, that and the illustration itself, which showed the cat standing unperturbed inside the box, wearing a complacently smug expression, as if it knew its part in the experiment, as if it understood perfectly what was going on, what law of physics it was demonstrating.

My father would show the illustration around the house, scorning the inane terms in which the experiment was couched, pointing at the cat as if to say that this was what physics had come to, cats inside of boxes, cyanide capsules, as if this sort of thing was the very stuff of physics these days, cat-based, cat-inspired thought experiments, and it was therefore no wonder he found it impossible to understand and therefore, too, only sane that he give up trying. He never really did, however, much to my mother's consternation.

To the paradox of Schrödinger's cat he opposed the straightforwardness of Prendergast's cat, which stated that, until it died, a cat was alive, and when it died, a cat was dead.

That what he was trying to figure out were things other people had already figured out and that this was the source of his frustration I never really understood. I knew that books were the source of these theories and conundrums, but where books came from I had no idea. They might have occurred naturally for all I knew, my father the only man on earth engaged in their decipherment. He would summarize at the dinner table as much as he thought he'd been able to understand of the Theory of Relativity, pointing out that, according to quantum physics, relativity was old hat; finding the point where, as he said, "they" lost him, whoever they were, he would read aloud from there, emphasizing those sections he found especially difficult, repeating certain phrases, holding the book in one hand and, extending his other hand, moving it up and down, preacher-fashion, to emphasize each word, as if to impress upon my mother that *here*, here was the gist of it, here was the part that, if one could only understand it, explained relativity.

All the while he was reading, my mother, her hands in her lap, would have a kind of "I'm with you so far" expression on her face, nodding her head ever so slightly now and then, or sometimes moving it from side to side. All this was meant to indicate not comprehension, but admiration for the sheer inscrutable complexity of what he'd read, and for him, as if it was a credit to him merely that he tried to understand such things. "Whew," my mother would say when he finished, smiling and shaking her head, as if to indicate not only that she was suitably mesmerized and confused, but that she could see why he had been and why he wanted her to hear the passage. This notion, that these theories existed not so much to be understood but as edifying demonstrations of the inscrutability of science, that they existed to be gawked at with open-mouthed astonishment and nothing else, that they were humbling examples of immensity in exactly the same way that waterfalls and mountains were, drove my father crazy. It especially galled him that she acted as if this were the point that *he'd* been trying to impress upon *her*, that he shared this view of hers. At this, my father, sighing loudly, would close the book and put it aside. He would sit there, arms folded, shaking his head for a few minutes, then finally launch into an attack on books that purported to explain things like relativity in layman's terms. The fact that there was a new such book every year was a testament to how completely each one failed, my father said. Every year, my father said, a new and uniquely incomprehensible explanation of relativity or quantum physics hit the bookshelves. Was it that the so-called experts were constantly having to revise downwards their notion of how stupid "laymen" were, each year releasing a more simplified book only to find that even that was over their heads? Or was it, as he suspected, that no scientist on earth knew how to write, how to express himself clearly?

On and on he would rant, all the while addressing my mother so that it was hard to resist the notion that it was really her he was mad with, her view of the world he was assailing, her he was criticizing. This so often seemed to be the case that his tirades often ended with my mother in tears and saying it wasn't her fault he couldn't understand such things, why was he shouting at her? Did he think, she'd ask him, that if he wasn't married to her he would be able to understand them? Was she keeping him back in some way, was that it? Did he regret having a wife and a family, did he wish he'd gone to graduate school or something? He could go back to school if he wanted to, there was no need now for him to work if there was something else he'd rather do.

"I'm not going back to school," my father would say, "and no, I don't regret anything I've done." But more often than not, my mother was unappeasable, saying it was ridiculous that a husband and wife should have a falling out over quantum physics.

2

My mother was fond of saying that we were living in the age of television, but for us, it was still the age of the Gillingham. The only thing I could imagine our set making obsolete was eyesight.

We did not own a television set, my father said, we owned a Gillingham, an obscure rival of the television set, invented around the same time, an alternative technology in which only he and a few other people had had the foresight to invest. The Gillingham, my father said, was superior to the television set in every way but that of requiring almost constant maintenance. As soon as Mr. Gillingham got this one minor flaw worked out, he would be a rich man, he said.

Mr. Gillingham was our TV repairman, though I preferred to think of him the way my father did, as the inventor of the Gillingham, every existing model of which he had to service. He would pull up in the driveway in his station wagon, from the back of which he would drag out an enormous suitcase. It was like some sort of vaudeville suitcase, an oversized prop for some bit about travelling salesmen. He was not an actual repairman, just a kind of general fix-it man who didn't charge as much as the others and who, my father insisted, was not the reason that our set kept breaking down. The problem, my father said, was with the set itself, and since we could not afford a new one, the best we could do was keep calling Mr. Gillingham.

There seemed to be no end to the number of ways that the Gillingham could break down. There might be a gradual shrinking of the picture from the sides. Or the horizontal hold would start to slip, at first about once a minute, then more rapidly. Sometimes we had the picture but no sound, sometimes the sound but no picture. Sometimes the picture disappeared from the middle outwards so that, for days, a black hole at the centre of the screen kept getting bigger. Or a lot of these things would happen all at once and night-time would find the three of us sitting within a few feet of the set, squinting while a snowy picture about the size of a snapshot flipped over constantly. Now I understand how TV is going to make books obsolete, my father would say. People are going to go blind watching it. We would go on like this for days before, finally, my father would call Mr. Gillingham.

He wore a raglan and, beneath that, a rumpled suit, the two parts of which did not quite match. He also wore a grey fedora, to the felt band of which a little red feather was attached. He never took off this outfit, not even his hat, while he was working, always looking as though he had either just arrived or was just about to leave, which is not a bad way to look when you're charging by the hour.

What a strange array of tubes his suitcase held. He would open it out on the floor, then cover both halves with paper diagrams like the ones in boxes of chocolates that identify the flavours. He seemed to work by trial and error, replacing every tube until he found the one that was burnt out.

I remember my father calling the television set one of the first inscrutable inventions. Up to the time of the coming of TV, he said, you could form at least a vague notion of how something worked just from looking at it. Or there might be someone around who was willing to explain it to you, however badly. Cars, planes, phonographs, even tape recorders made at least some sense. But no one, it seemed, not even the people who fixed them, knew how televisions worked. There was a difference, Mr. Gillingham assured me, when I asked him to explain television to me, between knowing how to fix something and knowing how it worked, though to my mind he did not illustrate that distinction nearly as well as he did the one between knowing how to fix something and not knowing how to fix it.

Our worst fear was that the picture tube would go. It never did, but once, to get at some other part of the set, Mr. Gillingham had to remove it. It was not until he was just about to leave that he informed my father that, although the set was working properly, the picture tube was upside-down. That is to say, although the reception had never been better, the picture itself was upside-down. He had discovered his mistake too late to do anything about it today, he said, but he assured us that he would be back first thing in the morning. In the meantime, he said, it would do the television set no harm to turn it upside-down and watch it that way. He left in such a hurry that my father doubted that turning the TV upside-down would work, but in fact it did, though it seemed strange having the screen begin about an inch from the floor.

The only thing about which Mr. Gillingham was not as good as his word was coming back first thing in the morning. As day after day went by, the television set lay upside-down in the living room, its legs, until my mother removed them, sticking straight up in the air like some sort of antennae. My father kept calling Mr. Gillingham, who kept promising to come, but it seemed that, because we had at least some sort of picture, we were low on his priority list.

When we hadn't seen him for a couple of weeks, my mother said that, if he showed up at the door, she would tell him where to go. She never got the chance, for Mr. Gillingham never did show up, nor did she bother phoning him to cancel. My father said he was probably too embarrassed to come back or else wasn't sure that he could put the picture tube right-side-up without breaking something else.

"I've had it with him and that television set," my mother said. "That's it, no more repairs. When we can afford it, we'll buy a new set." We eventually did buy a new set, a colour set in fact, on instalments, but only after two months of making do with the Gillingham, my father and me watching it, my mother refusing to.

The day the new set arrived, my mother started making plans to get rid of the Gillingham but I pestered her into letting me keep it, on the understanding that not one red cent more would be spent on it.

"If it breaks down, if something goes wrong with it, that's it, it stays that way, O.K.?" she said. I nodded. My father and I lugged it into my room and set it up on the floor across from my bed. I re-attached the legs, for even upside-down it looked incomplete without them. At first I mostly watched the colour set and only every now and then, for the novelty of it, switched on the Gillingham, usually late at night, with the lights off and the curtains closed. The time I spent in front of the Gillingham gradually increased, however, until soon I watched it more often than I did the colour set.

Mr. Gillingham may have been right about what had been causing all the problems, for none of them returned. Reception was flawless, a fact my mother attributed to how much less the set was being used than before – with normal use, she assured me, it would break down in a week. But the Gillingham did not break down, at least not until years later, by which time we could well afford to have it fixed. It was my first television set, the first one I ever watched, owned, or, as would soon be the case, saw myself on, all of which had something to do with my wanting to keep it, as did the fact that it was upside-down. But mostly what I liked was switching it on and peeking in through the perforations on the back, turning down the volume so I could hear the faint hum from the tubes; there was a smell that, it seemed to me, went with this sound, was inseparable from it, that of the dust warming on the tubes inside each of which you could just make out a filament of orange light. My father would come in sometimes while I was kneeling there with my face against the wooden panel, looking in.

"Most people like to watch it from the other side," he said.

Then "Rumpus Room" happened. That's the best way I can think to put it. One of my mother's scripts caught the eye of someone at one of the studios and "Rumpus Room" happened. My mother signed a contract with the network to write and produce thirteen episodes.

Though the show started out merely as a local children's television program, seen only in the Toronto area, it was syndicated in its second year and it wasn't long before it was being seen, not only across Canada, but in the U.S., the U.K., as well as in dubbed or subtitled versions in many non-English-speaking countries, including the U.S.S.R., where, my father liked to imagine, they must be using it for some revolution-boosting purpose, perhaps as an example of the depths of decadence to which the West had sunk, or perhaps it was dubbed in such a way that the Bees seemed to be engaged in some sort of lively, ideological debate.

If you were born between 1962 and 1970, chances are that my mother and I were part of what one of the show's few detractors called your "introduction to indoctrination."

My mother was Miss Mary, the sole proprietor of "Rumpus Room." She decided that I would play both Bee Good, whom children at home were encouraged to model themselves after, and his alter ego, Bee Bad, a cross-looking bee, the brat bee, my father called him, who was forever misbehaving.

On each show, there were short clips of the Bees illustrating the do's and don'ts of childhood. They never spoke. Instead they acted out their tips on safety, hygiene, and good manners in a kind of manic pantomime, making it look as though the film was running a touch too fast, while Miss Mary did the voice-over, explaining to those at home what was going on.

Although my torso was contained, mascot-fashion, by the suits, the bee faces consisted partly of makeup and partly of attachables, including a set of microphone-like eyes through which, if you looked closely enough, my real eyes were visible. Sticking out of the bulbous black and yellow torso, and absurdly skinny by comparison with it, were my arms, on which I wore black elbow-length gloves, and my legs, on which I wore black stockings, with black elfin boots, curled up at the toes, on my feet. To my back was attached a pair of plastic wings, while a set of coiled antennae, with little yellow balls on the ends, were fastened to my head, bobbing every which way at the slightest movement.

The set was both a playground and a rec room, with swings and slide, sandbox, oversized building blocks arranged to spell out RUMPUS ROOM in a V-shape that framed the area where Miss Mary and the children played. It was meant to resemble a nursery school. The floor was solid white tile, designed to make even the footsteps of the visiting children audible so that, as Miss Mary led them from one section of the set to another, it would seem − or was at least intended to seem − that they were walking a long way. The playground was a kind of stylized outdoors, with papier mâché trees and a cardboard sun suspended from the ceiling. There was the Book Nook, where the children gathered around Miss Mary as she read to them from a storybook held open on her lap, Miss Mary's house, a collection of unwalled, miniature rooms in which, while playing, the children learned good manners, good posture, and good hygiene. And finally, there was Bee Good's Place, a beehive painted on the wall, with an opening in it through which both Bee Good and Bee Bad came and went, ideal for their dramatic entrances because it was dark inside the hive and it was not until they came jumping out that the audience could see them.

I loved making that jump out of the darkness onto the set, through the archway into television land, which was characterized for me by how brightly, how intensely it was lit. Everything on the set was so finely detailed, so heightened that it seemed to me that this was television, this was its peculiar, distinctive quality, this super-illumination and that what later showed up on the screen was something else, a dimmed, compressed approximation.

It always seemed strange, going back to being Henry Prendergast, sitting down in front of the TV and watching myself cavort about on the screen. What did he look like, the real me? I was not all that fat, but I was at an age when being only a little overweight can make it seem you have no chest; I seemed to have only a kind of featureless, pear-shaped torso that, as I walked, would swivel slightly from side to side, as if it was hanging from my neck by a string. I had black, lotion-slicked hair that made my face seem even paler than it was. I sometimes, at my mother's insistence, wore bow-ties, which accentuated the narrowness of my shoulders, as did the white, long-sleeved shirts my mother liked me to wear and which, no matter what time of year it was, were always soaked to the point of transparency with perspiration. "The boy is always too warm," my mother would say, looking mystified at my father as she felt my forehead. "Always. Even in the middle of winter. He works up a sweat just watching television. And yet, when I take his temperature, it's normal."

This, my father would tell my mother, was because of my essential "bee-ness." My father liked to pretend that I had lately become a superhero. "Bee Boy," he called me, saying that I was once an ordinary boy who, because of some freak accident involving radiation, had had his genes fused with those of a bumblebee, leaving him part boy, part bee, and with a schizoid, Jekyll and Hyde type of personality.

I was alone when I saw the first episode of "Rumpus Room," when I first saw myself on TV. I told my mother I wanted to watch it on the Gillingham and said that she and my father should watch it on the colour set. She'd been looking forward to the three of us sitting down together for the show's debut and told me that, if I were to watch it by myself, she'd be very disappointed. My father came up with the compromise that I would just watch the start of the first episode on the Gillingham, then come out and join them.

I lay on the floor in front of the Gillingham, my face just inches from the screen. When Bee Good came leaping out of his hive, however, when it hit me that it was myself that I was watching on the screen, I went round to the back of the set and looked inside, peering through the little grid of holes, not with any expectation of seeing myself in there or figuring out how the workings of the set produced my image on the screen, but just in sheer bewilderment, sheer wonder that some version of me could be in there. It seemed hard to believe that on the other side of that loudspeaker-shaped picture tube, an image of me exact in every way except for size was moving about. I remember first seeing the little ruby-coloured light and wondering what it was for; and there was the smell of the dust that was warming on the tubes, and a faint hum from within when I put my ear against the side of the set, the wood of the television warm against my cheek.

Then I knelt down at the front of the set and, putting my face so close that the hairs on my cheek would stand up, I tried to look sideways through the glass to see how thick my image was, to see what it consisted of, only to have the whole thing dissolve into a mass of teeming dots, as though I had light itself beneath a microscope.

"Rumpus Room," in addition to coming on every weekday morning at eleven, came on at noon on Saturdays, and, after that first episode, the three of us would always watch it together. In the beginning, we would all cheer loudly when Miss Mary or the Bees appeared. "Here he comes," my father would say, as I, dressed as Bee Good or Bee Bad, came tearing onto the set, or when a Bee Good film clip was shown. "Who's this, boys and girls?" Miss Mary would say, and the kids in the studio audience would scream "Bee Good" as I nodded and, like the Pope on the Vatican terrace, held out my hands to acknowledge their applause.

Soon, however, my father and I, to my mother's bemused disapproval, ended up booing Bee Good, whose niceness we said we found boring, and cheering for Bee Bad, exhorting him to misbehave.

I loved the moment when, faced with some temptation, Bee Bad paused and looked sideways at the camera, which would zoom in to show him contemplating crime. Then, without further hesitation, he would make for the nearest box of matches or bottle of detergent, or, his hands haughtily on his hips, step onto some crosswalk without looking at the light, or start climbing the fence of some electrical enclosure, only to be saved at the last second by Bee Good, who would suddenly appear in an inset in the upper right-hand corner of the screen and wag his finger at Bee Bad, shaking his head, the little antennae bobbing censoriously up and down, until Bee Bad would skulk away, head bowed in shame.

The two bees were never on stage at the same time. The moment the one who was on stage heard a buzzing from off-stage, he fled as though in mortal terror. My mother didn't think it would be a good idea for them to be played by different actors and have them appear on stage together, for the children on whom they had first tested this idea had always wanted some sort of fight or confrontation to take place between them. (This was why they ought not to be on stage together, my father said, but was not a reason for them both to be played by the same actor. He said my mother just didn't want someone not a Prendergast to play a part on the show.) As soon as I was off camera, while the children in the audience were cheering or booing in anticipation of Bee Good or Bee Bad respectively, Carol, the stage manager, would make me over; the Bees were distinguishable by the black, burglar-type eye mask worn by Bee Bad and the superhero-like insignia that was emblazoned on Bee Good's chest – "BG", it said, in large block letters. Also, Bee Bad's stripes were more narrow, making him look like some sort of cartoon convict, though my mother assured my father that it was only so children could tell the two bees apart at first glance that she had given Bee Bad narrow stripes.

I liked playing Bee Bad more than I liked playing Bee Good, if only because Bee Bad had more to do. It was sometimes offputting, though, upon making my dramatic entrance as Bee Bad, to be met with such an avalanche of boos from the children and their parents.

Though my mother wanted the studio audience to register some sort of disapproval of Bee Bad that the home viewing audience could hear, she didn't want me to think, she said, that it was me that they were booing, nor did she want them to boo so loudly as to frighten me, so she had the stage manager speak to the studio audience before every show, instructing them not to overdo it; throughout my time on stage as Bee Bad, whenever it seemed the booing was getting out of hand, the prompter would hold up a sign saying "Shhhh," and the audience, for a while at least, would settle down.

When we were taping a scene in some public place, Bee Good would be instantly recognized. "Hi, Bee Good," children would scream, as soon as they saw him. Cars going by would blow their horns. People on the sidewalks would stop to watch, lining up with their kids during breaks in the shooting to get autographs or to have their pictures taken with him. Even when dressed as Bee Good, I was not allowed to remove my bee head, my mother telling me that it wouldn't be appropriate for Bee Good to be seen half out of costume. Nor out of character for that matter. Because Bee Good never spoke on TV, I was not allowed, when meeting the public, to say anything, but could only stand there, nodding my head and waving, miming amusement, appreciation, gratitude for whatever people said to me, holding my stomach sometimes to indicate that I was laughing, signing autographs while wearing my black gloves. All the while, my mother, still in the role of Miss Mary, stood there, jumping in when I was uncertain about what to do, interpreting my sometimes vague gestures to the children. "Bee Good likes you," my mother would say. "Bee Good thinks you're very sweet."

I was only ever Bee Bad when the camera was rolling, the Bee Bad part of my costume coming straight off once a scene was finished. Bee Bad made no public appearances, nor was I even allowed to talk about him when I was out of costume, my mother deeming it appropriate for Bee Bad to keep as low a profile as possible. On location, when I was dressed as Bee Bad, I was always hurried off the set after every scene, hustled behind a tarpaulin to change over to Bee Good while Miss Mary stayed outside to meet the public. Bee Bad was not allowed to sign autographs, nor to have his picture taken with anyone – not that there was any great demand for either one. On the contrary, when efforts to keep me out of sight were not diligent enough and I was spotted by someone, a chorus of boos would start up, dying down just as quickly when I disappeared.

The problem of Bee Bad was never far from my mother's mind. She would come home with a large dufflebag of fan mail every week and my father and I would help her sort it into piles according to which of the show's characters it was addressed to. There would be a Bee Good pile, the largest, a Miss Mary pile, a miscellaneous "Rumpus Room" pile, and, smallest, a Bee Bad pile, which my mother never quite knew what to do with.

She would go through the mail piece by piece in her spare time, composing replies while she watched TV or at the dinner table, and often, to my father's chagrin, reading aloud those letters she found most charming or most sincere. Purportedly from children, most of it was of course ghost-written by their mothers or fathers, the children merely scrawling their names and ages at the bottom in letters intermittently inverted and randomly capitalized.

Most of these letters expressed affection for Bee Good, extolling his virtues, and telling him to watch out for Bee Bad. Likewise, the replies, supposedly from Bee Good, were ghost-written by my mother. But Bee Bad got some letters, too, many of them begging him to change his ways or asking him "Why are you so bad?" or "Why can't you be good?" or "Have you always been so bad?" My father wondered what sort of answer the parents who wrote these letters on behalf of their children could possibly expect to get from Bee Bad. It hardly seemed possible that they wanted him to reply in character, which is to say defiantly, or even abusively, but how else, being Bee Bad, could he reply? Letters straightforwardly and, in some cases, vociferously denouncing Bee Bad, letters to which, it was obvious, no answer was expected, were one thing, my father said, but letters to Bee Bad that did expect replies were something else.

To the boys and girls who wrote to Bee Bad, my mother sent a form letter, thanking them for watching the show, along with autographed photos of Miss Mary and Bee Good. No photographs of Bee Bad were sent out, though my father imagined children all over the world tacking them to dartboards. (No photographs of me dressed in what my father called civilian clothes were sent out either, though there were plenty of requests for such photos, to which my mother would reply that it was "Rumpus Room" policy never to show Bee Bad or Bee Good out of costume. My name did not even appear in the credits at the end of every show, my mother saying she thought it best for a boy my age to avoid publicity and fanfare as much as possible.)

The Bee Bad letters, and a few others addressed to her from parents who thought there should not be a Bee Bad, generally sent my mother into a crisis of conscience. She sometimes wondered herself if it might not be better simply to show Bee Good being good and leave it at that. She worried that some children might not be able to distinguish between the two bees, between what one should and should not do, or that they might be imitating both of them indiscriminately. But somehow, she said, the scripts without Bee Bad fell flat, the children they tried them on lost interest after only a few minutes. She was likewise worried about the effect playing both Bees would have on me. She was forever considering alternatives – having a grownup play the Bees, for instance, or having some other boy play Bee Bad. The first idea she dismissed because of my protests, and because, at any rate, she didn't think a grownup would be right for the parts, the second because she couldn't, in all conscience, she said, pawn off on someone else's child a part she wouldn't want her own child to play. She would often take me aside and remind me that, when playing Bee Bad, I was showing children "not what they ought to do, but what they ought not to do." "I hope he remembers where that 'not' goes," my father said, adding that my mother needn't worry, that either Bee Good and Bee Bad would cancel each other out in my mind, leaving me completely amoral, or I would alternate back and forth between them, developing a kind of Jekyll and Hyde personality. My mother's next project, my father told me, would be a dramatization of *Paradise Lost* in which I would play both God and Satan.

My father would assure her that Bee Bad was an important character and would tell me that playing the embodiment of pure evil was a responsibility not to be taken lightly. He

29

reminded me that, when I played Bee Bad, I was a role model for evil people everywhere. I was, he said, the most popular pin-up in correctional facilities. I was being watched, closely scrutinized. The slightest slip-up, a moment of weakness resulting in an act of decency or kindness, and those who looked down to me would be forever disillusioned. My father's interpretation of "Rumpus Room" was that Bee Bad was the hero, the doomed recidivist whose nemesis, Bee Good, would always win, but who, like some stoic psychotic, would nevertheless keep trying, persevering, never giving up the bad fight, no matter what the odds. It was this, Bee Bad's tenacity, he most admired, his dedication to the cause of awfulness.

My mother's favourite part of the show was the "I See" segment. Holding in front of her face "Miss Mary's Looking Glass," which was in fact just the frame of an oval, hand-held mirror from which the glass had been removed, she would list the names of children she could "see" at home. First, her face would be obscured by a spinning red and white swirl like those used by hypnotists. After sufficient time had passed for Miss Mary to go into her clairvoyant trance, the swirl would disappear, showing Miss Mary's face, framed by the mirror.

My mother spent a lot of time compiling her lists of names, agonizing over them in fact. She wanted, she said, to be as fair as she possibly could, while at the same time, "making contact," as she put it, with as many children as possible each day. Gender was the main determining factor, there being always an equal number of boys and girls on the list, but after that, it was not so easy to decide how the list should be comprised. At first she tried lists of names all beginning with the same letter, designating Monday as 'A' day, Tuesday as 'B' day, etc., but found that children felt left out more keenly if, on "their" day, their names weren't on the list than they did when the list seemed to have been chosen at random. She took this notion of being fair to great extremes. She had someone get her a breakdown of the population of her broadcast area according to ethnicity and tried to make her lists reflect it as closely as possible. She found out which were the most common names of each ethnic group and included them most often. She had many books of names and, on Sunday afternoons, would spread them out on the kitchen table, poring over them, compiling her lists for the coming week. She had a book of Italian names, a book of Chinese names, a book of Indian names. Backlists of names previously used, along with the dates on which they'd been used, were at her fingertips, so she could avoid repeating certain names, or be sure to repeat more common names like John or Mary that made the list once or twice a month; children were more likely to keep watching, she said, and to "benefit" from the program if, in the I See segment, their names kept cropping up. My father wondered if all this was fair to the Xaviers and Loyolas of the world, but my mother assured him that, sooner or later, such names would turn up on the list and that, at any rate, as far as fairness went, she was being fair to more children by doing things her way.

The only name that made the list more often than, according to her method, it should have, was mine. (My father said that I was named Henry after Longfellow and that "Wadsworth," Longfellow's second name, had been in the running for a while. It was just as well they'd chosen Henry, my father said, for it would have raised some suspicions if Miss Mary had claimed more than once every millennium that she could see someone named "Wadsworth.")

About twice a week, my mother would mention "Henry" during the I See section, saying, when my father teased her about showing favouritism, that Henry was a fairly common name. Still dressed as either Bee Good or Bee Bad, I would watch her from offstage as, looking through the glassless frame of the mirror, looking away from me and at the camera, she would say "I see Henry." Later, when a show was aired, when, gone back to being Henry, I was sitting with my parents, watching it, my mother would look at me to see how I reacted when Miss Mary said my name. I would smile and try to look as tickled by this tribute as I knew she wanted me to be, though in fact I found it unsettling. There was first of all the eeriness of it, my mother on the screen, saying "I see Henry," watching me, while at the same time my mother in the room was watching me.

This double-mother effect was made that much worse by my father, who pointed out that Miss Mary was a kind of all-seeing mother figure. Sure, the boys and girls at home got a kick out of having Miss Mary "see" them, my father said, but there was more to their fascination with the I See segment of the show than that. Miss Mary was a reminder to the children that, as he put it, "Big Mother is watching." Miss Mary, he said, was Big Mother, every child's own mother, writ large on the screen. There she was, their own omniscient mother, watching them, naming them, seeing everything they did, their own mother, from whom they could keep no secrets. No wonder the phrase "I see so-and-so" seemed to have such an effect on them.

My mother said that this was nonsense. She denied having had anything like this in mind when she first came up with Miss Mary. Miss Mary was nothing more than what she seemed to be, my mother said, a kind of mother-figure, yes, though in fact more like a teacher. She pointed out that her character's name was Miss Mary, not Mrs. Mary, signalling the fact that she was unmarried and therefore not yet a mother. The I See section of the show, she said, was intended, among other things, to make children feel that they were being watched over, overseen, taken care of, that they were safe, not that they were being spied upon.

But my father would merely shake his head and assure her that even if everything she said about Miss Mary was true, so was everything he said about her.

"Big Mother is watching," my father would say whenever Miss Mary went into her looking-glass routine. It seemed strange to think that, when other children were contemplating misbehaviour, it was my mother who, at the behest of their consciences, appeared before them. It was as though my mother were the source of everybody's guilt, not just mine, which I doubted would do very much for my popularity among my classmates in the long run.

It was hard for me sometimes not to think of my mother as Miss Mary, for she altered her appearance very little to play the part. In some ways, the most significant thing she did, and which no one watching at home knew anything about, was remove her wedding ring before each show. What little makeup she did put on was intended only to keep television from distorting her appearance, so that she looked, on screen, almost exactly as she did in real life. Her hair she wore exactly the same, almost shoulder-length, curled inwards at the bottom, with a simple bang across the front. She had a costume, of sorts, in that she wore the "same" dress day after day, a light-green pleated knee-length summer frock with a wide collar and a small-buckled belt; though she did not wear one identical to it offscreen, it was very much like the ones she wore, which made me further disinclined to distinguish between Miss Mary and her.

3

My father continued on with his substitute teaching, working on his book when he had the time. My mother kept pointing out to him that he was the only one of us not involved in the show, neither in front of nor behind the camera. My mother wanted to make the show a family project, and was always trying to "bring him in," as she put it, but he declined, telling her that, for his liking, "Rumpus Room" was too subversive. Though my mother wanted at least to include him in the credits as adviser or consultant, both of which titles, in her opinion, he deserved for having been what she called a "sounding board" for her ideas – something my father said he could not remember having been – he again declined, saying it was fine with him if we took all the credit. In fact, he said, it was fine with him if, on the street, we pretended not to know him, and if we told the neighbours he was boarding in the basement.

What if his name didn't actually appear, my mother said, what if the credits at the end read something like "Concept by the Prendergasts"? Twenty years from now, my father said, when the show business communist witch-hunt had been revived and "Rumpus Room" was being denounced as the

Marxist propaganda that it was, a sentence like "Concept by the Prendergasts" could mean his doom. The only credit he would accept, he said, would be a discredit, something like, "Not involved with this program, nor acquainted with anyone who is: Peter Prendergast."

My mother once asked him if he would like to be a guest on the show. Every Friday, there was a guest who talked about his or her job and she wanted my father to come on the show and talk about being a writer. My father declined, saying he didn't think a writer would be of much interest to five-year-olds or would fit the format of "Rumpus Room." It wasn't as if children had regular contact with writers. It wasn't as if writers were instantly recognizable by their distinctive uniforms, or went from door to door collecting short stories of theirs that people had put out for them and leaving new ones. "All right," my mother said, "all right. I was merely asking."

She kept after him, however. Television needed good writers, she said. He wouldn't have to work on shows like hers. She could get him involved, she said. She could get him in on the ground floor. She could bring him in.

"Why don't you let me bring you in?" she'd say.

"I don't want to be brought in," my father would say.

The phrase always conjured up for me an image of my father, standing in the rain on the doorstep of my mother's life, too proud, too stubborn, as my mother liked to say, to come inside. All he had to do was say the word, she said, that's all he had to do.

This offer was so often repeated, became, in fact, so routine that, after a while, my father didn't bother to decline it, but would only smile at her. "Well, all I can do is try," she'd say, in turn smiling at me. "I can't do more than try, can I, Henry?" Her manner at these times suggested that my father was a "cause" on which, no matter what he said or did, she would not give up. "You'll come around," she'd say, as if the very rightness of her position lent her patience, gave her the strength to press on cheerfully where others would have quit.

"The future is in TV," my mother, heady with her new success, would often say, "there's no question about that." The only question, she said, was what sort of TV we would have. She wanted to make sure that television was used for the right purposes, to educate, she said, to educate, using the hand in which she held her pencil to emphasize the word. My father would tell her that, despite being a teacher, he was not altogether unfamiliar with the concept.

"I'm sorry," my mother would say, blushing, putting her hand over her mouth. "I know I'm getting carried away. I still haven't gotten used to the idea that the show is such a hit. I can't believe how fast everything is happening."

What especially concerned her, she said, was that TV was going to make books obsolete. "Don't get me wrong, I hope it doesn't," she said. "I hope, with all my heart and soul, it doesn't, but I'm afraid that it will."

It seemed important to my mother that TV be acknowledged to have this sinister potential. My father, for his part, said he had nothing against TV, and was not at all worried that it would make books obsolete, or at least, as he put it, "any closer to being obsolete than they've always been." Whenever he told her this, however, she would take it as a criticism, as a kind of belittlement of her medium.

"How can you say that, Peter," she'd say, "how can you say that?" The harm that TV could do if misused seemed to be a kind of inverse measure of the good that it could do if used properly. Good TV would keep books from becoming obsolete, she said, but my father would say it was good books that would keep books from becoming obsolete.

My mother seemed to relish these little debates. It became a cherished notion of hers that she and my father were friendly rivals of some sort. My father, for various reasons, did not enjoy these exchanges nearly as much as she did. What most got him going was her new attitude towards teaching. It was as if, now that she was no longer a teacher, she could not imagine anybody being one, as if she assumed that, when she left it, the profession itself had been discontinued, abandoned by all as unsatisfactory, unviable. That there were still some people whose lot in life was to do what she herself had outgrown she seemed to find hard to believe, hard to credit. When my father talked about something that had happened in the class-room, she would give a mock shiver and shake her head, as if to rid herself of the memory of the time when her own life had revolved around such things.

"Are the students still throwing spitballs?" my mother would say.

"Yes," my father would say, "they are. And surprisingly enough they still have arms and legs."

Just as irritating to him was the habit she had when engaged in conversation of closing her eyes to listen and open-ing them to speak. She would turn her head towards whomever she was speaking to but she would close her eyes, and only when she began to speak would she open them. My father said she had not even been conscious of doing it until, one day, he brought it to her attention and, even then, she had been unable to stop doing it for any length of time. What was most offputting about it, especially when you had a closeup view of her face, was that, though her eyelids were closed, her eyeballs, like those of someone dreaming, kept moving back and forth, darting about beneath the lids in a way that made it almost impossible to concentrate on what you were saying. During their talks, she would sit beside my father on the sofa, leaning towards him until, eventually, their faces were about a foot apart. With much fluttering and blinking, as if she had just had a blindfold removed, she would open her eyes to ask him a question to which, while trying not to notice what her eyes were doing, he would stammer some reply. Sooner or later, exasperated with the effort of trying to keep up his part of the conversation while her eyes were darting about in this manner, he would storm off, leaving my mother to think he had done so because he'd been about to lose the argument.

But there was one "Rumpus Room"-related thing we did together. We would drive around the city, scouting locations for the safety segment of the show, scouting, that is to say, potential safety hazards, no-nos, as my father called them, anything dangerous to children, especially anything that, to the average toddler, might look appealing or intriguing – ravines, water reservoirs, electrical enclosures, subway tunnels, railway tracks, fire escape ladders, garbage dumps, the waterfront, the fence around the airport, the fence along the freeway, construction sites, freight yards, loading docks. The city, it seemed, was a landscape of no-nos, hazards, forbidden zones, danger signs. It was a strange way of looking at the world, of seeing the sights, being taken on a guided tour of places you should stay away from, the lowlights of the city. It was as though my mother thought there was a finite, controllable amount of danger in the world, a finite number of hazards, perils and, once these had been identified and marked, you had only to avoid them, which it would always be within your power to do. She compiled hazard maps of the city, charting it as one might a minefield.

I remember well those Sunday morning drives (Sunday was the best day for no-no hunting, for there was less traffic on the streets), the three of us in the car, my parents in the front seat, me in the back, usually standing on the seat, ignoring my mother who would ask me if I had forgotten the episode of "Rumpus Room" that dealt with the perils of standing on the back seat while the car was moving. What would children think if they knew that Bee Good didn't practise what he preached? "Physician, heal thyself," my father would say, looking at me in the rearview mirror.

A lot of the time I acted, inadvertently, as a kind of no-no detector, for almost everything in which I showed a natural curiosity or interest was forbidden, off limits to me for one reason or another. Forgetting the purpose of our tour, I would kneel on the seat, my hands and face pressed against the window. "What's that?" I'd say every so often, usually pointing to something bearing a skull and crossbones, or with KEEP OUT or DANGER signs plastered all over it. My mother, while explaining to me what "it" was, would jot down the location on her clipboard, adding it to her list of possible safety tip sites. My father would tease her about it, saying that my danger detector was infallible, telling her that, when he and I were out walking, I would suddenly assume the pointing position, stopping and indicating with my outstretched arm in which direction danger lay and staying like that until he had found whatever I was pointing at. Mind you, he said, this sort of behaviour earned me a lot of strange looks from passersby, but being taken for a lunatic by total strangers was a small price to pay for safety.

4

My mother was trying to shield me from the effects of stardom, saying there was no reason that I couldn't have a normal childhood. I was ten by this time, the show was in its fourth year and well on its way to becoming a classic of its kind. We never appeared in public as what my father called "civilians," she refused all offers for me to star in other programs, turned thumbs down on any and all ideas for spin-off products. There were no "Rumpus Room" board games or record albums, no clothing or paraphernalia bearing the "Rumpus Room" logo. There was only the show itself, pure and unadulterated, in the closing credits of which the name Henry Prendergast still did not appear.

But stardom, if you could call it that, had its effects on me. It gave me insomnia, for one thing. My mother's theory was that I got so worked up during a taping, what with all the excitement, the cameras, the audience reaction, and so on, that afterwards, I couldn't sleep.

At any rate, every little thing kept me awake, but especially clocks. As long as my parents were still up and making sufficient noise to distract me from or drown out that of the clocks, I could get to sleep. But once they were gone to bed, the ticking of the clocks would wake me up. So it was that the last thing my father did before going to bed each night was clock-proof the house for me. Luckily, the alarm clock they relied on to wake them up every morning ticked quietly enough that I couldn't hear it from behind the closed door of their room. But not every entranceway in the house could boast a door, so most of the clocks were a problem. I could hear the clock in the hallway well enough, for instance, so it had to be unplugged. There was, in the living room, a mantel-piece clock that not only ticked loudly but chimed on the hour, so that had to be unplugged. In the kitchen, there was a clock, the cord of which ran down behind the stove to an outlet so much of a nuisance to get at that, each night, instead of unplugging the clock, my father would simply take it down and put it in the stove, still ticking. My mother was convinced that, someday, my father, forgetting it was there, would cook the clock, but he never did. Upon going to bed and being asked by my mother if he had remembered about the clocks, my father, who said her question always reminded him of Tristram Shandy's moment of conception, would say, "God's in his heaven, the clock's in the stove, all's right with the world." The first thing every morning, my father would go about the house, restoring the clocks to their usual posi-tions, resetting them. Father Time, he called himself.

It wasn't long before, even with the house clock-proofed, I couldn't sleep. My mother, on the advice of doctors, tried all sorts of things with me, including bio-feedback, which seemed to be working for a while. I would come home from my ses-sions at the clinic saying I had never felt so full of energy, so rested. As if to prove it, I would bound around the house, up and down the stairs, jauntily swinging my arms as though I was playing the part of "Pep" in some public service announcement about the benefits of exercise. I stayed up late several nights in a row – you didn't need as much sleep when you were doing bio-feedback, I said, explaining that, according to the doctors at the clinic, a half an hour of bio-feedback-induced relaxation was worth four hours' sleep. "Yes, well, we won't sell your bed just yet," my father said, a remark which proved to be prophetic, for I was soon back to normal, or rather, what with having fooled myself into thinking I had energy to spare and having gone on such a spree of hyper-activity, I was worse than ever, overdrawn on my adrenalin account, my father said, to the point where I was incoherent with exhaustion.

Most children require a night light to get to sleep, but it turned out that all I needed was a night noise. We had one of those swivelling electric fans and my father put it on a night table at the foot of my bed, aimed away from me so that the blast of air wouldn't bother me. It looked as if it was not so much drowning out noise as fending it off, blowing it away, sweeping back and forth like some radar dish, a little cycloptic sentry at the foot of my bed, standing guard while I slept. And there it stayed, for though it took me a while to get used to it, it got to the point that I couldn't sleep without it. It became a permanent, distinguishing fixture in my room. When my mother came to wake me in the mornings, all she had to do was turn it off. Invariably, the instant the fan began to wind down, I would open my eyes. I took it with me when we travelled, found one as much like it as I could when, after breaking down for the umpteenth time, it proved unfixable. The sound of that fan appeared as a kind of background noise in all my dreams.

(Interestingly, my parents had some sleep-related problems of their own about this time. Though they still slept in the same room, they did so in separate beds, the reason being that my father had gotten into the habit, when he was asleep, of raising one arm straight up in the air. He would roll onto his side and, as if this was one of the standard things that people did to get comfortable in bed, he would slowly raise his arm, the hand hanging limp, the arm itself swaying slightly back and forth. Separate beds kept my mother from getting hit when, as it was wont to do, the arm went limp and dropped. But she would wake sometimes, in the middle of the night, and there it would be, looming eerily above the bed, sometimes casting a huge and by no means sleep-enhancing shadow on the wall.)

In addition to my insomnia, I developed what my father said amounted to a sense of doom. My mother, telling me that we should begin preparing now for the day that I would appear unmasked on camera, the day that I would play, not Bee Good/Bee Bad, but some human character, had me fitted with an especially cumbersome pair of orthodontic braces. For no reason whatsoever, I fastened on to the notion that I would have to wear, in addition to the glasses and braces I already wore, a hearing-aid of the sort the man next door wore. My father, perhaps thinking to cajole me out of my anxieties, made matters worse by teasing me about my nose, wondering if my nostrils were not too far apart and if some sort of "nose clip" might not be necessary. The thought that even my nose needed some sort of boosting, that with this "clip" the obliteration of my face by prosthetics would be complete, was more than I could bear. I begged my mother not to make me wear the nose clip. It took her a long time to convince me that there was no such thing as a nose clip, that my father had only been joking. In fact, for days afterwards, I was suspicious, watching my parents closely for any sign that some awful truth was being kept from me. "What are you looking at Mom like that for?" I'd say, if my father happened to glance at my mother.

I became adept at spotting inconsistencies in any argument designed to reassure me. When my parents tried to convince me that things were no more and no less than they seemed to be, I concentrated especially hard, not only on what they were saying, but on how they were saying it, watching their lips, their eyes, looking for the slightest hint of insincerity or doubt. Perhaps, my father said, some rigorously logical, sub-clause proliferating argument devised and read aloud, poker-faced, by some philosopher like Hegel or Wittgenstein would have satisfied me, but anything less would only make matters worse, for I would follow around for the rest of the day anyone so foolish as to try to reassure me about anything. My father said that my favourite three words were "But you said." "He got me on a technicality," my father would say after failing to convince me that, for instance, the doctor who'd just examined me had found nothing whatsoever wrong with me.

My mother would always include among our Christmas gifts what she called a "family gift," a gift from the whole family to the whole family, as she put it, from "us" to "us," though no one but her laid eyes on it until she had my father open it on Christmas Day.

The first family gift was our cat, Cooper. It was as if, in between sightings of Cooper, my father forgot we had a cat. Certainly, a man who did not have one would not have been more startled to see one walk across the floor in front of him than my father always was. "God almighty," my father would say, putting his hand on his heart, at which Cooper would go bolting from the room. Cooper, my father said, belonged to the species *beeline domesticus*, so named because of its habit of taking the shortest path between two points, no matter what obstacles, human or otherwise, lay in the way.

Often the family gift was what my father called a "safety gift," like a first aid kit, my mother saying that introducing such items to the household first as Christmas gifts would impress upon all of us how important they were. We spent a good part of every Christmas morning learning how to use such things, forbidden to open the rest of the gifts until my mother demonstrated the proper use of some fire extinguisher or smoke alarm.

Once, the family gift was *Dr. Heimlich's Home Guide to Emergency Medical Situations*, a paperback the size of a phone book, on the cover of which a woman was shown administering the Heimlich manoeuvre to a man, her arms around him from behind, as if she had him in some wrestling hold from which no escape was possible. The faces of both the man and the woman were featureless, completely blank, presumably because any expression appropriate to their situation would not be the first thing someone running to consult the book would want to see. The blank faces terrified me, for I had some half-formed notion that face erasure actually occurred during medical emergencies. My father, declaring the book "defaced," defaced it by re-facing it, that is, by drawing faces on the man and woman, having a lot of fun with that play on words while giving the Heimlich-performing woman a look of diabolic glee and the man a look of startled fright as if she had crept up and grabbed him from behind. Upon seeing what he had done to it, my mother declared the book spoiled, threw it out and, as soon as the stores were open after Christmas, went out and bought another one.

On another occasion, the family gift was a molecule of water, H_2O, one of those ball-and-stick models on which my parents, represented by hydrogen, were red, and I, represented by oxygen, was white. The molecule model of the family, my father called it when my mother said that we should display it as a kind of family symbol. "Without Henry, we'd be nothing but gas," my father said, adding that it was a good thing that they had not given in to the "propagation propaganda" of the fifties, for if they had had two children, the family symbol would have been H_2O_2, or hydrogen peroxide, and the family would have been symbolized by bleach.

My mother said that, just because I was a child television actor, there was no need for me to become some sort of "television child," which, it seemed to her, because of my insomnia and sense of doom, I was well on the way to becoming. She put my father in charge of instilling in me what she called "a love of books," which she regretfully admitted that she herself did not have.

It was with this in mind that she came up with the most memorable of all her family gifts, *The Lifetime Reading Plan,* a list of Western Literature's best one hundred writers, the Best West List, my father called it, compiled and annotated by one Clifton Fadiman who, like my father, had been a high school teacher. Fadiman was like some ultimate substitute teacher, the ultimate layman, a jack of all subjects and a master of none, a kind of anti-specialist, the closest thing to a Renaissance man the twentieth century had yet produced, my mother said. In Fadiman's Utopia, people sat around in bars and barbershops discussing Aristotle's *Ethics*. A world in which Plato was as popular as Agatha Christie – why not? said Fadiman. On the back of "The Plan," as my father called it, there was a picture of Fadiman, cherubic guru, bespectacled and smiling, looking every bit the evil genius my father, by way of asserting that Fadiman was out to rule the world, said he was. How Fadiman would achieve world domination by having people read *Thus Spake Zarathustra* was not yet clear, my father said, but you could tell just by looking at him what his real intentions were. Perhaps what Fadiman had in mind was a kind of global lowering of self-esteem, my father said. Perhaps he hoped that, upon failing to get through even one of the books on a list which, according to him, should have been "well within their range," people would be so convinced of their stupidity, so demoralized, that they would agree to anything. Imagine, my father said, going through life thinking that you were alone in finding Hobbes' *Leviathan* unreadable.

My mother made matters worse for herself by ordering and having specially bound all one hundred books on the list. She said the books were for all three of us but especially for me. She bought an adjustable bookstand on which she arranged all the books according to their places on Fadiman's list, starting, on the far left, with *The Lifetime Reading Plan* itself, then stretching, left to right, from the *Iliad* to *Nineteen Eighty-four*. She displayed the books prominently, as one might a set of encyclopedias, on a coffee table in the corner of the living room, the books tilted back on the slanted stand to make their bold-embossed titles legible from across the room, a banker's lamp throwing light across the spines. My mother assured us that the books were not just for decoration but for reading and that we could borrow one at any time as long as we put it back in the right place when we were finished. She had numbered each of the books, she said, on the top right corner of the title page, so we would know, without having to consult the Plan, what order to replace them in.

She either hadn't noticed what sort of books were included in the Plan or, never having heard of most of them, didn't realize how difficult they were to read. She seemed to have had in mind a kind of treasury of classics, books of the "best-loved" variety, like *Huckleberry Finn*, *David Copperfield*, *Gulliver's Travels*.

These books and a few others like them were on the list and perhaps fooled her into thinking that the rest, though she was not acquainted with them, must be similar. In fact, the list was mostly made up of books like *Ulysses*, *Remembrance of Things Past*, *Tristram Shandy*, the *Interpretation of Dreams*, and also included works of philosophy, psychology, and history.

My father could just imagine it, he said: a winter's night, a roaring fire, the whole family gathered in the living room, him in the easy chair, smoking his pipe, my mother and me gazing fondly at him as he read aloud our favourite passage from Hegel's *Phenomenology of Mind*, or gave the traditional

Christmas reading from the abridged and illustrated version of Kant's *Critique of Pure Reason*, including that heart-warming section in which Kant first demonstrates that noumenal knowledge is impossible.

"It doesn't matter if Henry can't read all the books now," my mother said. "He'll read them when he's older."

"You can't get that old," my father said, assuring her that not even Einstein had read such books when he was older. My mother tried gamely to demonstrate their readability by reading them herself, or, at least, by trying to look as though she was reading them, leaving them lying around the house, open, face downwards. Great benefits could be had just by reading small portions of such books, my mother said, by dipping into them from time to time.

She seemed to have had a notion that all classics were uniformly great and was confused when, after she had extolled the virtues of one of the books on the Plan that she had "dipped into," as she put it, my father made disparaging remarks about it or dismissed it altogether. She grew more and more unsure of herself, having no idea whether or not she was choosing what, in his mind, were the right books or the best books. She would watch him closely when he glanced at some book she had left lying around, clearly wondering whether she should chance some remark about it or venture an opinion. Any book at which he snorted with derision or hardly seemed to notice was soon back on the stand. My father, who clearly saw how embarrassed she was, how awkward she felt about having recommended as family reading books she had no hope of understanding, seemed inclined at first not to give her a hard time about it. But the more she tried to talk about the books, the more irritated he became, the less able to resist taking her up on some remark she made. What irritated him most was the notion she seemed to have that books were things to be dabbled in, that they could form the basis of that near-mythical long-sought-after joint pursuit of theirs, some common area of interest like gardening, to be enthused about over coffee on Sunday afternoons. I would see her reading the backs of the books, or the author information page, or, if there was one, the introduction, trying to find some clue as to how the book was widely held, some pithy and, she must have hoped, representative description of it, some typical summing up of its merits. Eventually, she stopped choosing books from the Plan, though she couldn't bring herself to move it to a less conspicuous part of the house, leaving it instead on the coffee table where, from then on, as though it were some emblem of their incompatibility, they pretended it did not exist.

My father put *The Lifetime Reading Plan* to use in supplying me with what my mother thought of as a kind of antidote to television stardom, "a good grounding in the classics," but he didn't go about it in the way she'd had in mind.

Some of the fictional characters from some of the books in the Plan would turn up, in altered form, in the stories he told me at bedtime. I complained that I was a little old for bedtime stories. "Not for this kind," my father said.

James Fenimore Cooper's "Natty Bumpo and Chingachcook" became "Fatty Rumpo and Spinach Cook." Bumpo was also known as "La Longue Carabine," Rumpo as either "Le Petit Pistol" or "La Grosse Derrière."

"Moby Dick" became "Moby Baby," an infant of gargantuan

proportions that crawled about with the initials MB emblazoned on its diaper, and whose adventures sometimes coincided with those of Fatty Rumpo and Spinach Cook. Spinach Cook was the very opposite of Rumpo. Like Popeye, he ate nothing but spinach, but this made him skinny and came not from a tin but from a pot he carried, forever boiling, on his back, the perpetual flame beneath the pot fuelled by the gas he was always giving off, making him a kind of human Bunsen burner. The stench of spinach from him was such that not even Rumpo could stand it.

"The Saga of Eric the Red" became "The Saga of Gregor the Green," a description of the epic bout of seasickness suffered by Gregor on his way to the New World.

One of the few classics that, at my mother's insistence, my father read to me in its original form was "The Rime of the Ancient Mariner," my mother thinking, wrongly as it turned out, that I would be able to follow the literal meaning and enjoy the poem as an adventure/ghost story. My father discovered, after several readings, that whenever he said the word "albatross" I thought he was saying "Albert Ross," as in: "Why lookst thou so? With my cross bow / I shot thee, Albert Ross." And "With his cruel bow he laid full low / The harmless Albert Ross." It was my belief that, throughout most of the poem, the Mariner was walking about with the rotting corpse of a man named Albert Ross hung around his neck.

"The Rime of the Ancient Mariner" and various other classics in which I was getting such a good grounding launched me on a year-long binge of misconception.

From explanations which he swore were as simple and as lucid as he could make them, and which I had asked for after he finished his recasting of the opening scene of *David Copperfield* in which Copperfield is born, I formed a kind of ship-in-the-bottle theory of reproduction, whereby Copperfield's father, using what most people would have thought was the least dextrous part of the male anatomy, put Copperfield together, assembled him piece by piece, inside his mother. Nor did I feel in the least compelled to reconcile this with my other theory, generated from my father's retelling of *The Scarlet Letter*, according to which, to make a baby, Hester Prynne and Arthur Dimmesdale had to do it every night for nine months, the reason that Hester's stomach got gradually bigger being that she was slowly, incrementally, filling up with sperm.

"No doubt about it," my father said, "the classics are doing him a world of good."

My mother thought enrolling me in a better school might do the trick. She surprised my father and me one day with the announcement that I had been accepted into U.C.C. She looked eagerly at me.

"What's U.C.C.?" I said.

"You've never heard of U.C.C.?" my mother said.

"Well, that's no crime, Audrey," my father said.

"I bet Henry knows what U.C.C. is," my mother said, "he's just never heard it called by its initials before."

I waited.

"U.C.C. stands for Upper Country College," my mother said, pronouncing the words very carefully, as if to emphasize the fact that they had not registered on me the first few thousand times I'd heard them.

"Also known as Upper Crust College," my father said. "Its graduates are known as Upper Crustaceans and..."

"Yes, well, a lot of people who never went there but wish they could have talk that way about it." my mother said. My father was about to make some remark, but my mother put up her hand to stop him, nodding her head as if to say, "Let's consider your next remark already said, shall we, and call it even."

"I don't think Henry is too crazy about the idea," my father said, looking at me, doing a kind of double take when I did nothing to indicate that I agreed with him.

"Your mother's not saying you have to go, Henry, just that you can if you want to," my father said.

"Oh, of course, sweetheart," my mother said.

My father kept looking at me, waiting for me to say something. I was embarrassed because I liked the sound of U.C.C. and wouldn't at all have minded going there.

"Well, what about it, Henry?" my mother said, clapping her hands lightly together. I looked at my father and we both shrugged at the same time.

"Then it's settled," my mother said.

I avoided making further eye contact with my father, who seemed surprised at my having spurned him as an ally. Later that night, when I had gone to bed, I heard my parents arguing about U.C.C., my mother saying that my father ought not to let his own biases get in the way of my having the best education available to me.

"That's got nothing to do with it," my father said. "I'm worried he won't fit in, that's all. What about −"

"You don't give Henry enough credit," my mother said, and after that all I heard was whispering.

My mother swore it was just coincidence but, not long after I began at U.C.C., we started getting fairly regular visits from reporters. At first, because of one photographer who snapped a picture of us from the doorway without her permission, my mother would send my father and me to the bathroom when the doorbell rang. Holed up, out of sight of the front door, we would sit on the edge of the tub, our backs to the frosted window as if we were not convinced of its opacity.

My father would pretend that it was him that the reporters were primarily interested in, telling me that he would never have gone into the high-profile profession of substitute teaching if he had known it would have this kind of effect on his family. It was one thing, he said, to have a camera crew waiting for you outside your school every morning when you went to work. He had come to accept that as part of the price one paid for teaching Grade Ten Geography. But to have them follow you home, to have them outside your house at night, demanding to know, in voices loud enough for your wife and son to hear, if it was true that you were contemplating adding biology to your list of subjects was something else again. Was there no depth to which these people wouldn't sink, my father said, assuring me that this biology thing was just a rumour.

After politely deflecting several requests for interviews, my mother decided we might just as well pretend that we were not home when they came to call. She stopped answering the door, drew all the drapes in the house and told us that, if the phone rang, we should let her get it. As soon as we saw someone coming up the driveway, we would hide, though I would often peek out at them from behind the curtain in my room. I remember one man, who looked like he was playing a reporter on a TV show, what with the press card he was wearing in his hat, knocking on the door and, when he got no answer there, tapping on the windows, trying to see inside, saying, "Anybody home? Yoo hoo, anybody home?", his tone half-puzzled, half-aggrieved, but also solicitous, familiar, as if he was a friend of ours who had been led to expect we would be home and who knew we wouldn't mind him taking certain liberties to find out if we were.

A couple of times, as we were backing out of the driveway, we were startled by this same man who seemed to appear from out of nowhere, behind the car, tapping on the trunk, standing there, blocking our way until my mother rolled down her window. "What do you want?" my mother said, barely turning her head. Still he stood there, looking in through the back window at me, smiling, nodding, not so much to say hello as to indicate he recognized me, to acknowledge the minor momentousness of seeing in real life someone he had long been acquainted with through television. "There they are," his expression seemed to say. "That's them. Miss Mary and the boy who plays the Bees."

"Just a few questions, Mrs. Prendergast?" he said. When my mother told him we were not granting interviews, he stepped aside and allowed the car to pass, bending over to peek inside as it did and waving as if we had come to visit him and he were seeing us off.

It turned out that this man worked for a tabloid called *The Television Set*, as in the Jet Set or the Smart Set. It wasn't long before we were among that publication's favourite subjects.

What suddenly made them notice us, whether it was my switching to U.C.C. or not, we would never know.

It was *The Television Set* that dubbed my mother "Mary Queen of Tots," a nickname that, to my mother's great displeasure, was soon picked up by all the other tabloids and by the general public.

The Set took to calling us "The Perfect Prendergasts." It got so that hardly an issue went by in which we were not mentioned at least once. My father was portrayed as an embittered failure who was jealous of my mother and me, what with being despised and ignored by everyone, while we got all the fanfare. I was described as lording it over him every chance I got, mocking him for making less money than I did, while my mother, it was said, made him do, in exchange for his paltry allowance, menial, janitorial tasks on the set of "Rumpus Room." My father and I got a big kick out of these stories. "Dad," I'd say, from time to time, "let's pretend that you're my slave." My father was willing, but my mother would object, saying it was bad enough that they were writing such things about us, we didn't have to play along with them.

My mother hated *The Set*, in which she was usually portrayed as a shrewish, child-exploiting stage mother who kept me docile and tractable by spiking my soda pop with tranquillizers, switching to amphetamines when the taping schedule required that I go an especially long time without sleep.

The Set had a lot of fun with me. They said Bee Good/Bee Bad were played by "the brothers Prendergast" who started out in life as Siamese twins joined at the tonsils, sharing one tonsil, in fact. They ran photos purportedly showing what they called our "separation operation" and a story in which there occurred sentences like "the removal of the Henry tonsil proved to be especially difficult." In another photo, twin boys who looked nothing like me, but were dressed as Bee Good and Bee Bad and holding the heads of their costumes beneath their arms like astronauts holding helmets, were likewise identified as the brothers Prendergast. My mother wanted to take *The Set* to task in some way, but my father said that that was what they were hoping we would do and that the best thing we could do was nothing.

Often, I never actually saw the photographer who took my picture. Photographs that seemed to have been taken without the subject's knowledge, that were just sufficiently blurred and obstructed to suggest that someone had gone to great lengths to obtain them, were a favourite with *The Set*. People who could just as easily have walked right up to me and snapped my picture did so from behind hedges, from passing cars.

The reporter for *The Set*, however, who said his name was "Larry" and carried his camera in plain view, took a different tack. He would wait for me outside the U.C.C. gates and as I made my way to the bus stop would walk along with me, taking pictures, asking questions.

"How's everything at school, Henry? Any problems? Ya like Upper Country College, do ya? What are the boys like? Pretty snobby, I suppose. How about the teachers, are they nice? Any you're not too crazy about? How's 'Rumpus Room' going? Does your mother make you come here like she makes you do everything else? What's the story, Henry?"

I ignored all his questions and spoiled most of his pictures by looking obligingly and cheerfully at the camera, smiling as though for publicity shots. His tone was always exasperated, as if my behaviour confirmed for him that what *The Set* said about me was true – I really was uppity, superior, standoffish.

I didn't tell my parents about Larry, for I knew I wouldn't like whatever measures my mother might take to keep me away from such people, and I was also worried that she might think it was best that I no longer be the star of "Rumpus Room."

As time went on, Larry changed his tactics. He would jump out in front of me or sneak up behind me. In either case screaming "Boo" as loud as he could, snapping as many pictures as he could before the look of fright wore off my face.

One day, he showed up with an associate, a man who looked like he might have been a boxer and who was wearing what must have been one of Larry's suits, so badly did it fit him.

"This is Tommy," Larry said, as the two of them walked along with me. "Larry, Tommy, and Henry," Larry said. "Hey, Henry?"

Larry got in front of us, walking backwards, snapping the occasional picture, then Tommy got in front of me and held out one of his massive hands to block the lens of Larry's camera.

"That's it, Tommy," Larry said. Then Tommy began shaking his fist at the camera as Larry, still walking backwards, snapped his picture. When I stopped, they stopped, Tommy shielding me, holding out his arms as if to keep Larry at bay and, when Larry reminded him to, saying things like, "No pictures, buddy, I warned you, no pictures," scowling at the camera. I was trying to get away from Tommy who was so close I was afraid he would fall over me; he kept looking back to see where I was, every now and then grabbing hold of me to keep me still, his broad back inches from my face as he shuffled about, following Larry who was following me and trying to include me in each shot, the three of us going round and round in a way that must have looked quite odd to passersby. Though I knew the whole thing was being staged and for what purpose, though no harm was actually being done to me, I was frightened, for the violence, phony though it was, was escalating, Tommy breathing ever more loudly through his nose, our shoes scuffing and rasping on the sidewalk, Larry coming closer and closer with the camera. Tommy had just begun faking some sort of an assault on Larry when I turned around and, evading a lunge from both of them, got away and ran back to Upper Country, where I waited in the library until I knew my father would be home, then called him and had him come get me in the car, telling him I'd lost my bus fare.

I didn't let on to him or my mother that anything had happened, but a few weeks later some pictures of Larry, Tommy, and me turned up in *The Set*, captions identifying Tommy as my bodyguard and the accompanying story claiming that *The Set* was suing Audrey Prendergast for turning Tommy loose on Larry.

The day the story appeared marked the last time I ever made my own way home from school. From then on, my father dropped me off at the school steps every morning and picked me up there in the afternoon. A couple of times, we saw Larry hanging around outside the gate. He ran along with the car once and snapped our picture but soon after that he disappeared.

5

For a while after our "discovery" by the tabloids, we continued to live on St. Clair, though the house, as my mother put it, was "modified" to give us more privacy. (There were some purely aesthetic changes. On either side of our front doorstep were stone lions, each with its mouth wide open and with one paw raised in a kind of hailing or else yawn-suppressing gesture, giving visitors what my mother never tired of pointing out was a roaring welcome. "How's that for a roaring welcome?" she'd say, whenever she met people at the door.)

The façade of the house was open to the street, but otherwise our property was surrounded by a solid, palisade-type fence too high to see over except from a distance, and even then all you could make out was the upper storey, half-obscured by trees. My mother had signs that, as my father said, definitely did not constitute a roaring welcome put up on the fence: PRIVATE PROPERTY, TRESPASSERS PROSECUTED, PREMISES PROTECTED, KEEP OUT.

We thought we had made some progress in regaining our privacy until there appeared in *The Television Set* a series of photographs of the various rooms of our house. There was my bedroom with the fan at the foot of my bed (why a fan in late November in Toronto, wondered *The Set*, especially a fan facing the wrong way?), my parents' bedroom, the kitchen, the living room. But most of the pictures were of my TV room, showing the armchair and the upside-down Gillingham from various angles. *The Set* claimed the pictures had been taken over the course of a month, throughout which time the TV had always been upside-down. That it was not just some sort of non-functional heirloom was apparent, they said, from the TV guide that lay on top of it, so what was the story here? An upside-down TV, a backwards-facing fan? Did Henry Prendergast have some sort of reversal fetish?

"My God, how brazen," my mother said. "They must have come right over the fence."

My father said they had obviously taken the photographs sometime when we were out, but my mother said she wouldn't put it past them to do it in broad daylight when we were home.

"They must have used a ladder," my father said, but my mother wondered if our neighbours might not be co-operating with the press, accepting money from them in exchange for phoning them whenever we went out and letting them take photographs from the upper storeys of their houses or from trees in their yards. My father said he doubted that anything like that was going on, but my mother said you'd be surprised.

I wondered if Mr. Gillingham would see the pictures and tell the tabloid the story behind the Gillingham. "Not if he wants to stay in TV repair," my father said. But *The Set* would want to know about the television set, he said, as would all the other tabloids.

He was right. For a while, there was more than the usual number of Larry-like characters hanging around. They came knocking on the front door, requesting interviews, asking my mother if the pictures in *The Television Set* were faked, if that was really our house, and if so, why was the TV set upside-down. Did the guy from *The Set* break in and turn it upside-down? Here was a chance to set the record straight, they said. They wanted a picture of me watching my upside-down TV, each one of them assuring her that he was not from *The Set* and was not the one who had trespassed onto our property.

My mother refused all requests for interviews, but more pictures of the Gillingham appeared, in *The Set* and in other tabloids. One writer claimed we watched it while standing on our heads. Another speculated that, to satisfy some eccentric whim of ours, we had had the set altered in some way or custom built. The set was mentioned whenever we were. "The brothers Prendergast" surfaced again. "The upside-down TV has become the trademark of the brothers Prendergast," said *The Set*, three weeks after pictures of the Gillingham had first appeared.

My father said that an upside-down TV might not actually be such a bad trademark and suggested that it appear at the start of all episodes of "Rumpus Room" and any other programs my mother might come up with in the future, as well as on all our stationery, but my mother said she didn't think it was such a good idea.

There was an avalanche of letters addressed to us care of "Rumpus Room" from children curious about the set. Every correspondent was sent an autographed picture of us and a letter of thanks in which there was no mention of the set.

We had to do something about these pictures of the house that were appearing everywhere, my mother said. My parents settled for closing their drapes at bedtime and when we were going out, but I put up blackout curtains on the windows of my room and the TV room because I not only didn't want whoever might be watching to see me, I didn't want them to keep tabs on me, to know when I was up, when I was watching TV, or if the light was on or off. The curtains hung from the ceiling to the floor and stretched from wall to wall so that, my father assured me, light could not escape even around the edges.

The pestering continued, however. Curiosity about the Gillingham didn't die down as we'd hoped it would. "This is ridiculous," my mother said, "a twelve-year-old with blackout curtains on his windows."

She said that, now that we could afford it, we ought to buy a bigger house with a bigger yard, a house with "grounds," for that was the only way we'd get any privacy, but my father was against it, saying the house we had was big enough, especially now that there was no one living in the basement.

We could live in a nicer neighbourhood, my mother said, but my father said the one we lived in now was nice enough.

My mother said he was acting as if nothing had changed. We had bought this house because it was the sort of house we could afford back then, not because we thought it was the best house in the city. Now, as recent events had made plain, we needed to move.

My father said that, while it might not be the best house in the city, it was the only one he had lived in for the past ten years and therefore his favourite. He was just being sentimental, my mother said, not to mention stubborn. My father told her he had no interest in upward mobility, downward mobility, or even lateral mobility.

He realized, he said, that this would be a nuisance to those who operated guided tours, that, when they were conducting tours of the homes of the rich and the famous, getting to our house would involve quite a detour and they might have a tough time convincing people that we lived here, but that was their problem, he said, not ours.

He remembered the rich and famous from his childhood, he said, coming through his neighbourhood on that "Tour of the Homes of the Poor and Obscure" that had been so popular back then, gawking at him from the windows of the bus, taking pictures of him.

My mother wondered what he thought we should do with the extra money we were making. Burn it?

"Only when the furniture runs out," my father said.

"I'm serious," my mother said. When my father said that we should buy a better cat and put behind us forever the days of having to make do with Cooper, my mother lost her temper. She wondered if it was making money, or her making money, that he objected to. My father nodded, humbly, penitently, as if, now that his secret was out, he might as well own up to it. He threw up his hands as if to say, "That's it, you've put your finger on it."

He was either jealous of her or ashamed of her, she said, she couldn't decide which. Perhaps he just didn't want to spend money made from something so crass as television, was that it?

My father said they should compromise. We would stay put, he said, but we would renovate, redecorate, refurnish, refurbish, remake, reconstitute, replace the house bit by bit so that, in the end, while we'd still be on the same site, not a stick of the old house would remain. That way, they'd both be happy.

My mother persisted, however. She said that, according to her real estate agent, with whom she had recently had a lengthy consultation, we were able to afford "something" in Rosedale.

"Rosedale," my father said. "Why in God's name would we want to live in Rosedale?"

"What's wrong with Rosedale?" my mother said.

"What's wrong with it? It's Rosedale, that's what's wrong with it," my father said.

"Could you be more specific?" my mother said.

"I'd feel out of place there."

"Why?"

"Why? Because the number of people in Rosedale who made their fortunes from substitute teaching is at an all-time low, that's why."

My mother said that, until we had taken a look around, we shouldn't rule anything out. So take a look around we did. On the weekends, we would go for drives around the city, wondering where we should live, looking for that elusive neighbourhood that both my parents liked. It reminded me of going hazard hunting in the early days of "Rumpus Room," the three of us in the car, my parents in the front, me in the back. My mother was still in the habit of looking back every so often as if to make sure that I was still there. We could live anywhere we wanted to, my mother told me. According to her real estate agent, there was not a neighbourhood in Toronto that was not within our means.

"Just because we can afford a place doesn't mean that we should live there," my father said. It wasn't until our third time out that my mother got round to insisting that we take a drive through Rosedale, just to see what it was like, she said. We drove along Roxborough Drive, my mother and I craning our necks to get a glimpse of some tree-shrouded mansion while my father, as if he wouldn't deign to look, kept his eyes on the road. We took a wrong turn into what proved to be the driveway of a sprawling grey-brick house that, because of a palisade of blue spruce, was invisible from the street. The house did not come into view, in fact, until we were nearly upon it, not to mention nearly upon a family having a patio lunch beside their pool. There were some awkward moments while, under the scrutiny of a man wearing tennis whites, who had gotten up from the table and come a few steps forward, my father turned the car around; there was room enough to turn a truck around, but my father manoeuvred as if we were in a tight spot, or rather, as if the tires of our car must not come into contact, must not be so presumptuous as to take liberties, with one more inch of this man's driveway than was absolutely necessary. I could hear the tires grinding gravel underneath, the brakes squeaking as my father turned the wheel. I could tell, just from looking at the back of her head, that my mother was mortified. I slumped down in the back seat and remained that way until, after alternating half a dozen times between forward and reverse, my father finally got the car pointed toward the street and we set off, at a kind of matter-of-fact, genteel pace, back the way we came.

My father's reaction surprised me, as it did my mother I think. I'd never seen him frantic with embarrassment before; in fact, I'd thought he lacked the capacity to be embarrassed. None of us said anything for quite some time. My father kept driving aimlessly through Rosedale, up one street, down another, but my mother and I were no longer gawking at the houses.

"I don't want people like that thinking I wish I had what they have," my father said at last, as if one of us had just asked him to explain himself.

"What makes you think that's what he was thinking?" my mother said.

"I don't like being mistaken by someone like that for someone who gets some sort of pathetic, vicarious thrill out of driving through Rosedale on Sunday afternoons. I hate it when someone like that gets the wrong impression of me."

"I don't know what you mean by 'someone like that,'" my mother said. "You keep saying it, but I have no idea what you mean. And I'm sure he didn't get the wrong impression."

"Then who did he think we were, what did he think we were doing? Obviously, he would have assumed we'd come to gawk and gotten lost," my father said.

"We could have been visiting someone in the neighbour-hood for the first time," my mother said. "Or we could have been doing what in fact we were doing, which was taking a look at Rosedale to see if we'd like to live here. It's not like the car would have made him think we were tourists or something. It's as good as any car you'll see around here, that's for sure."

"Oh, for God's sake, Audrey," my father said, "why do you care about what these people think?"

"You're the one who cares about what they think," my mother said.

"Do you really think that you – that we – could feel at home here?" my father said.

My mother replied that not everybody in Rosedale came from long-established families. There were people here like us, she said, self-made people who had been poor starting out.

"We were never poor," my father said.

"We were poor," my mother said. "But so were a lot of people who live here. Or at least their parents and grandparents were."

My father said that that was doubtless one of the standard lines that real estate agents fed the *nouveaux riches* to make them think they could be happy in a neighbourhood like Rosedale.

"All right, all right," my mother said, "we're not good enough for Rosedale, you've made your point."

"That's not my point and you know it," my father said. "People who win the sweepstakes don't live in Rosedale, why should we?"

"How do you know where they live?" my mother said, asking, as though as an afterthought, if that was how he viewed her accomplishments, as the equivalent of winning the sweepstakes.

"I was just talking about people who come into money unexpectedly," my father said.

"Well, anyway, there are plenty of other neighbourhoods left," my mother said, her tone clipped to signal that Rosedale was no longer a subject for discussion.

There were indeed other neighbourhoods, many others, and eventually we toured them all. Sunday after Sunday we went driving, though the mood in the car was never much different than it was that day in Rosedale.

We tried the Old Post Road – the houses and the lots were bigger so you would never have to see your neighbours if, for some reason, you didn't want to, my mother said; my father, while allowing that he would sooner live there than Rosedale, said he didn't like it.

We tried Forest Hill – just a far-flung piece of Rosedale, my father said.

Lawrence Park and Leaside, he said, were not too bad – he could stand to live in either one of them. My mother didn't like them. Or rather, she said, she liked them, but they didn't make sense for people who could do better. We drove and drove; when we exhausted all the possibilities within the city limits, we tried the suburbs and beyond. We drove through neighbourhoods that we knew we would never live in, as if my parents were merely looking for fresh examples, fresh illustrations of their divergent tastes. They conducted purely hypothetical arguments about whether or not places like Don Mills, Scarborough, Etobicoke, and Mississauga were worth living in. We kept going on these drives until we more or less forgot why we'd begun them in the first place. After a while, it seemed that the point, on a Sunday afternoon, was simply to drive, to pile wordlessly into the car and drive in a straight line away from where we lived, out of the city, out of the suburbs, into the farmland and then the countryside, taking the less-travelled roads until the pavement ended and there were not even summer homes along the way. These drives always set us off making earnest resolutions about the future, got my parents talking in a kind of vaguely optimistic way. They promised each other they would compromise and settle on a place for us to live. There we were, all of us together in the car, all headed in the same direction, moving in consort, our destination agreed upon by all, the country we were travelling through devoid of anything familiar – it's no wonder they talked this way. It would always seem that, by the time we got home, the whole question of where we should live would be settled. Things were going to be just fine and how could we ever have imagined otherwise. And yet no sooner would we have turned around to head for home than this feeling would start to fade, and, by the time we reached the outskirts of the city, we would have fallen silent.

Soon, these manic-depressive drives of ours were abandoned and it seemed the question of where we would live next had been likewise put aside until my mother told me one day at the dinner table that she and my father had reached a compromise which they hoped would satisfy me as well. Having concluded that the house did not exist that would please them both, they had decided they would buy a condominium. Or rather, my father, on the understanding that it was just a temporary measure, a way of securing our privacy until the mythical house was found, had reluctantly agreed when she suggested that they buy one.

We moved into a condominium called Pristine Place One, the most remarkable feature of which, from a distance at least, was its landscaping. There was a kind of moat of greenery around it – that is to say, not a lawn and some newly planted trees, but a chunk of mature forest that seemed to have been transplanted, earth and all, from somewhere else, its colours clashing with those of the nearby park. It was hard to resist the notion that, somewhere, there was a patch of forest the shape of the building, surrounded by an excavation the shape of Pristine Gardens, as they were identified by a sign above the entrance. It must have been somewhere in South America or Africa, my father said, for, although he knew his trees and shrubs pretty well, he could not identify most of these. The whole thing rose like an oasis of tropical lushness above its surroundings. It wasn't until you were almost at the gate that you could make out, on the other side of the high, barbed-wire-topped fence that ran around the grounds, a great assortment of what appeared to be exotic rocks, boulders in fact, from the same or some equally far-flung location as the trees, we assumed, for we had never seen their like before. It was only when we took a closer look, peering in through the fence, though taking care not to touch it because of a sign that claimed it was electrified, that we realized that the rocks were fake, gyp rock, so to speak. They were much the sort of thing you might see on a stage, bolted to the ground to keep them from blowing away. I couldn't help visualizing this prospect: fifty fake boulders blowing about the grounds like tumbleweed, with all the tenants looking down from their balconies.

The rocks were strewn along the banks of a stream that was also artificial, a kind of horizontal fountain, in fact, the same five-thousand-gallon supply of chlorinated water being circulated constantly around the grounds, as my mother, without so much as a hint of irony, explained to us later.

The gate, which my father said looked like the East Berlin border crossing, featured a double-sided booth, with a security guard on one side for incoming cars, a guard on the other side for outgoing cars, and on either side a red and white striped horizontal bar that was raised electronically to let cars through.

My father said he loved the place, just loved it. "A two-storey condo," my father said. "I didn't even know there was such a thing." He couldn't imagine, he said, how much work had gone into that horse-shaped hedge out back, nor what percentage of the monthly rent it represented. As for that weightlifting room, well, he was sure the effects of time spent there would soon be evident on all of us. And how convenient it was to have a ceramics workshop on the premises, he said, though he had to admit it made him feel a little guilty, what with the number of people who had to go to bed every night not having made a pot.

It was the most unusual of hideouts, my father said, a very high place in which to lay low – we lived on the sixteenth floor – but not a bad place from which to keep track of troop movements.

There were closed-circuit TV cameras everywhere, the management boasting that hardly an inch of the building, aside from the stairwells and the interior of the apartments themselves, was out of camera range. There were so many video monitors in the gatehouse that my father called it Mission Control. (We were like a threesome of astronauts, he said, calling down to Mission Control every other minute to ask them how some appliance worked.)

My father said my mother chose the place just so she could, at long last, get him on TV. It was strange, he said, that the only way to achieve privacy was to put yourself under almost constant surveillance. It was the people who might intrude upon our privacy who were under surveillance, my mother said, not us.

"I'm not saying it's the perfect place." my mother said. "But we couldn't agree on a house and we needed to move somewhere, we have to have our privacy, so let's make the best of it."

The day we moved in, my father and I went on a tour of the building, for we had given it only a cursory once-over when my mother first took us to see it. On the way back, we were about to board an elevator that was waiting open when we saw a man lying on his back on the floor of the car, polishing the underside of the brass rail that ran around the walls, emitting little grunts of exertion, one hand on top of the other as if he was pushing upwards on the cloth with all his might. He was wearing the Pristine Place maintenance uniform, a blue jumpsuit that zippered up the front, though his zipper was partway down, revealing the fact that he was wearing no shirt underneath – every now and then, as if something about polishing brass or lying on your back made you itch, he would take one hand off the cloth to frantically scratch the hair on his chest, then replace it, as if he was holding up the rail and couldn't spare the hand for more than a split second.

"Fingerprints on brass," he said. "There is nothing worse. Nothing. Keeping six elevators clean is quite a job, as anyone who's ever done this kind of work can tell you. You, for instance," he said, looking at me, "you've never spent an afternoon lying on your back doing this kind of work, have ya?" He winked at my father in a kind of send-up of the notion that they were fellow working men, as if to say, in a way that my father was meant to see through, "wasn't it something to be that age, wasn't it something not to be faced with work like this?"

I shook my head at his question, though I knew that it was my father he was having on. "No, I didn't think so," he said, smiling and shaking his head fondly at my father, as if to say that, far from begrudging me my sheltered existence, people of his and my father's age were cheered by the fact that young people nowadays had it so easy.

We took another elevator. My father called him "Mr. Brass 'n' Glass," for his job consisted solely of polishing the brass and glass in the elevators and the lobby. We encountered him every time we entered the building and were subjected, every time, to the same display of disingenuous humility, the same Uriah Heepisms, as my father called them. Mr. Brass 'n' Glass, literally and figuratively, was never on the level. He was always either on the floor or on the ladder and everything he said meant something else. I noticed that, while talking to him, people often gave him money. Something about the absurdity of a split-level conversation, with everybody having to look either up or down at Mr. Brass 'n' Glass, stand over him or under him, the money having to be handed down or handed up, seemed to capture perfectly the essence of the whole thing.

There were others in the building who hung about for tips as well, so many in fact that, whenever we were about to leave or enter the building, my mother would ask us if we were ready to run the gauntlet. She scorned those who tipped, those, she said, who paid a kind of toll to get into their own apartment.

There was Frank, who sat in what my father called the "troll booth," pushing the button that unlocked the front door, and whose response to everything my father ever said to him was "Yes, sirrr," the *r* dragged out in a way that was plainly derisive, as if to emphasize the fact that my father was a pretender to Pristine Place status, putting on airs when it was common knowledge that, if not for his family, he wouldn't have come within a million miles of the place.

Tower Two was an exact replica of Tower One, right down to the shrubbery in the lobbies and the wallpaper in the hallways, so exact that, one day, my father got turned around in the mailroom, left by the wrong door, rode the wrong elevator to the wrong Apt. 1606 where, upon finding that his key wouldn't fit, he began banging on the door. There followed a scene involving the elderly tenants of 1606, Pristine Place security, and my father which ended with him being escorted back to our apartment where he announced to my mother and me that the tenants of the other 1606 were exact replicas of us.

Relations between him and security were somewhat strained after that. He was stopped several times at the gatehouse when coming back from a solitary walk and asked by security men, who afterwards apologized for not recognizing him, to show them some ID.

Certainly, he was not your typical Pristine Place resident, forever going about the building, even if only to get the mail, with his Castro coat zipped up to his chin, the garment drawing a great many stares of disapproval in the lobbies and the elevators. Likewise attired, he would sit at a table on the terrace, in the shade of a blue and white striped umbrella, people all around him in their gleaming tennis whites or bathing suits, chatting and having drinks, stealing a glance at him from time to time. I would look down from the balcony sometimes and see him there, incongruous in their midst, absorbed, or feigning absorption, in some massive, impressively bound, ponderous-looking volume chosen for effect, sitting by him-self, hunched forward, his arms resting on the table, enfolding the book as if to keep someone from snatching it away, look-ing neither like a resident, nor the sort of visitor a resident might have, nor like a member of the staff. They must have wondered what he was doing there, though no one, doubtless to his disappointment, ever challenged him about it.

Once, not long after we'd moved in, when the three of us were getting off a crowded elevator at our floor, we heard someone say, just as the doors were closing behind us, "Those were the artists." My father looked back over his shoulder, but it was too late even to shout something back, let alone stop the ele-vator. There was no doubt that we were meant to hear this remark, the man timing it perfectly so as to make a clean, anonymous getaway, tossing his words out through the doors just as they were closing, not even waiting around to witness their effect on us, long gone by the time we even realized what he'd said. The remark had gotten no audible response from the other people in the elevator, the car afterwards ascending silently except for the faint whirring of machinery, the words, because of the silence, seeming to hang that much longer in the air, as if some definitive judgement upon us had been delivered.

"Those were the artists." It had been said with such rel-ish, such glee, as though the speaker knew that everyone on the car was thinking the same thing, as though they'd been dying for someone to say it. Just before the doors opened, my father had been leaning, legs crossed, on the rail, and might conceivably have looked to people who didn't know him as though he were trying to affect some sort of aloofness from his surroundings, taking the elevator up to his sixteenth-floor apartment like some Pristine Place artist-in-residence, surrounded by people just getting home from work, highly paid and doubtless hard-working professionals, careerists wearing suits, wearily clutching satchels, briefcases, their eyes following the lights along the row of numbers above the door.

For a long while we said nothing about it. Once inside the apartment we went our separate ways. My mother went to her room and, when she came out, she looked like she'd been crying. It was not until we had sat down to dinner that she mentioned it.

"That awful, horrible man," my mother said. "Did you see who it was, Henry?"

I shook my head.

"'Those were the artists.' As if he knows art. As if I don't know that 'Rumpus Room' is not great art." She looked at my father as if waiting for him to put in his two cents' worth or at least second her remarks, but he said nothing. She went on for a while, defending "Rumpus Room," defending me, wondering what sort of person would say such a thing or, worse yet, allow a child to hear him say it. My mother reached out her hand and brushed my hair back from my forehead, looking at me as if to gauge the effect the man's words had had on me, looking at my father, too, as if she hoped that, by thus pointing out that I had been included in this slight, she might prompt him to come to my defence and dismiss this elevator crank with some hilarious remark, but still he declined.

I thought it was me she was most concerned about until I saw the way that she was looking at him. It had been obvious, from the expression on my father's face when he turned around, that the words had stung him the most, that he had taken them to be aimed especially at him. He had felt bad for us, of that I had no doubt, but on the other hand he had been lumped in with us, the family of poseurs, pretenders, "the artists," as if it had been his idea that we live at Pristine Place, as if he had no more claim to be an artist than either of us did, as if it went without saying that his work was on a par with ours. But it was even more than that, for there he'd been, "the artist" as he might have been portrayed by some *Punch* cartoonist, seemingly, absurdly trying to pass himself off both as a writer and as Pristine Place material, a bearded, unkempt, overweight figure, ridiculously incongruous in such surroundings, thinking he could get away with riding the rush-hour elevator like everybody else, an unpublished novelist, living off his wife and son in the lap of luxury, supposedly toiling, though without apparent result, on some would-be masterpiece.

The artists. He'd been a sitting duck, he'd walked right into it. Did he blame my mother, if not for whom he wouldn't have been there in the first place? I could tell that she was wondering about this, perhaps even wondering if he altogether disagreed with the mystery man's assessment of her, if it was because he thought that, of the three of us, he alone was undeserving of such scorn that he was saying nothing. What my mother wanted from him was a show of solidarity with her and me. She wanted him to act as if we had all three suffered the same slight and would laugh it off together, and she wanted it more for his sake than for hers and mine, for she knew the remark had stung him most, but she didn't get it and she resented him for it.

She swore, in the days that followed, that she would never forgive "them."

"It was just one wise guy," my father said. "There is no 'them.' Let's not make a big thing out of it."

My mother said that it wasn't just one wise guy, that it was clear to her that he'd been speaking for all of them, for everyone on the elevator and, in all likelihood, for everyone in the building. She'd felt, she said, that, although the others had remained silent while the doors were open, they'd all had a good laugh about it once they were out of earshot.

"You're imagining things," my father said.

I think it was as much in protest of my father's reaction to it as of the incident itself that my mother vowed that she would never again set foot in an elevator at Pristine Place.

"We live sixteen floors up," my father said.

"I don't care if we live a million floors up," my mother said, "I'm not getting on that elevator again."

The whole thing made me a little elevator-shy as well. I often wondered, when I stepped onto an elevator going down, if one of the men already on was *him*. I would steal glances at them to see if they were looking guilty or smirking or exchanging winks with one another or their wives. Perhaps they'd been on the elevator that day, witnessed what happened, or perhaps they'd merely heard about it. I felt like asking them if they knew who he was, knew what apartment he was in, but what I would do if they told me I had no idea.

I was spared this sort of thing from time to time, if you can call having to climb sixteen flights of stairs being spared.

It was my father's idea that, if one or both of us arrived home with her, we would join my mother in climbing the stairs. We would come and go by the rear entrance to the building which, though monitored by TV cameras, had no guard beside it. Thankfully, there were no cameras in the stairwells, or else we would have been a source of great amusement to the men of Mission Control. For my father, who was so much over-weight, it was an especially arduous climb and my mother would warn him not to do it, to which my father would reply that, if she wanted him to stop climbing the stairs, she should take the elevator. "Suit yourself," my mother would say, head-ing off across the lobby towards the stairwell, my father and me following behind. My mother would take the lead on the way up, keeping far ahead of us as if to emphasize the fact that this was her protest and it was entirely up to us if we wished to come along. We would lose sight of her eventually, but every so often she would shout down, "Henry, are you staying with your father?" I was under orders to stay with him no matter how slowly he walked or how often he stopped to rest, which he did frequently. So earnestly intent were my father and I on the climb in front of us that no conversation took place between us. By the time he'd climbed sixteen flights, he would be red-faced and breathing heavily, his clothes so wet with perspiration the dry parts looked like stains. Luckily for him, he and my mother only rarely arrived home together and on all other occasions he took the elevator.

Sometimes, it was just my mother and me climbing the stairs, but still, to drive home the fact that I need not be gov-erned by this protest of hers, she would keep just ahead of me. I got so used to it that, after a while, I would hang back a bit to make it easier for her, making sure there was always a gap of five or six steps between us. You could see the stairwell from outside the rear of the building, however, and I often tried to imagine what we looked like to people watching, my mother and I, climbing, plodding at our slightly staggered pace, the gap between us constant as, with heads down, we scaled slowly upwards, two lone figures on a stairway that, otherwise, along its entire length, was empty. I remember that image as a kind of mother-and-son tableau from our early days at Pristine Place.

At times, when our eyes met, I could see that my father wondered if I was ashamed of him, if I shared the world's opinion of him, if even to me, his son, a man who, while his wife and child were out earning his living, spent his nights working on some never-ending novel seemed pathetic. That was what he imagined he saw when he looked at me, perhaps, his son who had once worshipped him merely for being his father starting to see him through other people's eyes, starting to measure him against the fathers of his classmates – doctors, lawyers, businessmen, "men of the world" as he called them, as if he had mixed feelings about not being such a man himself.

I was not ashamed of him, or trying not to be, at least, for I didn't often mention him among my classmates, nor did they, taking their cue from me, ever mention him, our very avoidance of the subject a source of awkwardness between us. I was not ashamed of him, but I knew he thought I was, perhaps even that I ought to be, not because he thought he deserved it or was ashamed of himself, but because he thought that for a boy my age to sustain complete faith in his father under the circumstances was expecting too much. Sometimes, when I caught him looking at me, I would blush as though I'd been caught out in something and he would look away, in his eyes a kind of wistful appeal, as if he believed, but had no way of making me understand, that this was just a phase that I was going through, that a time was coming when my faith in him would be restored, and he wished he could ask me to withhold judgement, put off making up my mind about him until the book was finished, or perhaps only until I was old enough to understand what made him want to be a writer. "Just give me a chance," his expression seemed to say. "Don't make up your mind about me yet."

I wanted him to know that I would think no less of him if he was not a writer, or failed at being one, but I could think of no way of saying it that would not make it sound as though I expected him to fail, which, in a way, I did, for though I really knew nothing about such things, something in his manner when he talked about his book made me doubt that he would ever get it finished. I wondered sometimes if he really wanted to be a writer, or if it was just some dream, some infatuation of his youth that he was stuck with now, having built up everyone's expectations about it, his fear of being seen by the world, and especially by my mother and me, as a failure keeping him at it long after he realized he didn't have it in him, or simply didn't want, to be a writer.

6

"Rumpus Room" was six years' running, I was thirteen and wrestling with whether or not to play the Bees for one more season.

My father summed up my dilemma this way: "To be the Bees or not to be the Bees, that is the question."

There was a coming-out party for me when I decided it was "not to be," a party to celebrate my coming out from inside the suit, a party to celebrate, my father said, my retirement, my passage from childhood.

From a part of childhood, my mother said, and certainly not my retirement from television. "Rumpus Room" would continue with the Bees played by someone else, but she intended, she said, to build a new show around me, invent a new role for me in which I would at last have the chance to demonstrate my acting talents.

I would be like one of those stars of the silent movie era, my father said, having to make the switch to sound, but with the added pressure of having to show my face for the first time.

It was at this coming-out party, attended by almost everyone who had ever been connected with the show, that I made my last appearance as Bee Good, Bee Bad not having been invited. I was reluctant to do it, but my mother managed to talk me into it, saying it would be a nice gesture to all the people we had worked with over the years. Luckily, I didn't have to remain in costume throughout the entire party, but only for the first little while, though as always when dressed as Bee Good, I was forbidden to speak. People kept shaking my black-gloved hands and hugging me as best they could, colliding with my bobbing antennae.

I had my picture taken with each member of the crew, and then was allowed to change back into Henry Prendergast. It was strange circulating the second time around, for everybody said goodbye to me all over again.

My mother, unwilling, "just yet," she said, to give up her alter ego, stayed on as Miss Mary. In the timeless, changeless world of "Rumpus Room," where Bee Good and the audience of screaming five-year-olds, and even Bee Bad, the one fallen figure in that kindergarten paradise, all stayed the same, she alone grew older. And yet, in a way, she didn't; in a way, she too was ageless, for as my father pointed out, "Rumpus Room" was not the sort of program that any one child would watch for years on end. One wave of children was always growing out of it, another coming along to take its place, the new children assuming that Miss Mary had always been her present age.

Even after I left "Rumpus Room," I kept watching the show. There she would be, my mother, herself grown older, but the world of "Rumpus Room" the same, the world off camera, it was easy to imagine, still the same as it had been when I started on the show, so that, when she came home, it was always something of a shock to see her back from our past.

Shortly after it was announced that I would be leaving the show, the Smithsonian Institution contacted my mother about doing some sort of "Rumpus Room" display. The show was itself an institution, according to the curators, who said they were making their request now because they were concerned that, what with changes taking place in the cast, some of the original "artifacts" might be lost.

My mother was very excited, expecting a kind of salute to "Rumpus Room," I suppose. She enthusiastically complied with their request for "artifacts," sending them my original bee suits, one of Miss Mary's first dresses, and Miss Mary's looking glass. She included with these a letter to the museum curators, assuring them that, although she was glad to comply with their request for artifacts, "Rumpus Room" would continue for many years to come, a fact she trusted they would make clear in their display, which might otherwise lead people to think the show was finished.

Perhaps she expected an official opening or launching of the display which we would be invited to attend as ribbon-cutters or some such thing. Although the museum sent word as to when the "Rumpus Room" display would open, no such invitation was forthcoming, her disappointment over which she downplayed, saying she had to remember that this was the Smithsonian after all, a great museum not given to hoopla of the sort she'd had in mind. To be "enshrined" in the Smithsonian, she said, was a great honour, much greater than our inevitable induction into the Television Hall of Fame, at which there would doubtless be enough hoopla to last a lifetime.

It was as though she thought the Smithsonian's stamp of approval, as she called it, had elevated "Rumpus Room" to classic status, putting to rest whatever doubts she had about it, conferring upon it a certain air of dignity, respectability, refinement, sophistication, all those qualities she liked to think that, in spite of her humble beginnings, she possessed or at least knew the value of cultivating and was able to appreciate in others, this trait in itself a mark of refinement. Perhaps she hoped all this would impress my father, make him see the show in a different light, make him see that there was more to her than he realized. She still hoped to "bring him in" and thought that her next project, because it would be aimed at an older audience, might do the trick. It must have occurred to her that, after seeing the Smithsonian display, he might be more disposed to write for television. She talked about the start of a new stage in our family history, and it was clear that she wasn't just referring to the fact that we were about to start a new show.

The Smithsonian trip would be a watershed event for all of us, she said; it would give us a sense of a new beginning. For me, she said, it would be a kind of rite of passage, for though "Rumpus Room" might not be ending, my part in it was, my childhood was, a fact which seeing this display, with its mementoes of our early years, would help me realize.

We decided to drive down to Washington, my mother saying that it would be more fun that way, more of a family occasion, a rare opportunity for the three of us to do something together, spend time together and talk.

Throughout the journey, however, my father was not in the best of moods. We were hardly on the road before he was

complaining about the distance he had to drive when we could
have been there in two hours by plane.

"I just thought it might be nice," my mother said.

"Nice if you're a passenger, I guess," my father said, at
which my mother was so miffed that we passed most of the rest
of the trip in total silence, feigning interest in the countryside.

Things did not improve much upon our arrival. It soon
became apparent that the Smithsonian had wanted to do the
display because they thought that, despite its continuing
popularity, the show's time had passed. They had prepared,
not a "Rumpus Room" display *per se*, but a display tracing
what they called the "evolution" of children's television. My
mother was disappointed with the dry, non-committal, and,
to her mind, faintly critical, even disapproving, tone of the
exhibit captions. The word "phenomena" kept cropping up,
as if the very existence of "Rumpus Room" was unaccount-
able, the hold it had on children something of a mystery, an
historical curiosity, as if "Rumpus Room" was a period piece
or fad that typified the 1960s and somehow still endured,
though at a lesser level of popularity, a kind of anachronism.

The captions described contemporary children's television
shows like "Sesame Street" as having "evolved" from "Rumpus
Room" and even earlier shows like "Howdy Doody," at having
her show lumped in with which my mother cringed, since it
was not one of her favourites. In fact, the exhibit traced the
course of this evolution in much the same manner as exhibits
in other parts of the museum traced the evolution of life
itself, prompting my father jokingly to equate "Rumpus
Room" with rotifers, which did nothing to improve my
mother's mood.

Another caption explained that the show was a phase through which children's television had passed on its way to maturity. "'Rumpus Room' typified its era," another caption read, so that from that point on, "Rumpus Room" was a kind of catch name for a whole host of children's programs, most of which my mother didn't care for. They had been her competition when the show was getting started and she still thought of them that way, gleefully pointing out as she went by their exhibits that most of them were no longer on the air.

There was even reference made to the show's "authoritarian" approach to education, with its "emphasis on hygiene, posture, obedience, politeness."

The "artifacts" were in an upright glass case, and did indeed look like artifacts. It was as though, since we'd last seen them, they'd been subjected to some sort of aging process, the opposite of restoration; they might have been articles of clothing from the previous century they looked so old, bee suits that were all the rage in 1843. They seemed, out of their television context, so mundane, so lightless that most people gave them only a quick glance before moving on. Objects brought back from television land, they were ordinary now, as disappointingly so as the moon-rocks which were on display elsewhere in the museum.

It was just the dim museum lighting and the fact that they were displayed museum-style that made them seem so old, my father said. "They ought to have the Gillingham in here," he said. I imagined it, a family artifact, the Gillingham behind glass, upside-down, a caption explaining how it got its name, what had happened to the picture tube.

There were several display cases devoted to "Rumpus Room," more than to any other program, my father pointed out, in an effort to cheer up my mother. In one of the cases, the Bee Bad suit was on the left, Miss Mary's dress in the middle, the Bee Good suit on the right, all of them stapled to the wall and somehow looking as though the people who'd worn them were long dead. It was something of a shock, though I can't imagine what we were expecting, or how else they could have looked. Dispelling this air of decrepitude, at least somewhat, were black and white photographs from the early years of "Rumpus Room," stills from the program, most of them showing Bee Good chastising Bee Bad, wagging his forefinger at him from the inset in the top right corner of each photograph while Miss Mary watched.

Other photos, taken from backstage, showed not only us, but the cameras and the 1960s-attired audience as well. In the centre of the exhibit, a photo showed my mother and me in street clothes, my mother behind me with her hands on my shoulders. The caption read: "The Prendergasts: Henry (Bee Good/Bee Bad); Audrey (Miss Mary)." I couldn't remember posing for the picture. We looked as if we epitomized, were a throwback to, the goofy wholesomeness of television's early days, the two of us smiling, son and mother, mugging it up, looking as though we were trying to crowd each other out of the picture or fighting to get closest to the camera, as though we had converged in that pose for a fraction of a second, though my mother remembered that they had had to stand me on a chair to get it right. How eager, how earnest, how enthusiastic we seemed, as if we'd been born into show business, though "Rumpus Room," at that time, was barely three months old.

My mother said she didn't think the caption should read "The Prendergasts" as if there were only two of us, as if my father was not a member of the family. My father pointed out that the caption said "The Prendergasts" not "All the Prendergasts" or "Both of the Prendergasts" or "Every Last One of the Prendergasts," but just "The Prendergasts." What was meant, and he assured my mother that people would understand this, was "the Television Prendergasts."

My mother said she would have a word with the curators, telling them either to use a photograph of the entire family or no photograph at all, but my father talked her out of it, saying he didn't want to be the first person to make it into the Smithsonian by having someone put in a good word for him. He imagined one of the captions of the exhibit reading: "These are the overshoes of Peter Prendergast, which his wife said we had to include if we wanted to get the rest of this stuff."

My mother said that surely people would be interested to know what the father and husband of the "Rumpus Room" cast looked like. It may have escaped her attention, he said, but the Smithsonian had a policy of not including in exhibits the personal effects or photographs of famous people's obscure relatives. Imagine, he said, a caption reading "This is the actual pipe smoked by Thomas Edison's first cousin George, who had nothing whatsoever to do with inventing the lightbulb."

My mother, ignoring him, said she hoped that in five or ten or fifteen years' time, when we returned to the Smithsonian to take in a display featuring her next television program, there would be a photograph of all of us, my father included.

My mother said he was welcome to take part in her next project, which would be more appealing to him, for it would not be a children's show but one designed for children and adults alike. He could help with the writing or rewriting of scripts, she said, he could be a kind of press spokesman for us if he wanted to. There were any number of things that he could do.

My father, perhaps not picking up on the fervour with which she spoke, seemed to think this was just another one of her dutiful attempts to bring him in. He said he was going to be a "conscientious objector" where television was concerned. He would not be "conscripted into writing scripts, nor drafted into writing drafts, nor pressed into dealing with the press." His reasons, he said, were entirely selfish. That suspension of disbelief that came so easily now and allowed him to become so emotionally involved in "Rumpus Room" would be forever impossible if, even once, he went backstage and saw how TV was made.

It was a bad time, the worst of all possible times, in fact, to bring the matter up, but I suppose that, such was her disappointment with the "Rumpus Room" display, my mother couldn't help herself. She blurted out her plans for what she called "Prendergast Productions," our own company, she said, perhaps some day our own studio, a lifelong family project that would not only keep on producing television programs, but would branch out into movies, and perhaps even into book publishing, and would, of course, involve itself exclusively with worthwhile projects of our own design. What excited her most about it, it was obvious, was the idea of keeping all of us together, keeping the family intact, putting off indefinitely, perhaps forever, the day when I would go my own way and she and my father would be left alone. Here was a way of bringing my father in, a never-ending family project that would give me a reason to stay when other boys my age were leaving home. It must have seemed to her that the end of family life, the end of the Prendergasts, need never come. She assured me that, when I was older, I would be free to work on projects of my own, eventually earning equal partnership with her and, if she could talk him into it, my father, whom she saw as being head of the publishing side of Prendergast Productions. We would all be equals, she said, sometimes collaborating, sometimes working independently, but always equal. And everything we did, she said, would have the Prendergast stamp on it, everything would be instantly recognizable to the public as a "Prendergast Production."

We stood there, in the Smithsonian, in front of the "Rumpus Room" display, my father and I listening with heads bowed as my mother, who had obviously intended to unveil Prendergast Productions at a more propitious time, later that evening, perhaps, at dinner, in the afterglow of our enshrinement in the Smithsonian, went on and on, her tone almost one of panic as if, even as she was making this pitch to us, she realized that it was hopeless. She reached into her purse and thrust at my father a small gift-wrapped package, this year's family gift, she said, a few months early, but never mind.

"Go on then, Peter," she said, looking nervously at me, "go on, you might as well open it." My father did as she said, untying the ribbon, taking the box out of the paper, lifting the lid off the box, throughout which my mother couldn't help smiling hopefully. She stood beside me and put her arm lightly around my shoulder, as if she were going through the motions of a scene she'd rehearsed over and over in her mind, determined to see it through, no matter what. My father stared into the box, eyebrows knit in puzzlement as if he could not make out what it contained.

"It's going to be the trademark of Prendergast Productions," my mother said, as though by way of telling him that, whether he was part of it or not, there was going to be a Prendergast Productions. "Remember you mentioned we should have a trademark. It's going to be our trademark from now on."

"It," I saw, as my father handed the box to me, was a bronze plaque consisting of three circumscribed interlocking letter 'P's, beneath which were engraved the words "Prendergast Productions."

My father, despite the fact that my mother's intentions were obviously good, despite her vulnerability at that moment, seemed as unable to resist making matters worse as she had been. He was miffed at what he seemed to see as an attempt to manipulate him. How could he say no when an invitation of this sort was extended to him? But say no he did. In fact, he said a great deal more than no.

"The family gift," my father almost shouted. "More like the family brand." He said that, down on the Triple-P ranch we would all be branded with it, as would any children I might have, and their children. Henceforth, all Prendergasts would bear the Triple P, my father said, and bear it proudly.

"Must you make fun of everything?" my mother said, grabbing the Triple P away from me and storming off towards the nearest exit.

We followed her outside to the car. Once we were all inside she started crying, waving my father away when he made as though to put his arm around her.

She looked at him. He had once speculated, she said, as to why Miss Mary was unmarried. Well, for his information, it was because he had refused to play a part on "Rumpus Room." It had been her original intention, as the pilot script she had at home would prove, that "Rumpus Room" be presided over by a couple known as John and Mary, John to have been played by my father, whom she'd modelled the character after, she said. Before she'd had a chance to tell him about and invite him to play the character of John, however, it had become apparent to her, from certain things he said, that he would decline her invitation, so she dropped John and made Miss Mary single, rather than have someone other than her husband play the part.

My father didn't quite seem to know how to react to this revelation. His face went blank, as if he dared not chance any sort of remark for fear of how she'd take it.

"Go ahead," my mother said, "make fun of me. I know you're dying to. You must have a million witty things to say about this. Tell me how naive and foolish and silly I am, go on. You too, Henry, like father, like son. Tell me I mustn't know you at all if I think you would ever agree to such a thing."

The trip back from Washington the next day seemed even longer than the trip down had. Guiltily, I had exactly the kind of thoughts she had attributed to me. How could she possibly have imagined he'd play any part on "Rumpus Room," let alone that one? I imagined my mother, holding in her mind, all these years, a kind of – if you'll pardon the redundancy – idealized version of "Rumpus Room" in which Miss Mary was not alone, but shared the screen with John. I doubted that she had ever quite given up on this character, on the notion of "bringing him in" some day.

I could just see it: Miss Mary announcing that she was married and out, from backstage, pops my father, dressed – well, it
was hard to imagine how he might be dressed – bounding out
jauntily to take his place beside her while the audience of children cheered, shouting in unison, at the prompting of the cue
card man, "Hi, John," an historic moment in children's television, John instantly accepted by the children, an overnight hit
with them, in fact, marking the start of a new era in the history
of "Rumpus Room." Every time, over the years, that she had suggested that he be a Friday morning guest, or help write a script,
or do some rewriting, or tell her what he thought might be done
to improve the show, she must have had at the back of her mind
the thought that, if he co-operated, this could be the first step
towards his at long last joining "Rumpus Room" as John.

Could she really still entertain such notions, I wondered,
could she really still think the man my father was and had
shown himself to be since they were married would one day
relent? I could not myself imagine my father playing, let
alone inspiring someone to create, such a character, my father
on television all these years, his John as famous, as much of an
institution by now, as my mother's Miss Mary.

I wondered what my mother meant when she said she'd
"modelled" the character after him, which of his traits could
possibly have seemed to her appropriate to children's television, to the world of "Rumpus Room."

"Rumpus Room" was never the same for me after that. It
was as though one member of the cast was missing, as though
they were forever having to make do without him. Even when
I watched reruns of the show on which I appeared, it seemed
that something was missing, that there was a gap in the script

that we were trying to camouflage, to work around. I had never thought of Miss Mary as being alone before, or else it had never bothered me that she was alone. But now I saw her with the phantom character of John beside her, an absence, Miss Mary incomplete without him, trying to get through life without her ghost co-host, John, by whom, it seemed to me, she'd been jilted, abandoned, though to the memory of whom she'd remained faithful, staying single all her life. This put Miss Mary in a whole new light, gave a kind of context to her existence, introduced, into the paradisical world of "Rumpus Room," all sorts of things, sadness, lone-liness, regret. I would watch my mother on the screen, Miss Mary with a secret, a secret hurt, surrounded by children, Miss Mary watching the antics of Bee Good/Bee Bad. There was to have been another character; my father was to have played him.

It was John who, at the Smithsonian, was missing from the "Rumpus Room" display, not my father. No wonder she cried the way she did when he made light of Prendergast Productions. It must have hit her then that it was too late, that "Rumpus Room," no matter how many years it had left, would run its course without him.

II

THE PHILO FARNSWORTH SHOW

"In 1922 at high school in Rigby, on the Upper Snake River in Idaho, he staggered his science teacher by asking advice on an electronic television system he was contemplating. The boy said he had been reading about systems involving mechanical wheels and considered those doomed; covering several blackboards with diagrams to show how it might be done electronically, he asked, should he go ahead? The baffled science teacher encouraged him.

. . .

"Philo had his first success in 1927 when he transmitted various graphic designs, including a dollar sign which . . . jumped out at us from the screen."

– Erik Barnouw
Tube of Plenty:
The Evolution of American Television

7

My mother's new project would be called "The Philo Farnsworth Show," in which I was to play the eponymous hero, the inventor of the first electrical television set. There had really been a Philo Farnsworth, as it turned out. In the 1920s, in Idaho, when he was still a teenager, he had come up with blueprints for the first electrical TV and had presented them as his high school science project.

My mother had taken a picture of the life-size photographic cut-out of Philo Farnsworth that was part of the Smithsonian display on television. The picture caught the reflection of her camera flash on the glass case, so that Philo appears in a melodramatic burst of white light, holding out on the palm of his hand his rudimentary and, presumably, just invented picture tube. The reflected flash gave the black and white photograph a kind of gloomy, twilight look, as if Philo, at the end of a day in his lab, has stepped outside to have his picture taken, his back to the sun, the glare of which accounts for the lack of any background in the photograph, nothing appearing but Philo and his tube, devoid of context, floating freely.

My father pointed out that, though it was true that Philo Farnsworth had invented television, it was also true that no one had ever heard of him. He wondered why this was the case, why no one seemed to know who invented the television set. Everyone knew that Bell invented the telephone, the Wright brothers the airplane, Edison the lightbulb. There was a name to put with every major invention of the last two hundred years except the television set.

My mother said it would soon be common knowledge that Philo Farnsworth had invented TV. She wondered, however, how she could drag out the invention of TV to get a continuing series out of it.

My father told her that, once TV had been invented, the rest of the series should be about the successive refinements that Philo had made to his invention. He could just see it, he said: Episode Three: "The Vertical Hold"; Episode Four: "Philo Solves the Snowy Picture Problem"; Episode Five: "Volume Control"; and, the one my father said he was looking forward to most, Episode Six: "They Said It Couldn't Be Done: The Non-storage Pick-up Tube Which Operates Without a Scanning Beam."

My mother's original plan was to make Vladimir Zworykin, who had been Philo's chief rival in the race to invent TV, Philo's archenemy the way that Bee Bad had been the archenemy of Bee Good. Zworykin, who had a Ph.D. in engineering, worked for RCA and was in his fifties when Philo, at seventeen, was designing the first picture tube, was seen by many people, though my mother was not among them, as the co-inventor of the television set. My mother saw Philo as an heroic innocent doing battle with the worldly Zworykin, who had behind him the backing of a giant corporation.

She was soon convinced by the network lawyers, however, to abandon the idea of portraying Zworykin as a villain. They said they doubted that Zworykin's children and grandchildren would share her enthusiasm for it.

It was hard to believe that people could be so small-minded as to object to having their father portrayed as evil incarnate on a weekly television program, my father said, but there you go. Why, they might even think that it would be adding insult to injury to present him in this light on the screen of his very own invention. "Some people," my father said, shaking his head, telling my mother not to let the "philistines" get her down.

She replied that she certainly didn't think of Zworykin's descendants as philistines and that she realized now that portraying him as a villain might not be right. The network lawyers were even worried about Philo's family, pointing out that, while everything said about him in the pilot script was complimentary, not all of it was true. Now that beat all, my father said, people objecting to strangers telling lies about their forbears on nation-wide TV. What next, he wondered.

My mother would not yield on the matter of Philo, however, and it was eventually decided that a disclaimer that left nothing to chance, and appearing at the start of every episode, would do the trick.

My mother decided to leave Zworykin out altogether. If there could be one boy like Philo, inventing gadgets that would change the world while other boys his age were chasing girls, there could be two, my mother said, by way of announcing her decision that Philo's nemesis, instead of being the middle-aged Zworykin, would be a boy Philo's age named Victor Valensky.

He should have been called Vanquished Valensky, for Victor he would never be. In his run-ins with Philo Farnsworth, he always lost, always, the way that Hamilton Berger always lost to Perry Mason. The name Victor was intended to be ironic, my mother said, but my father said that characters whose names began with V were always villains.

At first, my mother planned to have me play Victor, for I looked so much unlike the real Philo Farnsworth that she didn't think any amount of makeup would make me seem right for the part.

When I protested, my father took my side, so to speak. It was typecasting, pure and simple, he said, the old, familiar story. You start out playing both the good guy and the bad guy, but you do such a good job of playing the bad guy that, for the rest of your life, all your mother will give you are bad-guy parts. If he had a dollar for every fourteen-year-old who told him that sob story, he'd be rich, he said. It was going to be like this forever, my father said, for my mother was simply unable to stop seeing me in terms of pure evil, evil incarnate, the epitome of evil, call it what you want, but once you've made up your mind about someone, it's hard to change. It wasn't fair, but there you were. He, on the other hand, he said, had a much higher opinion of me than this. He was very proud of me. For a boy who, throughout most of his childhood, had been a metaphor for evil, universally despised by parents and by kids my age, I hadn't turned out too badly.

He told me to cheer up, assuring me that bad-guy parts were more interesting than good-guy parts anyway, for there were far more ways of being bad than there were of being good, being good essentially consisting of doing nothing.

It seemed that he was making things worse for me, but then he half-jokingly reminded my mother that, upon going out in public, actors who played TV villains were often verbally abused or even physically assaulted by TV viewers. In no time at all, my mother was saying that perhaps it didn't matter that I didn't look like Philo.

"Of course it doesn't," my father said, pointing out that I didn't look like Zworykin either. Mind you, Zworykin was fifty-five years old, but still –

"All right, Peter, all right," my mother said. "We'll try Henry as Philo and see how it goes."

My father took to calling me Philo and asking me how the invention of television was coming along. "If you hit any snags, just let me know," my father said, pointing out that there was a television-shaped object in the living room that might give me some ideas. "TV invented yet?" my father would say. I would smile as if to say, "You're still on about that, are you?" "You're all around it," my father would say, "I can sense it. You've invented rabbit ears, the television guide. You're so close, Henry."

Philo. Short for philosopher, I assumed. Philosopher, lover of knowledge, the inventor of the television set who was not to blame for the uses to which his invention had been put. Here was a Philo worth following, worth playing. He fell into the "curiously overlooked" category of genius. That he had been overlooked, neglected, made him all the more appealing to me, confirmed for me his authenticity. His had been a genius of a sort that only other geniuses could appreciate. Although chapters in books about the history of television were here and there devoted to him, there was only one book that dealt exclusively with him, *The Story of Television: The Life of Philo T. Farnsworth*, first published in 1947 by George Everson, who had been a close friend and business associate of Philo's and who had believed in him and lent him financial backing when no one else would, when Philo was hardly more than a teenager. I read and reread George Everson's book, which was more of an homage than a biography, though I read it uncritically, taking every word of it to heart. To me, as to Everson, Philo was an heroic pure-hearted genius who could do no wrong, a David who had done battle, a patent battle, with the RCA Goliath and had won – but not my mother's kind of bland, featureless, over-simplified, invincible hero, whose accomplishments were effortless and whose life was free of suffering of any kind, but a hero in the great tradition, an individualist, a maverick who would not compromise his principles to suit society and who succeeded only by overcoming great odds and enduring great hardships.

I read everything about Philo that I could get my hands on, which admittedly wasn't much. I even read the Horatio Alger novels of which Philo was said to have been such a big fan, books with names like *Ragged Dick* and *Mark the Matchboy*. I read my mother's scripts and imagined myself in the part of Philo, pictured how I would look as Philo on the Gillingham, rehearsed my lines until I knew them so well I would recite them to myself at school, in the classroom, standing off by myself on the playground, my back against the wall of the school, as oblivious to my surroundings and schoolmates as if I were living in the world of Philo Farnsworth, boy genius, teenage inventor.

At home, I would look inside the Gillingham and try to imagine a boy not much older than me coming up with that, masterminding that. I could not even begin to understand how all those tubes and wires worked together to produce the picture on the screen. The picture tube, to which the glass screen was attached and which was shaped like a loudspeaker, was the masterstroke, it seemed to me. Philo had come up with it first, then built his television set around it. It was a kind of funnel for electrons, except they came in through the narrow end, and at the same time as they were being mysteriously restored to their original configuration, they were dispersed evenly across the screen, by what means I had no idea.

My mother came home from the studio one day and told me that there was a problem with my screen test for "The Philo Farnsworth Show." With screen tests, you couldn't always tell right away what the problem was, so the test would have to be studied carefully, frame by frame, she said, so gravely she might have been saying that something suspicious that would require further tests had showed up on my X-ray. She said it was probably the kind of thing that, off the screen, went unnoticed but, on the screen, was only too apparent.

While I was waiting for what my father began calling the "diagnosis," I could think of nothing else. On that three minutes of videotape, something otherwise unnoticeable about me had registered: some intrinsic and heretofore imperceptible flaw, some basic shortcoming, some essential inadequacy of mine that even my mother had not known about had been revealed.

The results came back. I was deemed deficient in pronunciation, enunciation, elocution, though even after my mother explained it to me, I had only the vaguest notion of what the difference was between them.

The people at the network, after watching my audition many times, said that I slurred my words, often running them together and even stuttering now and then, all of which flaws were noticeable, to a much lesser extent, in my normal conversation, but seemed much worse on screen. There was also, my mother said, a problem with my voice itself, which when recorded seemed expressionless, monotonous. All of these problems, according to someone at the network, had to do with self-consciousness, and there was no doubt whatsoever that they could be corrected, my mother said – people who had had far more serious problems were now stars of their own television programs. But it would take a little time, she said.

My mother said that, for as long as was necessary, I would be taking lessons three times a week from a woman in the city named Mrs. Madgett, originator of the "Madgett Method," which the network seemed to swear by. She was a speech therapist, acting coach, and elocution expert rolled into one, a highly qualified woman who would have me camera-ready in no time.

When it was announced that taping of "The Philo Farnsworth Show" had been delayed, *The Television Set* said that Henry Prendergast and his mother had had a fight, which had ended with her telling her teenage son, "I'll see to it that you never work again." Other tabloids ran other stories, which my father and I, much to my mother's consternation, read aloud. Henry Prendergast was said to be mute / stuttering / missing, his whereabouts unknown / under sedation / threatening to kill himself / refusing food / hospitalized / paralyzed. My mother wondered if reading such things about myself was going to put me in the right frame of mind for sessions with Mrs. Madgett.

Face unexpressive, voice monotonous, could all this have anything to do, my father wondered, with my having spent my entire acting career to date miming from inside a bumble-bee suit? My mother said he was right, she was to blame, she ought at least to have noticed that my speech was slurred and done something about it before my first speaking part came along. "I can't believe I didn't notice it," my mother kept saying. "It's entirely my fault, entirely my fault."

My father told her it was no one's fault, not hers, not his, not mine, but my mother kept going on about what I was having to go through because of her. "I should have done more to get him ready," my mother said. "It was just that he took so readily to 'Rumpus Room,' I just assumed ..."

"Now remember, honey," my mother told me, "none of this is your fault." She said she didn't want me developing some kind of complex about the way I talked. She told me she didn't want me thinking that I talked funny, or that anybody else found my way of talking funny. It was only when I was on TV that this very minor problem was even noticeable, she said. It was like the camera making a person look heavier than they really were, she said; in the same way, a person's voice, on a recording, sounded different than it really was. Speech therapy wasn't just for people who had some sort of speech impediment, but for anyone who would like to be able to speak more clearly.

My father also tried to cheer me up, though, to someone without an ear for irony – someone like my mother, for instance – it was not always obvious that this was his intention. The truth was out, my father said. Miss Mary had carried the Bees for years. Miss Mary had made both Bee Good and Bee Bad look good but now the jig was up. It was obvious now, looking back at the old shows, he said, that Miss Mary had the talent and the Bees had merely been along for the ride. "Hit the bricks, pal," my father said. "Beat it, scram, you're washed up, you're through, you hear me, you're through."

In one way, my father seemed somewhat relieved that, for the time being at least, I would not be acting. For a long time, he had been the only one of us not involved in television and, though this had been by his own choice, he must have felt like the odd man out.

"Welcome to obscurity," my father said, telling me that I was now "a part of the great unwatched." He said we should try to get my mother's autograph, or maybe an eight-by-ten glossy signed by her.

My father would go with me on my after-school visits to Mrs. Madgett. The waiting room, her white coat, her consulting-room-like office, all combined to give the impression that she was some sort of doctor – the actor doctor, my father called her.

All the while I was in her office, a video camera was trained on me and my image appeared on a television set situated where we both could see it. She would look back and forth between me and my image on the screen, comparing them, taking notes. Sometimes she focused the camera so that my mouth or my eyes, eerily magnified and isolated, filled the entire screen. This, my father said, was just the trick for me, just what I needed to ease me through the awkwardness of adolescence. What better way to rid me of my self-conscious-ness than to have me spend a couple of months looking at close-ups of my various facial features?

We would sit in facing chairs, Mrs. Madgett and I, knees touching and, holding my mouth between her thumbs and forefingers, she would work it into all sorts of shapes, all the while telling me to watch the screen to see what my mouth was doing when I spoke certain words. Sometimes, she even took hold of my tongue while I was speaking, making it behave, she called it, moving it the way it was supposed to move or holding it still. She would pronounce a word "cor-rectly," then have me pronounce it.

I could see right away that I was in an absurd predicament, trying to learn correct pronunciation from a woman who, as far as I could tell, pronounced words no differently than I did.

As the weeks passed and I was making, at least in Mrs. Madgett's estimation, no progress whatsoever, all sorts of things began going through my mind. I kept asking my father what was really wrong with my audition, for I won-dered if maybe there had been a lot more wrong with it than they were letting on. Did my mother really think I'd ever be good enough for speaking parts, was the speech therapy just an excuse to keep me off the show, something to keep me busy until they thought I was ready for the truth, which was that I would never act again?

Walking home, I was often on the verge of crying with frus-tration. The thought that my return to television depended on my pronouncing words to the satisfaction of this impossible-to-please elocution expert, that, while I was there, day after day, making, at least in her eyes, no progress whatsoever, the network might be auditioning other actors for my part was more than I could stand. How, I asked my father, was I supposed to modify my pronunciation to match hers when, to my ears, they matched already? I couldn't bear to think that, after all the preparation I'd been through, after memorizing the scripts and immersing myself in the facts of Philo's life to the point where I was already half-living the part, someone else might get to be Philo because Mrs. Madgett didn't think that I was good enough.

Mind you, I had more problems than just Mrs. Madgett. Larry, the photographer from *The Television Set*, was often hanging around outside Mrs. Madgett's, parked just up the street perhaps, or around the corner. As we were leaving, he would come running to meet us. In spite of my father's presence, he would snap my picture, our picture, asking questions as he pedalled backwards in front of us. "What's wrong, Henry?" one man said. "Failed your screen test, did ya? Too bad. Couldn't make Mom's grade. Runs in the family, or so they say."

Then there was the treatment I was getting at Upper Crust. Things there had been all right at first, but now that I was going around in such a funk all the time, some of the older boys had begun taking notice of me, declaring that I was getting on their nerves. The idea of a boy thinking that being a TV star gave him some sort of status at a place like Upper Crust, or was a legitimate reason for putting on airs, or for being, as it seemed to them I was, haughtily reserved, they found hilarious. I believed myself too good for boys who, in fact, were my superiors in every way that mattered, they said. Perhaps, as my father said, their being envious of me had something to do with it, though I found it hard to believe that anyone could envy me my part on "Rumpus Room."

I took a lot of teasing about having played the Bees, and having flunked the audition for the first real part that came my way. On one especially bad day, my English teacher spent the morning demonstrating onomatopoeia, focusing on a line from "The Princess" by Tennyson: "And murmuring of innumerable bees." That, as my father later put it, got the whole school buzzing. A great swarm of boys followed me around the grounds of U.C.C. at lunchtime, chanting over and over, "And murmuring of innumerable bees," so that it was all I could do to keep from running. My hair was cut fairly short at the time, in what my father aptly called a "blushcut," so when I blushed you could see my scalp turning increasingly pink. "Watch out, boys, he's gonna blow," the Upper Crustaceans would say, concluding their routine by scattering in all directions as if I was on the verge of exploding.

Reports of the teasing I was getting somehow got back to my mother, who inadvertently made matters worse by complaining to the principal about it. He in turn announced over the school public address system that Henry Prendergast should be "left alone," a choice of words I have often thought was disingenuous, the principal perhaps having come to the conclusion by this point that Upper Crust would be better off without me. It had been mentioned several times in stories about me that I was enrolled at Upper Country College and I doubt that he thought that frequent mention in the tabloids was doing a school like Upper Crust any good.

At any rate, the boys of Upper Crust took him at his word, for I was left alone, more or less completely alone, spoken to only when it was unavoidable, and otherwise ignored.

It had become my habit, before failing my screen test, to watch the Gillingham in my room late at night, with the lights off and the blackout curtains closed, the spooky, gloomy effect that I was after enhanced by the fact that the picture on the screen was black and white. I discovered that, so impenetrable were the blackout curtains, I could achieve this effect even in the daytime. I took to spending a lot of time in the "Dark Room," as my father called it. I wasn't always watching television, but I was almost always in there. When I did switch on the Gillingham, I switched off the light.

I felt those days, what with Larry and his cohorts following me around again, the treatment I was getting at school, and the afternoons I was spending being scrutinized by Mrs. Madgett, that I was under constant observation, the result being that, even when I was alone, I felt self-conscious, unceasingly self-aware, as though I were sitting face to face with a mirror. About the only time I could lose myself was while watching the Gillingham. It was better for what ailed me than watching the colour set, on which things looked all too realistic. I much preferred the Gillingham's other-worldly black and white. You could never for a moment forget that what you were watching was make-believe. Nor, for the purposes of escape, did it hurt that the set itself was upside-down, its four legs sticking up like that.

It wasn't healthy behaviour, my mother said, this spending so much time in the Dark Room. It looked to her like some sort of withdrawal from the world, morbid self-absorption. "I don't want him becoming some sort of television hermit," she told my father. He told her there was nothing to worry about.

"Then why is he in there?" my mother said.

"The mass of boys lead lives of quiet masturbation," my father said.

"Be serious, Peter," my mother said.

My father said that sitting in a dark room with a flickering TV set was the sort of thing boys my age liked to do. It was just a phase that I was going through. And as for those pictures of Howard Hughes, Greta Garbo, and J.D. Salinger on my walls, she should just ignore them.

What bothered her most about it was that, by spending so much time in the Dark Room, I seemed to be setting myself apart from them, shunning their company, boycotting the rest of the apartment as though in protest of something that one or both of them had done. It was not her idea of how families should act in what she called "a time of crisis."

"Everyone should pull together," she said. "The three of us should help each other."

"Talk to him, Peter," I heard my mother tell my father, "really talk to him, O.K.?" as if it was for want of a father I could really talk to that I had taken to sitting in a dark room watching television.

Those afternoons that I did not spend at Mrs. Madgett's, late November afternoons with darkness falling and a cold wind blowing leaves across the yard, my father and I sat in front of the Gillingham, not having the kind of earnest conversation she imagined we were having, but merely sitting there in silence, watching suppertime reruns of the early episodes of "Rumpus Room," which we found hilarious, and which made us feel nostalgic for our own early days. We would try to remember what we had done the day the episode we were watching had been taped. Most of the time we were guessing or pretending to remember, but now and then we were certain we remembered, one of us agreeing instantly with the other's recollection. We'd remember having gone to Fran's restaurant afterwards, eating ice cream sundaes while sitting on the stools along the counter, spinning the stools, going so low that the man behind the counter couldn't see us. Sometimes, the TV images called up memories in such detail that I even felt the way I felt back then, as if the things that had happened since had really not yet happened.

It was hard not to believe that the rest of our past was just off screen, peripherally recorded, attached to what was on screen, trailing along with it, but out of sight, inaccessible, our younger selves, our former lives, off in the wings, still going on while we sat there, watching.

My father did his best to cheer me up. He said my mother was holding auditions for our real-life roles and that, if we weren't careful, both of us would be replaced. Why, just the other day, he said, he had come home to find a fat man with a beard and a boy about my age tap-dancing in front of our mother in the living room, while similar twosomes were lined up halfway around the block.

He went on calling me Philo, ignoring me when I said that I doubted I would ever get the part. He said that, though he hadn't quite figured out what it was yet, there had to be some connection between the fact that a teenager had invented television and the amount of television watched by teenagers. He made up his own version of the invention of the television set. Like any teenager, he said, there was nothing Philo Farnsworth would rather do than watch television, but since it was 1924 and TV had not yet been invented, he had to do that first. It was his original intention to invent it in, say, six months, then spend the rest of his teenage years sitting slack-mouthed in front of it, eating junk food. Had he succeeded within that length of time, Philo would not only have been the inventor of the television set, but also the world's first couch potato, but it took him longer to invent it than he thought it would; he faced opposition from every corner. No one doubted that he could do it, they just thought that, even though it was not invented yet, television was harmful to children and would result in a lot less homework being done. So it was that, while most teenagers are forbidden to watch television, Philo was forbidden to invent it. His teachers and parents were forever on the lookout for his blueprints, many of which they destroyed. All this interference slowed him down. By the time he was finished, he was almost thirty, by which time there was nothing he would rather do than make money, so he sold the patent of the television set to RCA.

Incidentally, my father said, the couch potato was named in honour of Philo's home state of Idaho, the staple crop of which was potatoes. Had Philo been from Iowa, the name for people who vegetate in front of television sets would have been couch corn. If he'd been from Georgia, it would have been couch peach.

My mother began to lose patience with both of us. Here I was, in danger of losing the part of Philo Farnsworth; here was my father, who was supposed to be "really talking to me," and, when she got home from work, all she could hear coming from the Dark Room was laughter.

She opened the door without knocking once and was taken aback to find us slumped in the near darkness in our armchairs, which were surrounded by several days' worth of candy bar wrappers, chip bags, pop cans. She said nothing, just slammed the door and went down the hallway to her room, from which she did not emerge all evening.

As what we would remember as "the Madgett months" passed, I spent more and more time in the Dark Room. My mother saw it as the reason I was doing so poorly at Mrs. Madgett's, though, to me, especially now that my father was joining me in there, it was one of the few good things I could look forward to each day.

It wasn't just losing the part of Philo that I was afraid of. There was the intolerable idea of my mother going on without me, leaving me behind, and the thought of how disappointed she would be. I didn't want to spoil her plans for Prendergast Productions.

"You don't blame me for your not getting the part, do you, Henry?" she'd say, putting her hands on my shoulders. I assured her I didn't, but she was not convinced.

"Then why are you spending so much time in there?" she said, pointing towards my room.

I shrugged.

"If it was up to me you'd have the part," she said, "but it's not just up to me, sweetheart. Mrs. Madgett was their idea, not mine. You know that, don't you?"

I nodded.

"Do you want to stop going to see her? You can if you want to, you know. No one's forcing you to go."

"But then I wouldn't get the part, right?" I said. She shook her head sympathetically. "Then I'll keep going," I said.

My mother, perhaps hoping to counter what she thought of as the well-meant but harmful influence my father was having on me, decided that she and I should spend more time together.

"You'll have to entertain yourself today, Peter," my mother would tell my father at the breakfast table. "Henry and I have things to do and places to go. Hey, Henry?"

The sight of two people so awkward with one another setting out, like partners in doom, to spend the day together so tickled my father that, as he was seeing us to the door, it was all he could do to keep from laughing.

We went to movies, museums, planetariums, all of which I enjoyed, though my mother would not take my word for it, mistaking my reserved manner for unhappiness. She was forever asking me if I was having fun, or if there was something else I would rather be doing.

Once, we went to Fran's, where my mother thought it might be fun to sit at the counter instead of in a booth. "How's the food, Henry?" my mother kept saying, raising her voice to a kind of cajoling half-shout. "It's good, is it? Is it good?" All along the counter, heads turned, the other customers staring, not at my mother, but at me, as if they were wondering what was wrong with me that I had to be addressed at such a volume.

My embarrassment at thus being made the centre of attention went unnoticed by my mother. Completely lacking in this type of self-consciousness herself, she was oblivious to it in others, and noticed only that I seemed to have grown even more discontented, which led to a renewed attempt on her part to cheer me up.

"It's good food, hey, Henry?" my mother said, to the turning of more heads, most of the customers by this time having recognized my mother as Miss Mary. My throat constricted with embarrassment as I tried to swallow, I nodded assent that, indeed, the food was good. It went on like this for some time. I heard some of the other customers saying, "That must be the boy, that's Henry Prendergast."

"Have you ever tasted better french fries, Henry?" my mother said. In an unnaturally loud voice that was meant to playfully mock my mother's, though it didn't quite come off, I said, "No, I never have," laughing to let the people in the restaurant know that it was my mother that was odd, not me.

The rest of the day went like that. By the time we got home, the awkwardness between us was so palpable that my mother seemed to be on the verge of tears. When we came through the door, my father made some quip that made me laugh. And his ability to do effortlessly what she'd been labouring all afternoon to do without success set my mother off. If we were assuming, she said, that just because she was our wife and mother, she would always be around to take care of us, we were wrong, and some day, she said, we would get an awful fright, because she would just walk out that door and never come back.

"In fact," she said, "there's no time like the present." She put her shoes and coat back on and, standing in the hallway where we could see her, she began fussing with her plastic bandanna, making it rattle as loudly as possible, tying the straps of it beneath her chin.

"I've had it," my mother said. "I'm trying to get us through this crisis and I'm getting no help whatsoever from either one of you. All you ever do is make jokes and make light of my efforts. I'm the only one who takes anything seriously around here."

"Now, Audrey," my father said.

"Call the cab for me, Henry," my mother said, her tone clipped, as if she would brook no dispute, as if, painful though this would be for us, it was our fault, we had brought it upon ourselves.

The cab. I couldn't believe that, though I was fourteen, this sort of stuff worked on me. For me, there was something especially sinister about the idea of my mother leaving home by cab, as if, somehow, it confirmed the worst, confirmed her seriousness, as if there was a kind of finality about it; and somehow, too, her choosing me to call the cab convinced me that she meant it, that not even the thought of leaving me, her only child, behind could make her change her mind. It was ridiculous, I knew she had no intention of leaving us, yet here I was with a lump in my throat, afraid to speak for fear of further antagonizing her.

"Henry, I want you to call the cab right now," my mother said. Not a cab but *the* cab, as if there was only one, as if it existed for the sole purpose of transporting to some nebulous elsewhere mothers whose families had taken them for granted.

"Well?" she said, looking at me as if she knew I wasn't sure that she was bluffing, as if she could see that she had hit home, that I was frightened. Feeling myself blush, hating myself because I knew she could see it, but determined not to give in, I shook my head, hoping I looked as if I were not so much saying I didn't want her to go as simply refusing to comply with her request.

My father sat there, looking shamefaced, as if he believed she was putting me through this because of him, and because he'd been derelict in his fatherly duty of keeping me in line.

"Call the cab." It was a masterstroke, a perfect choice of words, somehow implying, planting in my mind the possibility, that she would not be coming back, invoking the outside world, the world to which, standing in our family circle, holding hands, we turned our backs, the world out there, the world of cabs, a world in which mothers left home shamefully by cab, the presence of such a vehicle in the driveway a sure sign to the neighbours that something was wrong, a world in which mothers were driven in cabs to unknown destinations by total strangers, riding by themselves in the back seat, looking out the window.

When she was satisfied that I was not going to call the cab, she walked out the door, not to her own car, but out the door, down the sixteen flights of stairs. I went to the window and waited until I saw her leave the building. She walked, as though she knew I was watching, along the path that led down to the gatehouse, at the end of which she took a left and disappeared behind the hedge.

Where she went next we would never know. It was hard to believe she was not standing, just out of sight, behind the hedge, Miss Mary out in front of Pristine Place, just standing there, her purse on her arm, out of sight of her family, but in full view of the neighbours across the street, advertising even more forcefully than leaving by cab would have done that she'd been wronged in some way, shaming us in what might have been, for wives and mothers, some standard form of protest.

In her absence, a guilty silence prevailed in the house, broken periodically by my asking my father where I thought she was, when he thought she might be coming back.

"She'll be back soon, Henry." my father said. I looked at him closely, wondering if he knew something I didn't, or if he was harbouring doubts, or if he was keeping something from me.

I was in bed when she came home, not sleeping, of course, but lying awake in the dark. I was relieved when I heard her at the door and then the sound of her footsteps coming down the hallway, her slow, unhurried footsteps, to which she must have known we were listening. They seemed meant to sound as if, by coming back, she had not changed her mind or given in, but that she had all along intended to come back, that she had simply stayed out for as long as she thought was necessary and had then come home.

In the morning I woke to find that she and my father were up, apparently reconciled, though the tone in which my father said good morning made it plain that last night was not to be mentioned. She hadn't brought home with her anything that might have indicated where she'd been. I knew she would not have gone to a friend's house, nor to a relative's, for that would have involved explanations or, if she offered none, have aroused suspicion or speculation that, in the Prendergast family, something was wrong. Nor, for fear of being recognized, would she have passed time in a public place like a restaurant, much less a bar. Even going to movies by herself, given how concerned she was about our public image, was out of the question for Miss Mary/Audrey Prendergast, wife and mother.

The evening could not have been an easy one for her. It wasn't as though she could ride the subway or the buses all night long, or even pay some cabbie to drive her aimlessly about. I simply couldn't imagine where she went, how she'd passed the time, for she would never have put at risk our reputation by allowing people to see her doing anything that might be construed as inappropriate or give rise to rumours.

If her walkout had been staged partly to motivate me into trying harder at Mrs. Madgett's, it worked, for I did try harder, but the results were still the same. One afternoon, while sitting with my father in Mrs. Madgett's waiting room, I simply started crying, for no particular reason, as my father later explained it to my mother. I could no more have held back the tears than I could have willed away an attack of nausea or dizziness. I had never cried like that before and it frightened me.

I might have ended up going back to Mrs. Madgett's had she not phoned my mother the next day to tell her that further sessions with me would be pointless. My parents tried to keep a brave face about it, my father telling me that he wouldn't have lasted as long with Mrs. Madgett as I had so I shouldn't blame myself, my mother not saying much of anything, just smiling lamely at me from time to time. I wondered vaguely what the future held for me, what "civilian life," as my father put it, was going to be like, but mostly I was so dazed my mind was blank.

"Is there anything that can be done?" my father asked my mother.

"I don't know," my mother said, shaking her head. "I just don't know."

I was afraid to come right out and ask her if I'd lost the part, afraid she would think my asking was a sign that I was resigned to the idea. For a couple of weeks, throughout which my mother looked progressively more tired and careworn, none of us said anything about it.

Then, out of the blue one night, about two weeks after my last session with Mrs. Madgett, my mother came home from the studio and informed me that I had the part of Philo Farnsworth. Though I was overjoyed at the news, I was not all that surprised, nor did my father seem to be. Perhaps we'd all along assumed that, somehow, she would save the day. She always had before, in lesser matters, admittedly, but my father and I had come to expect this sort of last minute intervention from her. Perhaps it was our not being surprised that set her off. She called me over to where she and my father were sitting on the sofa. "You have to understand, sweetheart," she said, her voice suddenly breaking, "both of you have to understand, I can't work miracles, you can't depend on me for everything." She put her face in her hands. My father, taking her into his arms, winked at me to indicate that everything would be all right.

"I'd do anything in the world for you, I love you both so much," she said, letting go altogether now, pressing her face into my father's shoulder so that, muffled like that, her sobbing sounded even more forlorn, as if she'd forgotten he was holding her.

"We love you, too," my father said, stroking her hair. It was only then that it occurred to me to wonder how she'd done it, what she'd had to do, what she'd been through that had left her in this state.

Later, after she and my father had spent some time in their room, he came out and said she would not be joining us for dinner. While we were eating, I asked him if he knew why the network had changed its mind about me, but he would only say that this was something I needn't be concerned about. The part was mine, deservedly mine, and that was the important thing. I should just concentrate now on doing as good a job as I could of playing Philo Farnsworth. He made me promise never to ask her about what had happened.

My mother seemed to think she was sparing me something by keeping it a secret, but in fact not knowing made it that much worse. There was something noble about her not wanting me to know, not wanting me to feel indebted to her, not exacting from me a full measure of gratitude by telling me the details, but I felt guilty nonetheless, chastened that, whatever it was, she'd done it for me and had had to because I'd let her down. Its having to be withheld from me seemed to hint darkly at some grievous sacrifice on her part, some ordeal or humiliation so far beyond the normal that the burden of knowing that such a thing had been done on my account would be too great. I vaguely imagined all sorts of things. I thanked her over and over, though for what I didn't know, acting as though I were reconciled to not knowing, indifferent to knowing, hoping this might convince her that, whatever it was, I could handle it, but she said nothing.

Several nights in a row, I eavesdropped outside their bedroom, one night overhearing my mother say:

"No one gets a part without having someone pull some strings for them. And besides, the boy the network had in mind wasn't half as good as Henry."

And that was all I heard, for they seemed to have agreed that, even when they were alone, they wouldn't talk about it.

So my mother felt guilty about this boy whom the network preferred to me and who, if not for her, would have had the part. It was the kind of thing that would especially play on her mind, that a child had been involved, a boy my age with a mother who loved him as much she loved me. The knowledge that, for me, she had done him out of the role of Philo Farnsworth made me feel even worse, and I still had no idea how she'd done it. I knew that, if I heard his name, my guilt about stealing the part away from him would get the best of me. But she knew his name and would always know it. I wondered if I should refuse the part. I considered it, telling myself for days that it would be the noble thing to do. But for all that I knew that I didn't deserve it, I wanted the part of Philo Farnsworth too much to be noble about not getting it. I told myself that if that boy was as good as the network seemed to think, he would have no trouble getting other parts. Perhaps my mother would pull some strings for him. But for me it was Philo Farnsworth or nothing. And besides, the part had been written for me, my mother had had me in mind when she wrote it, she'd gone to great lengths to get it for me. It wouldn't be fair to her for me to turn it down.

8

"Philo took me into the darkened receiver room where we viewed, for the first time, the actual transmission of a motion picture film by electronic television. The picture was one of a hockey game..."

That was my favourite part of George Everson's book, *The Life of Philo T. Farnsworth*. I imagined the darkened receiver room to be much like the room in which I watched the Gillingham. I could picture the room dimly lit from the glow of that first set, the two men peering at the screen on which, barely distinguishable, looking as though they were playing in a blizzard, skaters darted electron-like, back and forth, swarming about, unaware of the camera.

This was the first transmission by television of a motion picture. The first ever television transmission was of the still graphic of a dollar sign that, according to George Everson, "jumped out" at him and Philo from the screen.

Among the other pieces of test film Philo used was that of Mary Pickford combing her hair in *The Taming of the Shrew*. "Mary Pickford," Everson said, "combed her hair at least a million times for the benefit of science and the development of television."

Sometimes, when I was watching the Gillingham and thought of Mary Pickford, it was my mother I imagined on the screen, my mother, Miss Mary, brushing her hair, staring at the camera just like Mary Pickford did in *The Taming of the Shrew*, a movie I made a point of watching whenever I could.

"Philo T. Farnsworth invented the first all-electrical television set, and gave the first public demonstration of it on June 13/1925, at 1519 Connecticut Avenue in Washington." This is part of the caption of an illustrated poster which I had framed and hung on the wall above my bed. The illustration shows Philo T. Farnsworth and several other men in Philo's laboratory crowded round the first TV, staring at a screen about three inches by two inches on which the first TV character, a ventriloquist's puppet known as Stookie Bill, is performing. The caption announces, not that Philo T. Farnsworth has invented television, but that he has "discovered" it, as though it had been there all along, as though he has merely found a way of converting to visual images some sort of pre-existent signal, the origin of which is still a mystery. It is as though not the apparatus but the image it projects has been discovered, invented, converted, as though it has always been there, implicit, latent, as though Philo T. Farnsworth has merely found a way of tuning in a channel that has been broadcasting from some unknown point of origin since time began.

That, at any rate, is the impression the photo and its caption have always made on me. The men in the photograph with Philo are U.S. government officials, the minister of

communications, etc. Such men, too, attend creation, I suppose. Not that the real Philo fit the image of the unworldly,
gullible, pure-hearted genius taken advantage of by worldly
men, a fact of which my father was always reminding my
mother and me. Philo negotiated such a good royalty contract
for himself when he sold the rights to his invention to RCA
that the RCA man is said to have left the session weeping. He
is also said to have taken great glee in the fact that his electrical television system doomed to early, indeed, almost
instant obsolescence the spinning disk mechanical TV which,
by the time of Philo's invention, was only two years old and
which a man named Nipkow had laboured decades to perfect.

My mother saw many parallels between Philo Farnsworth's
life and her own. Philo's had been a rags-to-riches story, "an
Horatio Alger type of tale," according to Everson. In fact,
Philo had been an avid reader of Horatio Alger, deriving inspi-
ration from the heroes of Alger's novels, self-made men who
achieved success through self-reliance and hard work. When
my mother, as part of her research for Philo Farnsworth, read
some of Alger's work, she declared that her own life was an
Horatio Alger type of tale, though she was quick to point out
that none of Alger's nineteenth-century protagonists had been
women. Nevertheless, my mother, too, became an avid reader
of Horatio Alger, recommending him to my father, who
assured her that Alger was not his cup of tea.

"There are more things in heaven and earth, Horatio, than
are dreamt of in your philosophy," my father said.

"Philo" was not, as I originally fancied, short for "philosopher," but meant "lover of, one who has an affinity for..." It
always seemed like half a name to me, a fragment, a prefix to

a name, nothing that one was a lover of or had an affinity for actually being specified. People thought my mother had made it up and that it was just a pretentious form of "Phil."

It's little wonder, my father said, that, with a name like Philo, he spent his teenage years in an attic inventing things, adding that you might as well name your child Anthrop as name him Philo, but my mother assured him that Philo was not all that unusual a name.

My father imagined some myopic misfit, holed up in his parents' attic, squinting at a slide-rule through glasses inches thick. He couldn't have been more wrong, as it turned out. In one of the books my mother acquired in her research, there were several pictures of Philo. In all of them he appeared either with his television set or with the picture tube that he perfected before Zworykin, dressed nattily in pin-striped suit and tie, his hair a kind of parody of good grooming, slick with lotion, the wave on the front several inches high. He had a long, thin face with classic features, slightly sunken cheeks, a sharp, jutting chin. It was hard to believe he had invented the picture tube and was not merely some model who had been hired to pose with it for advertising purposes. He looked, my father said, like a cross between F. Scott Fitzgerald and Rudolph Valentino. It was hard to imagine him wearing anything else, hard not to picture him in his laboratory, dressed as though for some affair of state, performing his experiments, his starched cuffs extending from his coat sleeves as he lit a Bunsen burner – the elegant inventor, my father called him. He must have stuck out like a sore thumb in the Idaho of the 1920s.

Zworykin, on the other hand, an employee of RCA, looked every bit the lab man, balding, stern-looking, bespectacled, staring grimly at the camera while holding in his hands a gadget that looked like a potato ricer. Zworykin looked as though he had arrived at his version of television incrementally, methodically, through umpteen repetitions of the same experiment, sweating day after day, month after month, in his lab, while Philo looked as though the invention of TV had not taxed him in the least, but had been the result of an afternoon spent musing in the shade.

One of the reasons the network had opposed my getting the part of Philo was that I looked almost nothing like him. I probably, at the age of fourteen, bore more resemblance to the middle-aged Zworykin than I did to Philo. Still, the makeup and costume people made the most of what they had to work with. I was made to look as though I had stepped straight out of some 1950s gangster film. I wore a double-breasted suit, black with white pin-stripes and with extra wide, flared out lapels, a pink silk handkerchief protruding from my pocket, a white, stud-collared, cuff-linked shirt, a flashy blue silk tie. My slacks were likewise black with white pin-stripes; baggy to the point of looking about three quarters inflated, they covered all but the toes of the wide, flat-soled Florsheims I would always wear as Philo. My hair, slicked with lotion, was combed straight back from my forehead. I was given sunken cheeks, prominent cheek bones. They managed, by a combination of makeup and camera and lighting tricks, to camouflage or at least tone down my Prendergast chin. Still and all, I thought the end result looked more like Henry Prendergast than Philo Farnsworth.

In the weeks leading up to the taping of the first season's episodes of "The Philo Farnsworth Show," we ran through all the scripts at home, in the evenings or on weekend afternoons. My mother did not have any on-screen role in the show, the network having told her that she was too well known as Miss Mary to play any other television part, even the one she wanted, which was that of Philo's mother, a very Miss Mary-like character. She didn't seem to mind much, saying it was just as well, since she had too much on her plate already.

My mother would go around the house a couple of hours before each run-through would take place, handing out the scripts, even giving one to my father who, for a while at least, was only too glad to take part. Our respective speaking parts were highlighted with different coloured pencil. My mother's colour was blue, my father's red, and mine green.

At first, my mother had had my father read the part of Mr. Farnsworth, but, as he refused, in her words, to take the part seriously, she demoted him to what he called the "bit parts," though she preferred the term "secondary characters." Therefore, the ratio of any one of the other colours to red in the script was always about twenty to one. There would be great blocks of green and blue, interspersed with little red one-liners, or even "one-worders," as my father called them. He would scan the script before the reading, complaining about the number of one-worders my mother had given him.

My father would make the most of his lines, however. While my mother and I would simply read, the point being merely to familiarize ourselves with the script, my father, as this would be his only chance to say the lines, would deliver them in the manner of some rude mechanical from Shakespeare, hamming it up, making great expansive gestures with his hands, adopting a Richard Burton kind of voice.

"Would you like me to check the oil?" my father would say, one hand upheld and quivering, looking around at the rest of us as though the question were unanswerable, imponderable, the last line of some soliloquy addressed to God himself.

"First house on your right after you pass the church," he'd say, with such vehemence it might have been a death threat, slamming his fist down on the table so that my mother and I would jump.

After a while, deeming his presence too disruptive, my mother told him he would either have to speak his lines the way that we spoke ours or not speak them at all. He promised to do the former but, after several times breaking the promise, was banished from the table. He didn't mind, he said, because now, not having read the script beforehand, he could watch the show on TV without already knowing what would happen.

The first thirteen episodes of "The Philo Farnsworth Show" were filmed at the network studios in New York over the course of ten weeks in the summer of 1973 and began airing that September. I was by no means living what I had previously imagined to be the life of a television star. In New York, all my mother and I did was work, all we saw was the studio and the hotel, at which we did nothing but eat and sleep – and after that we went back home, for my mother had got the network to agree that we not take part in any more than the bare minimum of promotional events and publicity. We watched the show's debut like everybody else, at home on our television set.

We would gather to watch "The Philo Farnsworth Show" on Tuesday nights, my father cheering for Valensky, my mother and I simply watching, smugly, my father said, there being no need for us to cheer, since Philo always won. My mother wondered if it might not be hurting my feelings that my father seemed to prefer Valensky over me, but my father said that playing an invincible character who every week was victorious and was loved by all the world should keep me from getting too depressed.

The only one of us who didn't know exactly how Philo would win was my father, whose reactions, therefore, my mother and I would watch closely. He was the nearest thing to a live audience we had. Indeed, it was hard to resist the notion that we made the program so that we could sit around on Tuesday nights and watch my father watch it. We would look at him after each gag to see if he laughed; throughout what he called my soliloquies, impassioned speeches in which the moral of each episode was plainly stated, we would watch him to see if he was suitably impressed, as we would during any big scene in which some sort of emotional outburst was called for.

My mother said my father watched me in the show the way other fathers watched their children in the Christmas play, just to get a kick out of seeing me in costume and make-up and to see how well I'd memorized my lines. As for the show itself, she said, he seemed to have no interest in it at all, though he assured her this was not the case. It was just, he said, that a suspension of disbelief was impossible when your wife had written the script and your son was acting it out.

The series began with Philo at school, a social outcast because of his intelligence, tinkering about in his attic laboratory, "discovering" TV, aware from the very beginning of the importance of what he was doing. He worked with the blinds drawn which, in the first episode, led to a raid by police, whose belief that drawn blinds were certain proof that a crime was taking place the audience was meant to be sympathetic with, though it was unfounded in Philo's case. When he explained to them the nature of his experiments, the two officers became his allies, vowing to protect him from as yet unspecified enemies until TV had been invented.

Subsequent episodes followed Philo through a kind of "agony of genius" period, the agony being signalled by him wiping the back of his hand across his forehead from time to time. After school and on his summer holidays, he grappled with his invention; in one episode, he took his blueprints for the first ever electrical television set to his high school teacher, known on the show as "Teacher Tolman," and who, in a departure from the historical record, renounced him as a dreamer who would never amount to anything.

It was my mother's plan that the series would culminate sometime in the, we hoped, distant future, with Philo winning the great television race and inventing TV. How she was going to play out the invention of television over so many episodes she still wasn't sure, but that she would somehow be able to manage it was borne out by the fact that, by the thirteenth and final episode of the first season, Philo was still being denounced as a crank by almost everyone he knew.

The show was popular right from the start, though there was no indication in that first year of just how big a hit it would eventually be or what form the adulation of the TV audience would take. Philo himself was an instant hit, not only with boys and girls his age, but with adults. He was hyper-moralistic, hyper-wholesome, the way superheroes are when dressed in civvies, an almost saint-like figure whose own parents, Mr. and Mrs. Farnsworth, were in awe of him, forever learning from him, forever being shown by him the error of their ways, shaking their heads in humble admiration at the end of every episode, giving each other a congratulatory hug for having been blessed with such a boy. Shyster lawyers, rapacious thieves, corrupt politicians, exploitative business-men, Philo walked unfazed through them all, remaining true to his work, his mission, which was first to invent TV and then to use it to make the world a better place.

The world of "The Philo Farnsworth Show" was a strange world, one in which nobody seemed to see anything unusual about teenagers owning laboratories or inventing gadgets that would change the world. It might have been how all inventions came about for the matter-of-fact way that everyone around them carried on. When Philo talked over with them the prob-lems involved in competing with a teenager backed by multi-millionaires, his parents never seemed the least surprised to hear of the existence of a teenager backed by multimillionaires.

It was the very corniness of all this that appealed to some people who, when interviewed, would say they knew the show was silly but that they loved it anyway.

The show was not a critical hit, however, mostly because of the way it played, as one critic put it, "fast and loose" with the historical record. My mother had decided it would be nec-essary to take certain liberties with the time scheme, setting the first episodes of her program in the late 1940s, so that the show would not have to jump the twenty-five "uninteresting" years between the invention of television and its widespread use in homes. It simply wouldn't do, after all, to have Philo eighteen in one episode and forty-three in the next. The main appeal of the show, she said, would be Philo's precociousness, the idea of a teenage inventor. He might not seem so remarkable when he was in his forties, no matter what he was shown accomplishing; nor would the story of how he had incrementally perfected his invention over the course of a quarter century make for good TV, so events of those twenty-five years would be shown as having taken place in one or two.

At the end of each episode, a disclaimer in print that my mother admitted was too small and went by too fast to read set out the real time scheme and explained why alterations had been made. The disclaimer was the network's doing and, though my mother complained to them about it, they refused to change it.

Critics pointed out that there was now, in the public mind, because of "The Philo Farnsworth Show," the widespread misconception that television had been invented in the early 1950s. One critic said it was ironic that my mother, who had so often said the purpose of her programs was to educate, was "systematically miseducating" the viewing public.

Then there was the question of the fairness of the character based on Vladimir Zworykin. In real life, Philo's and Zworykin's proposed television systems had been different but equally ingenious and related in the interesting way that neither quite worked satisfactorily unless aspects of the other's system were incorporated in it. It was because of this that there ensued between Philo and RCA a long series of patent negotiations and disputes which held up for years the commercial use of television, ending in 1939 when Philo won by signing with Zworykin's RCA a royalty contract, instead of selling his patent outright.

My mother, in what in fact was a gross simplification of the truth, chose to portray Philo as a kind of pure-hearted genius, the lone hero doing battle with and vanquishing the evil genius, Valensky, and his soulless corporation, RCA. How much sympathy was a man of Russian descent likely to get from a North American audience in 1973? Not much. There was always the faint suggestion that Victor was some sort of spy or infiltrator, though the word "communist" was never mentioned. He was forever returning from trips to some nebulous "abroad" with "ideas" that would put him temporarily ahead of Philo in the race to invent television; also, he was forever stealing, or trying to get a look at, Philo's blueprints, or sabotaging Philo's lab. Much hinting was done about Victor's "backers," though they were never named, sounding at times like ruthless capitalists and at other times like ruthless communists.

Philo, on the other hand, despite all of Victor's skuldug-gery, was forever suggesting that the two of them co-operate and forever being taken in by Valensky, who would play along at first, then double-cross him.

My mother, my father said, seemed to be trying to make the race for the television set sound like the race for the Bomb. Indeed, Victor seemed at times to be a kind of criminal-element Oppenheimer figure, with his lab in some secret Los Alamos–like location, only ever seen from the inside, and his team of swarthy, industrious assistants, forever putting together and taking apart on the bench in front of them apparatus that bore, even to the television sets of the early 1950s, no resemblance whatsoever. Victor would oversee their efforts, walking among them, with his hands behind his back, miming his approval of the progress they were making.

My mother, though pleased by the show's popularity and her successful transition from children's television to adult television, was stung by these criticisms and at first defended herself by saying that, because of the network involvement with the show, she did not have the kind of free hand that she had with "Rumpus Room." When this was dismissed as a mere excuse, when it was pointed out that, if my mother didn't approve of what the network was asking her to do, she could quit, no one was forcing her to make "The Philo Farnsworth Show," my mother released a statement she afterwards wished she had thought about more carefully in which she said that critical hits were almost always popular flops.

She coined the phrase "crit hit, pop flop" and touched off a great deal of controversy and debate about the attitudes of the people who were making television nowadays and about television itself. My mother was frequently called upon to defend this phrase of hers, which she tried to retract, saying she had over-generalized and spoken too hastily, that she was, of course, interested in producing quality television and placed a high value on art, a fact borne out, she said, by the fact that her own husband was a "serious novelist."

There began appearing in *The Television Set* pictures of us that could only have been taken from across the way in Tower Two, though from which apartment was impossible to say. My mother, who had been assured that, because of the careful screening of tenants, the proximity of Tower Two wouldn't pose any such problem, was indignant. She tried to find out if there were new tenants in any of the south-facing apartments on floors fifteen through eighteen of Tower Two, but management told her that such information was confidential.

At night, my mother would stand at the edge of the curtains in her bedroom, peeking out, trying to catch a glimpse of someone out on their balcony or at a window, aiming a camera in our direction. At the same time, she had my father and me sit in full view in the brightly lit living room; "the bait," she called us. My father doubted that our photographer would let himself be seen and warned my mother that if she wasn't careful it might be her the cops hauled in.

Every time a TV flashed across the way, my mother thought it was a camera. "I'll bet it's that Larry," my mother would say. "I'll bet that's who it is."

Sometimes, unknown to her, while she was keeping lookout, my father and I would chase each other round the living room taking turns wielding a baseball bat; we would run past the window, my father with the bat, chasing me, then, seconds later, reappear, the bat having changed hands, me chasing him. We also staged strangulations, me standing at the window, looking out, him creeping up behind me, his hands outstretched; he would grab me around the throat, at which there would ensue a mock struggle that would end with him dragging me, still kicking, out of camera range, my feet the last to disappear. Sometimes, as he walked around the room, eating from a plate he tried to keep hidden from me, I would follow him about on my knees, my hands clasped and held out in front of me as though I were begging him for food, my father with his back to me at all times, guarding the plate, looking at me over his shoulder, eating with his hands, greedily gobbling until, the food all gone, he would show me the plate as if to say that it had all along been empty, at which point I would fall prostrate in front of him, beating my fists on the floor.

What effect all this had on our photographer was hard to say, though anyone else looking out from Tower Two must have been surprised. No pictures of these mock murders turned up in *The Television Set*, but pictures of us acting normally continued to appear. My mother, who swore she wouldn't live with all the drapes drawn day and night, insisted there must be something we could do.

He or she was probably taking the pictures from behind or even inside something, my father said, suggesting that we should have the police check every south-facing apartment on floors fifteen through eighteen, the object of their search being any appliance or piece of furniture with a telephoto-lens-sized hole in it.

"It's not funny," my mother said. "We have to do something."

"We could move again," my father said, but my mother said that was out of the question. Pristine Place management said there was nothing they could do except put us on a waiting list for apartments that faced away from Tower Two, pointing out, however, that there was an only slightly more distant building facing that side too. My mother decided in the end that we would hang semi-transparent drapes and blinds and keep them closed for as much of the time as we could stand it and would otherwise just have to let whomever it was go on taking pictures.

Because I appeared on "The Philo Farnsworth Show" looking more or less like myself, I was often recognized when I went out as Henry Prendergast. Not that most of the people who recognized me called me by my real name. It was always "Philo."

"Look, it's Philo," people would say, pointing me out. Others would come right up and shake my hand or pat me on the shoulder, saying, "Hello, Philo," or, "Keep up the good work, Philo."

The fact that most people were very nice about it didn't make it any less offputting. My father assured me that people knew I wasn't really Philo; that is, that I wasn't Philo off the screen. They were either just having fun, he said, or they didn't know my real name.

It wasn't long, however, before my mother was stipulating that I not go anywhere alone, which is to say that I not go anywhere without my father, for I had very few friends. Any celebrity, "good guy" or not, was a possible target these days, she said. My father and I joked about how, from now on, I was his bodyguard and he was mine.

Sometimes, he would insist that we take the subway, just to prove to me, it seemed, that I could still do such things. We would ride it back and forth to school, often, at those hours, sitting among boys and girls my age, exposure to girls being something my father thought I could do with a bit of, what with my going to an all-boys school and not being, as he put it, the sort of young man anyone would ever nickname Romeo.

Those subway trips backfired, however. One morning, a girl about my age who, along with some other girls, was with a group of boys I knew from Upper Crust, performed a kind of mock swoon across my lap, saying, "Save me, Philo, save me," her hands clasped on her bosom. She looked up at me, fluttering her eyelashes like some damsel in distress. I looked at the boys for whose benefit, I suspected, the girl was show-ing off, being so daring as to tease me with my father there beside me. They were nervously laughing, looking at my father to see how he was taking it. When I looked at him, he smiled as if to say that I should go along with it. That, by doing so, or even just by laughing it off, I might have made myself more popular among these boys and girls, especially the girls, did not occur to me. Here was this one girl in par-ticular, still sprawled across my lap, and I was not sure what to do about it. I sat there with my arms hanging limply at my sides, as if I were waiting for someone who had fallen across me accidentally to extricate themselves.

"Save me, Philo, save me," the girl, a girl of the sort I dreamed about, kept saying, not minding much how her pleated school skirt was arrayed, a peek of white bra show-ing between the buttons of her blouse that, because of her position, was pulled tight across her body, her wide brown eyes looking up at me through fluttering lashes, her face just inches from mine – that I might have taken some advantage of this I didn't realize until my father hinted as much later. I did notice how intently she was watching my reaction and thought I would try a smile, at which her air of brazenness and self-possession gave way to something else, a look of uncertainty, self-consciousness, as if she had turned inward for just a moment, but then she looked away and, grabbing the subway pole with both hands, pulled herself up, receiving much congratulation from her group when she rejoined them.

That night, my father took me aside and assured me that, despite being a TV star, I could have friends my own age, girl-friends included. All those boys were jealous of me, he said, and all those girls were crazy about me. Not believing it, I rolled my eyes, at which he rolled his, and went on to say that, since I was famous, I might as well make the most of it.

But, though I nodded as if I knew all this was true, I couldn't imagine myself taking advantage of my fame the way he said I should; I remembered that, when the girl had got off my lap, I had turned towards the subway window, where I saw my face reflected. I wore a pinched expression, my brow knit, my lips pressed tightly together. This, I real-ized, was the face my schoolmates and their girlfriends had seen. My father might be right but also he might not be right and nothing short of absolute certainty would do for me. I imagined the going-over I would get at Upper Crust if, after asking some girl out, she turned me down. "The burden of being Philo," my father said, smiling at me.

He didn't know the half of it. He assumed that I was treated at Upper Crust much the way that I was treated on the sub-way, but in fact it was worse at school, for he was not allow-ing for the moderating influence his own presence and that of the girls had on my classmates.

At the school I had yet to live down my days on "Rumpus Room." I was still being "buzzed" by some of the boys, that line from Tennyson about the "murmuring of innumerable bees" having passed into school lore, so that it was now some-thing of an Upper Crust tradition for boys to "swarm" me on the playground. I imagined the masters at their windows, looking out and fondly smiling at the sight of yet another generation of boys chasing Prendergast around the grounds.

I did my best to ignore it, telling myself it was Bee Good/Bee Bad they were making fun of, not Henry Prendergast, but no matter how hard I tried to affect boredom, my full body blush would give me away. I suppose I was a kind of symbol to them of their kindergarten era and all the hokey, corny models of good behaviour and proper hygiene they had once been so gullible as to take seriously and for which they now had such gleeful scorn. They were getting their revenge through me, chasing their own outgrown, short-panted, snot-prone, satchel-toting younger selves around the fields of Upper Crust. And here I was, no sooner retired from playing the Bees, playing a model teenager, Philo Farnsworth, a boy who, in his hyper-earnest do-gooding wholesomeness, was a kind of sendup of the school ideal, a parody of what the masters wanted boys to be. It must have seemed to them that I would dog them forever, my alter-ego role models growing older with them, some new version of Henry Prendergast being held out for them to emulate at each new stage of their lives. No wonder they went into such spasms at the sight of me.

This time around, luckily for me, the boys didn't have any material as good as the Tennyson quote handed to them by their teachers, but had to rely on their own wits to come up with some sort of Philo routine. They would tease me about the fact that, while I played a genius on TV, I got only B's and C's at school. They kept asking me to explain to them how television worked. That this was pretty lame even they seemed to realize.

More successful, I have to admit, was their rendition of the theme song from the show which actually needed no altering to sound like a parody of something, but which they altered anyway, the original being "Philo, Philo Farnsworth, the boy who gave the world TV," their version being "Philo, Philo Farnsworth, the boy who gave the world V.D."

When I suggested to my mother one day that instead of going to school, I should have a tutor, and that my father would be ideal for the job, I was expecting her to reject the idea out of hand. Instead, she took to it right away. It was my father who was against it, saying that school was about my only social outlet, the only place where I could meet and be with other boys my age. My mother said that this "social outlet" seemed to be doing me far more harm than good and was not convinced when my father assured her that I was just going through a rough patch, after which things would improve.

She was as much concerned about my safety while I was going to and from school as she was about how I was making out there. She didn't approve of these subway trips my father had lately been insisting that we take, telling him it would have been much better for him or someone else to drive me to and from school as we had always done.

She pointed out that it was quite common for child actors to have tutors. It made sense, she said, given their special circumstances and quirky schedules.

"It was your idea that he go to Upper Crust in the first place," my father said. "It was supposed to be the perfect place. Now suddenly a tutor is the perfect thing. What will it be next week?"

My mother said that, since she first enrolled me at the school, circumstances had changed and that there was no reason to expect that a tutor would not work out, especially if my father was the tutor. "I'm surprised you're not jumping at the chance to be Henry's tutor," she said.

My father looked at me as if to say that he knew he was being manipulated and not just by my mother, knew that I had put him in the awkward position of having either to go along with the idea or seem to be rejecting me. "Well, if you're going to have a tutor, it might as well be me," he said, giving me a kind of smile of resignation.

If I thought that with my father as my tutor, I would get away with doing less work, I was wrong, he said, and my mother, as if to mollify him, was quick to back him up about this. I would still have to pass public examinations, she reminded me, so any slacking off I did would catch up with me.

"There won't be any slacking off," my father said, saying that at the slightest sign that I was not taking my tutoring seriously enough, that would be the end of it, I would have to go back to school, a different school, for they would never let me live it down at Upper Crust if, after quitting, I went back. Once again, my mother agreed, saying that our being at home didn't mean that we could act as if every day was a holiday.

My father, who was obviously disappointed in me for having, as it must have seemed to him, given up, continued to take a hard line even after he became my tutor. He said there was to be no clowning around during school hours, which would be from 9:00 a.m. to 1:00 p.m. each day. Getting individual attention, he said, I would do in four hours as much work as

I used to do in six. But it would be four hours of hard work, make no mistake about it.

So it was that my father gave up substitute teaching. I sometimes wondered if my mother saw the tutoring as a face-saving way for him to quit a job, the income from which was embarrassingly meagre compared to what she made or, indeed, compared to what I made. She may have thought she was doing both of us a favour by going along with my suggestion and that my father had only been putting up a token resistance.

My departure from U.C.C. was noted in the tabloids. It was variously reported that I'd flunked out, that I'd been expelled because my presence there was too disruptive, that I'd quit because I believed that, for someone who was making as much money as I was, school was a waste of time. It was also reported that my father was my tutor, though how they came by this information we were not sure.

We began to be referred to as "the self-sufficient Prendergasts," "the ever more reclusive Prendergasts." It was said in *The Television Set* that this "tutoring business" was, for both my father and me, just an excuse for staying home all day, "pent up in our penthouse suite," as one writer put it. It was hinted that my father was not my tutor, just a kind of playmate, the two of us whiling away our days at Pristine Place, "never coming down to earth, never venturing outdoors." Some of the tabloids said my mother was putting my father to work, making him earn his keep, the idea that he tutor me having been hers and hers alone. Others said that not even Upper Country College, the most posh school in the country, was good enough for the son of Audrey Prendergast.

The spare room, in which my mother had a small black-board installed, became our classroom. When she went off to work in the morning, my father and I would sit in our facing desks and begin the day's lesson. In a way, the arrangement was ideal for him, for it freed up his afternoons, which he spent working on his novel, which he kept under lock and key in his study and about which he would tell us nothing, no matter how often we asked.

I spent my afternoons in the Dark Room, supposedly reading but, as often as not, in front of the Gillingham, wondering what the boys at Upper Crust made of my leaving and what they were doing at that moment. I tried not to dwell on the fact that I had felt the need to say goodbye to no more than a few boys who had not really been close friends and who, in all likelihood, I would not be seeing much of in the future.

The tutoring marked the start of a short-lived resurgence of family togetherness for us. My mother was always asking us how it was going and said that she wished she was able to spend her days doing what my father was doing. She wished, she said, that she and my father could tutor me together, share the duties, that my education could be a joint project of theirs, the whole family constituting a kind of three-person school or classroom, she and my father the faculty and me what my father liked to call "the student body." "Well, if it isn't the student body," my father would say, or, "It's time for the student body to get some exercise."

But this arrangement was impossible, for she had too much to do, so my father was a faculty of one, my mother a kind of superintendent keeping tabs on him. One of the subjects my mother had taught in school was French, my grades in which she had never been happy with. She decided that her contribution to my tutoring would be to get me to practise my French with her. "I declare a French lunch," my mother, on Saturday or Sunday, would say, which supposedly meant that, throughout lunch, none of us was allowed to speak anything but French.

My father and I would groan and roll our eyes. "I declare Greek Week," my father would say. My mother would persist, however. She would say something in French, then point at me and say, "Converse or translate," eliciting further groans. There never seemed to me to be much point in choosing either one, for I usually understood next to nothing of what she'd said, and a series of pronouns and articles interspersed with ellipses struck me as being neither much of a translation nor much of a jumping-off point for conversation.

"Converse or translate," she'd say. I would choose translation, for I could usually get her to supply me with some of the words – giving me a hint, she called it – if I did an especially good rendition of having the answer on the tip of my tongue. She would say the first part of the next word, for instance, or a word that rhymed with the next word, as if rhyming and translating were known to be more or less the same thing. We would struggle, in this manner, through a few sentences, my father looking back and forth between us, his expression one of mock astonishment, as if some lightning-fast exchange of French were taking place, a veritable chess match of repartee by two masters of the art.

My mother and I didn't have many friends among what my father, borrowing the name of the tabloid, called the "television set." My mother put this down to the kind of programs she produced, saying that children's television, or television programs that, like "The Philo Farnsworth Show," appealed to both children and adults, were not taken seriously among the "television set."

Still, she felt obliged, because of the show's success, to throw an occasional party, but they were always dismal, weirdly staggered and abbreviated affairs, over in no time, with waves of people coming and going at roughly half-hour intervals throughout, as if they'd all agreed upon this strategy beforehand. Clearly, the idea that anyone could think that Pristine Place was "in," or that living there might be some sort of status symbol, was a source of great amusement to the "television set." My mother's guests paid her a lot of faintly tongue-in-cheek compliments about her own condominium, saying she'd done wonders with it, but seemed to think it was O.K. to be openly scornful of Pristine Place itself, pretending to think she shared their opinion of the place and was only living there because of the privacy and security it offered. "My God, Audrey, it must be like living in a shopping mall," they'd say, and my mother would laugh as if to say that, though she had her legitimate reasons for living here, she had to admit that the place as a whole was pretty hard to take.

Later, bidding my mother goodbye at the door, the guests would often say they regretted having to leave so good a party for one that, though it promised to be a crashing bore, they felt obliged to attend. They pronounced advance judgement on this other party with such vehemence that it was sometimes all too clear what they'd be saying about hers once her door was closed. My mother would try to join in the knowing, conspiratorial laugh they always gave as they were leaving, as if she was on their side against bad parties, having suffered through a good many crashing bores herself.

She switched, for a while, from parties to dinner parties, hoping she might better be able to manage a smaller group of people, but at such close quarters, things went even worse. It was a habit of hers to ask a guest a question just before putting a forkful of food in her mouth, then staring at them expectantly while chewing, her mouth moving slowly, deliberately, as if to impress upon them how intently she was listening, how she was savouring their every word. It was an affectation she had picked up somewhere, and I don't think she realized that she was doing it, let alone that there was something faintly disingenuous about it, as if she was feigning interest, or trying to mask a preoccupation with something else, or as if she already knew, or thought she did, what your opinion on any subject would be. "Do you really think so?" she'd say, a touch doubtfully, when the guest answered her, exactly, she must have hoped, as she'd had it said to her by the host of some dinner party she'd had to attend by herself. But however the person she was mimicking had said it, my mother always sounded as though she were feigning disagreement just to keep the conversation going. She meant nothing by it, but people who were unused to her found it irritating, as though her implication was that, with this particular group of people, such contrivances were necessary. That it arose, not from condescension on her part, but from feelings of social ineptitude, was not something that most people understood.

Consequently, her gatherings were marked by an almost excruciating awkwardness, with her guests feeling resentful, guilty, for each group seemed to fancy, from her manner, that her other gatherings must be more successful, that they were not only taking part in some rare failure but were somehow responsible for it, as if she had found them to be less interesting than other people, and therefore was withholding from them her vintage self. After an evening of long pauses and stilted conversation, people would end up leaving early, mumbling as she saw them to the door, my mother affecting a kind of mock dismay, laughingly accepting their apologies, saying, "Oh dear, the party's over," as if, in fact, the very opposite was true, as if the party was going so strong that whole droves could leave without affecting it.

She never openly acknowledged the failure of these gatherings, afterwards declaring each one a "mixed success." "Well, that was a mixed success," she'd say, as the three of us were cleaning up, but looking hurt, confused, as if she was wondering what it was about her that put people off, that made her such a failure as a hostess.

"People expect me to be interesting," she'd say, to which my father would reply, in a tone of mock reassurance, that no one who had seen her television programs would expect her to be interesting. "Thank you very much," my mother would say. "That makes me feel a lot better, it really does."

At first, my father would go out before these parties began and not come back until they were either over or winding down, but my mother kept after him to at least put in an appearance, asking him not to shun her colleagues so completely as to offend them or give rise to still more rumours about the Prendergasts. They might think that he was hiding something, or that we were hiding him, she said.

My father said he was not too concerned about what the "television set" had to say about him. Even so, my mother said, she couldn't help wondering what people thought of him, what they imagined his life to be like, or what they might think were his real reasons for staying away from her parties or, for that matter, her television programs.

Perhaps, my father said, they thought he must be so inept, so hopelessly untalented that not even the most menial job could be found for him in television, a fact of which he was so ashamed that he wouldn't show his face in public. Or perhaps, my father said, she should let slip at one of her parties that, in his youth, he had had a brief stint with the Royal Shakespeare Company who had let him go because he drank too much. Now, here he was, twenty years later, the wittily dissolute, ascot-wearing lush who, when she has company over, lies passed out in his room, though he was, he said, willing to come lurching out around midnight to deliver, in the manner of some ham tragedian, a soliloquy of bitterness and self-debasement, denouncing his family as mere television actors, unable to appreciate his talent.

"That should put an end to any and all speculation," my father said. My mother said that, all joking aside, there was probably a great deal of speculation about him and it would mean a lot to her if he would show his face at her parties from time to time. He eventually came round and she must have thought it was because of what she said, though in fact it was me who changed his mind by telling him how she was faring and being treated at these gatherings of hers.

He wasn't much help at first, though his mere presence had an enlivening effect on most parties. Sometimes, having been out to see a movie or a play, he would show up late, looking, without trying to, very much like The Husband come to crash the party, making such an impressive, glowering entrance that the guests, even after he had spent the better part of an hour standing off in a corner, more or less by himself, kept watching him, waiting for the scene to happen, which of course it never did, though the looks he got prompted my father to wonder what my mother told the world about him. An incongruous presence in almost any setting, and certainly at any gathering, he was something of a spectacle at these, leaving on his Castro coat though everyone else was there in suits, tuxedos, evening gowns. He described himself as looking like a man from a catering company run by homeless people, standing there, with his hands behind his back, intently, unnervingly watching everyone.

He would tell my mother, afterwards, when she upbraided him for not having spoken a word to anyone all night, that he had been doing what people expected him to do, which was to lounge about, looking bitter. Skulking and glowering came extra, he said. For the right price, he was willing to compose and recite drunkenly, while swaying back and forth in the middle of the floor, the sort of poetry he was rumoured to be writing, unpublishable, experimental, world-weary poetry, in which his wife was the central, mythic, enigmatic figure. He would, he said, drop hints about, cram his pockets to bursting with hand-written drafts of, recite excerpts from, a great world-encompassing, universe-containing cycle of poems collectively entitled the *Vast Wasteland*, by T.V. Eliot (his pen name). He was willing, he said, after having recited the famous "Imbibe, scribe, imbibe" passage from this poem, to point at the most meek and unassuming of her guests and roar accusingly, "the world's more full of weeping than *you* can understand." He would then, he said, allow himself to be calmed down and led muttering from the room, a shaking husk, all assembled would be given to understand, of the man he used to be.

Or else he could stagger in a drunken, yet somehow dignified, somehow defiant manner to the door, after opening which he would turn one last time to face the room, recite a poem denouncing all those whose annual income exceeded his, then slam the door behind him. He was willing to stand there, he said, eyes closed, spits of indignation flying from his mouth, with a drink in one hand, the other hand lashing out, cutting and thrusting as though he were skewering his enemies, describing in great detail how, on their way to the top, his wife and son had used him, stepped on him, how to them he was just another rung on their ladder of success, how he had been a kind of behind-the-scenes creative genius, the unacknowledged source of all their best ideas, and how, after stealing "Rumpus Room" from him, his wife had cut him loose, cast him aside, all of which, instead of destroying him, had given rise to what was perhaps the greatest of his poems, "Rumpus Room Revisited."

My mother said she would settle for his merely speaking to someone from time to time. She denied his assertion that she wanted him there merely as some sort of conversation piece. "I want them to talk to you, not about you," my mother said. "I want you to talk to them, to be yourself."

As it turned out, they talked to him first. Some people, men usually, began approaching my father at these parties and carried on with him as if they had him figured out, as if, in a way, they were kindred spirits, knew what he was up to and didn't blame him for it one bit. One man told him, in a supposedly tongue-in-cheek manner, that he'd done well to land Audrey Prendergast and that he should make sure not to let her get away, yes indeed. These people always seemed to assume that my father would agree with this assessment of himself, expected him to good-naturedly, ironically, own up to his being along for the ride, to be amusing about it.

At first, my father would let such talk go, though he would never give them what they were looking for, never play the life-of-Riley-living freeloading moocher. But they kept on at him about it. They pretended to think that, in their eyes, there was no shame in being a kept husband. In fact, they hinted, it seemed to them to be the ideal situation as if, somehow, the man was still in charge, as if it was really at his behest that his wife was making so much money and doing all the work, as if she was a kind of super-servant to him and he the canny one, letting her think that she was running things, letting her think that achieving worldly success made her the equal of men, when in fact, as everybody knew, it didn't.

For this was something, too: that my mother's success was seen by them as not being the real thing, not to be taken seriously; she wasn't the equal of a man but merely a woman aping men, a comic figure, doing things against her nature, performing tricks. It was as though it was for this, for the act itself, the novelty of her routine, that she was being paid, rewarded, as though a man, doing and saying the same things, would have got nowhere with it because it lacked substance, because it was just for show.

My father, though he kept his temper pretty well and didn't give these men who were pretending to pal around with him the kind of going-over he must have wanted to, eventually got round to exacting some measure of revenge for himself and my mother. He got into the habit, while circulating, of baiting one group after another into impassioned tirades with remarks about the awfulness of television or, worse yet, its "unrealized potential," a phrase which never failed to get the "television set" going, for they much preferred to think that television was intrinsically awful than that it could have been good but was awful because of them. He never argued with them, just got them going, then stood back and listened.

Except on those rare occasions when people my age had been invited, I followed my father around, standing beside him while he spoke. He started to do a send-up of the role people wanted him to play. He was our audience of one, he said. At one party, he introduced himself to someone by reading aloud a list of his aliases that he had compiled that day and that included "your public, John Q. Public, the man in the street, the average Joe, some poor slob, manservant Prendergast, the petit bourgeoisie, the rank and file, the great unwashed, the great unwatched, the little guy, the huddled masses, Joe Blow and John Doe." Someone had to keep the family anchored in reality, he said, adding that his job was to be a reminder to my mother and me of our humble beginnings. He was there so we could look at him from time to time and realize how far we'd come, he said. He, on the other hand, could say "he knew us when."

"Henry Prendergast," my father would say to some amused, though more often bemused party guest, "I knew him. I knew him long before his Bee Good/Bee Bad days. He used to hang around outside the bathroom in the old days. Quiet, never said much. We had this thing where he called me Dad. 'Hey, Dad,' he'd say, 'Could ya hurry up in there?' Ya see, ya see, even then, the signs were there. Imagine a six-year-old kid comin' up with that all by himself. I don't see him much anymore, of course. Times have changed. He has his own bathroom now. We bump into each other every now and then, in the hallway or in the kitchen, but it's not the same."

He said that, around us, he referred to himself as "your humble beginnings," and that he would leave notes for us around the house signed simply "Y.H.B." He informed my mother's party guests that he was now acting as our butler and chauffeur, these being the only terms on which we would allow him to go on living with us. We had gone on to bigger and better things, he said. Soon, no doubt, we would send him packing. He would be the figure from our past, a seedy wino in cut-off gloves who would show up on the doorstep at Christmas time, there to be given a good cuffing by his son who, upon going back inside, would swear to all assembled he had no idea who the hobo was. He could see it now, he said, like an episode from Dickens, the house inside all gaiety and merriment while outside he limped across the lawn, on his way to God knows where.

9

My father. There was a curious vanity about him when it came to certain things – his hair, for instance. Having gone bald on top, he had let what hair he did have, on the back and the sides, grow so long that, when he arranged it a certain way, not so much as an inch of scalp was showing. I could never decide if he did this for purely cosmetic reasons, or if he was actually trying to fool people about his being bald.

He would never have his hair cut in a barbershop; instead, despite her complaints that she could not do a proper job of it, he would have my mother cut it, to save money, he said, though that excuse wore pretty thin after "Rumpus Room" became a hit. He was too embarrassed to go to a barber, not because of the baldness *per se*, but because of the lengths, literally, to which he had gone to hide it, the length of his hair, the paleness of his bare scalp.

I can still see him, sitting on a chair in the kitchen, his shirt removed, a towel draped across his shoulders, his hair hanging, like some sort of reverse beard, down his back. How strangely bare, how vulnerable he looked with his hair down, his bald head showing. He didn't like me to see him this way and usually sent me off on some trumped-up errand when he was having his hair cut. But if the weather was bad or if I got back early, I would sit on the countertop and watch them. My mother would stand behind him, a pair of scissors in one hand, a long black comb in the other. Every now and then, as she was reaching around him to dip the comb in the pan of water he was holding on his lap, she would kiss him on the cheek.

My mother would trim his beard as well. He had what he called a "polar beard," the sort of beard that men who went on polar expeditions came back wearing. It was probable, my father said, that such an expedition would leave him clean-shaven. He had a deep, quavering voice, and it was hard to resist the notion that the beard somehow magnified his voice, hard to imagine any other sort of voice issuing from it.

It was to hide his Prendergast chin and not, as most people seemed to think, as some sort of compensation for going bald, that my father had grown his beard. The distinguishing family feature – double feature would have been more like it – was the chin, a double chin that no amount of dieting could get rid of. Prendergasts who, if anything, were underweight, had double chins. And woe betide you if you did put on some weight. My father estimated that, on any Prendergast, the first five extra pounds were stored, as though for future use, beneath the chin. If a Prendergast were lost, starving in the wilderness, my father said, his arms and legs would disappear before his double chin did. We must have started out in the womb as double chins, he said. The rest of the world, my mother included, was descended from apes, the Prendergasts from pelicans. We were like some send-up of family resemblance, my father and I, what with those chins of ours, his apparent even through his beard.

His Castro coat. I've mentioned it several times, I should tell you what it was. He always left it on when we went out so that people wouldn't see how fat he was, not that he ever owned up to leaving it on for that reason or even to being fat. Nor did we mention it. His habit of leaving his coat on was one of those never-to-be-acknowledged things.

He had found himself the perfect coat for the purpose. It looked like the kind of mid-length, all-season, buttoned-down-the-front cross between a jacket and a shirt that Fidel Castro wore, with a flared front collar that enhanced the shirt effect; though unlined, it was made of shiny, light-blue duffle-coat material, bulky enough to disguise the shape of his body; even up close, it could just barely pass for some sort of unorthodox dinner jacket. He also had a kind of perspiration complex, and it was to hide his sweat-soaked shirts that he wore the coat. He sweated even more while wearing it, of course, but at least it didn't show, so he suffered through the worst kind of summer heat rather than remove the coat. He would sit with his elbows on the table, the sleeves of his coat pulled halfway up his forearms; he always wore the lightest of short-sleeved shirts under the coat, the collar of which would be hidden by the flared coat collar, so that, with the hair at the top of his chest showing and his bare arms extending from his sleeves, he appeared, sometimes, to be wearing no shirt at all.

He hated being out in public places. The first few minutes indoors, before the air-conditioning, if there was any, began to have an effect on him, were the worst. Despite going to the bathroom first thing to throw some water on his face, he would, not long after coming out, begin to sweat, the coat, in spite of its bulkiness, clinging to him. My mother would reach over to take his handkerchief out of his pocket, mopping perspiration from his forehead, or in restaurants she would dip her napkin in a glass of water and apply it like a cold compress to his forehead, to all of which he would submit without acknowledgement of any kind, ignoring her the way we, while rehearsing our lines or receiving last-minute instructions from the show's director, ignored the makeup lady at the studio.

He would try to look as if his forehead didn't really need mopping, as if it was just to indulge his wife's tendency to fuss that he was allowing her to do it. My mother would carefully crease his handkerchief and place it in his pocket or restore the napkin to its former shape, then resume eating, taking a glance at him every few seconds to see how he was doing, her eyes peeled for that first bead of perspiration on his forehead, giving him a little touch-up now and then.

The body supports a large stomach by thrusting it straight out, the spine arching inwards so that there is less pressure on the neck and shoulders, one of the effects of which is to make the stomach look even larger than it is. So it was with my father, who would stand and walk as though he was piled high with heavy boxes, his head held back as if to allow him to see around them. He had the posture of a baseball park vendor, his stomach as he walked swaying slightly from side to side as though it were suspended from his neck by strings. All of this gave him a kind of permanent appraising aspect, as though he were constantly leaning back to get a good look at things, people especially, whom he would seem to be sizing up while he was shaking hands with them or talking to them.

My father's book. We'd been living with it, my mother and I, for years, but we had never seen it, never read one word of it, or even once heard him talk about it without first being asked, and even then he told us next to nothing. I had come to think of it as something he was tending, maintaining, each day ridding it of flaws that cropped up overnight like weeds, but never making any progress with it, nor wanting to. Sometimes, late at night, I could faintly hear the tapping of his typewriter from inside the study. I liked the idea of him in there, writing his book while the two of us were sound asleep.

He would go to his study in the afternoons as well, closing the door behind him while I went down the hall to watch the Gillingham, each of us in our sealed-off rooms, happily pursuing our solitary entertainments, or so it seemed to me.

My mother took his writing more seriously. She would ask him how the book was going and, if he told her it was going badly or slowly, as he almost always did, his voice full of irritation as if it had been five minutes since she last asked him, she would tell him what she did when her scripts were going badly.

"I often find a good walk helps," my mother would say, "or listening to music."

My father would reply that, as writing a novel was not the same as writing a television script, and as, in any case, no two people were the same, it was unlikely that what worked for her would work for him.

"Just trying to help," my mother would say, putting up both hands as if to say, "Don't shoot."

"Listening to music," I once heard him mutter to himself when she was out of earshot. "I wonder which one of Beethoven's symphonies gave rise to 'Rumpus Room.'" But when he saw that I had not only overheard him but that I was laughing, he looked contrite and, putting his hands on my shoulders, said "I don't want you laughing at your mother, Henry." When I protested that it was what he'd said about her that had made me laugh, he nodded his head. "I know," he said. "But that was just a joke."

My father wouldn't even let us see the book, literally see it, let alone read it. Nor would he tell us what it was about, except to assure us, when we speculated that it must be about us, that it was not.

Finally, after we had pestered him a great deal about it, he said the book was about a man like him in what he called "different circumstances."

"What do you mean, 'different circumstances'?" my mother said.

"Different than mine, different than these," my father said, shrugging as if his meaning was obvious and taking in the apartment, the whole of Pristine Place, it seemed, with a sweep of his hand.

My mother seemed put out by this, though she said nothing until after I had gone to bed. I heard them out there, talking, not quite arguing, not quite raising their voices, my mother, her tone half wounded, half accusatory, my father protesting himself innocent of something. They went on for a long time. Indeed, it was one of the longest conversations I could remember them having.

It came out in subsequent days that, among the "circumstances" excluded from this book that featured him was us, her and me, and it was *that* she didn't like, *that* she didn't understand, about *that* she was seeking reassurance, about *that* he was having to explain himself. Why would he put himself in a book and leave us out?

"I said it was about a man like me," my father said, adding that he'd left a lot of people out, not just us. The only person he was sure wouldn't mind being in the book was himself, and even he wasn't really himself. She was hard to please, he said, her greatest worry all along having been that he *was* writing about us, that he was writing some sort of barely fictionalized story of the Prendergasts. Now here she was complaining that he was not writing about the Prendergasts.

My mother said that, first of all, she was not complaining, just wondering why he was in the book and we were not. When he'd said he was not writing about us, she'd assumed he meant himself, too. He was one of us, wasn't he? Of course, my father said.

"Then why are you in the book when the rest of us aren't?"

"Because I wrote it that way," my father said, "because that's the way it came to me."

Was he married in this book, my mother wanted to know. If so, to what sort of woman? What sort of life did he have in this book? What were these other circumstances? If he was single, did he date a lot of women? Did he have children, how many, what were they like, were any of them girls, did he wish she'd had a girl? Did the man in this book live the way we used to live on St. Clair Avenue, was there anything in the book at all of the sort of life that we'd been living since then? If not, did this mean he wasn't happy with his life, that he wished his life was different? She was all the more anxious to see the book now, saying she couldn't understand why he didn't want her to read it.

My father said he'd be happy to have her read it, after it was published, after he knew for sure that it was good, that it was worth reading, after it had been edited and was in its final form. It was something of a superstition with him, he said, assuring her that no one else had seen the book yet either. And at any rate, he said, reading the book would do her no good in her present state of mind, for she was certain to read something sinister into everything that happened or didn't happen. It was a piece of fiction, he said, not some sort of veiled or coded expression of dissatisfaction with his life, not some personal fantasy of his in which everything was how he wished it to be. My father said reading the book would merely confirm what he had said: that we were not in it, that he was. What it came right down to was that he wasn't writing about us because he didn't want to.

When my father came down from his study one night to announce that, at long last, his book was finished, I was taken aback. I looked at my mother who, though she eventually recovered sufficiently to get up from her chair and congratulate him with hug and a kiss on the cheek, looked quite startled, even frightened at first. It was only then I realized that she'd been dreading the completion of this book for years, that she'd been watching for it, that, in all likelihood, she had not gone a day without wondering what would happen when this moment came. It bothered me, too, the question of what would happen next, for it was clear, looking at my father, that something would, that he was hoping things would never be the same. He'd been sustained by the thought of some day playing this trump card of his, and here he was, playing it and, with nothing in reserve, smiling as though he couldn't quite believe that he had done it. Because he'd been so secretive, we hadn't seen it coming, hadn't prepared ourselves as we might have if he'd told us it was almost finished. And this was how he wanted it, it seemed, for he was obviously tickled to see how surprised we were. One day, the book was as far from finished as ever, still the mythical "book"; the next day there it was, on the coffee table, done, real, material, an intervention in our lives.

"Here it is," he said, and dropped it from a height of about three feet onto the coffee table where it landed with a bang that made us jump. It was in a dark blue typing-paper box, the lid of which he removed with a kind of masterpiece-unveiling flourish. "Ta-dah," he said, as my mother and I gathered round to look inside the box. He hadn't as yet decided on a title, so there was merely his name on the first page; in the middle of the second page, however, there appeared a dedication, upon reading which my mother started crying. "This book is for my dear wife, Audrey, and for Henry, our son."

So that was that. The book, as though it had fallen from the sky, landed with a bang on the coffee table and suddenly our lives revolved around it, and there was no mention of anything except the book.

My father decided that, in his search for a publisher, he would use a pseudonym, not wanting his being one of *the* Prendergasts, as my mother liked to call us, to influence a publisher's decision. He even used a post office box in case someone twigged on our address. He knew he wouldn't be able to keep hidden forever from his publisher the fact that he was the husband of Audrey Prendergast, the father of Philo Farnsworth, but he wanted to be sure on what grounds his book was being accepted, so he planned to wait until after he had an offer to reveal his real name.

The pseudonym he used was R.P. Henderson, R.P. being the initials of his second and third names. My mother didn't like the idea of his using a pseudonym, any more than she had liked the idea of his excluding us from his book. It was as though a second version of him now existed from whose life the two of us had been erased, she said. There was the character in his book, whose name we didn't know, and there was this R.P. Henderson. He had used his own initials but had dropped the family name, my mother said. It was almost as though he was ashamed of us or would find it demeaning to be identified with us.

It wasn't that he was ashamed of us, my father said, just that he wanted his book to make its own way in the world. It was about time, he said, that he had an alter ego, what with my mother having had one for years and me already on my second one.

What name would appear on his book when it was published? my mother wanted to know. My father said he would probably use the pseudonym, the concerns he had about publishers extending to critics and to readers as well – he didn't want who he was, whose husband and father he was, to influence in any way how they received his book. When my mother said he should come right out and say what he meant, my father at first refused to talk about it, but she kept at him until he finally admitted to being worried that some people might be inclined to take his book less seriously if they knew of his television connection.

"I can't imagine why," my mother said, obviously offended. My father assured her that he was proud of his family's accomplishments, but that he simply wanted his book to live or die on its own merits. My mother wondered what sorts of preconceptions he imagined people might form about his book from knowing who he was.

"Well, for one thing, they might think I got published for the wrong reasons, that I didn't earn it, that I was just using my name, exploiting my family connections, to sell an otherwise unpublishable book."

My father, declining all offers from my mother to help him find an agent, eschewing, in fact, the very idea of agents, began sending his manuscript to publishers who, with almost churlish promptness, began sending it back. He went around the house, waving his first rejection letter, a form letter, assuring us that it was standard for a book to be rejected many times before being accepted; he made it sound as though this rejection letter was his first step towards publication, as though his ability to elicit such a letter confirmed that he was the real thing and one day would be published. He had four copies in the mail and hardly a week went by when one of them was not returned.

Perhaps nothing worth writing about had ever happened to him, he said. He began joking about his writer's C.V. not being up to scratch.

He said he had offered to drive an ambulance in the Spanish Civil War, but, as he was only six years old at the time, they turned him down.

The closest he'd come to burning, in a fit of rage, a manuscript that he'd been working on for years was crumpling up a sheet of paper that he'd been writing on for twenty minutes.

He said he especially regretted having passed up the opportunity to stand at the head of his own grave, facing a firing squad, only to have his sentence commuted at the last second to seven years' hard labour. "You can't put a price on experience like that," my father said.

My mother had once suggested to him, he said, that they line their bedroom walls with cork, but he had dismissed the idea.

Instead of taking mind-expanding drugs, he had eaten body-expanding food.

"'In Canada did Prendergast a stately pleasure dome decree' – it just doesn't have the same ring to it, somehow," my father said.

He had to admit it, he said: his youth had been wasted with frivolity. Not that, to some extent, he hadn't tried to acquire the right sort of experience. He had.

Instead of joining the Paris expatriates, he had joined the Toronto homebodies, a group of writers who met once a week in a local pub to talk about how boring Paris was.

"Now, I know what you're thinking," my father said, looking at me. "How could anybody pick the homebodies over the expatriates. Well, at the time, believe it or not, all the smart money was on the homebodies."

And then, he said, there had been that young man who had shown up on the doorstep one day and offered to follow him around for the rest of his life and write down everything he said, but he had turned him down. And so it was that

Krupnick's *Life of Prendergast* was never written.

And he had come so close so often, he said. It had just been a matter of bad timing, bad luck. In the 1950s, incredible as it may seem, just as a play of his called *Look Back in Pique* was about to be produced, a play called *Look Back in Anger* was produced in Britain and for some reason attracted more attention than his did. Consequently, the Piqued Young Men movement, which he had planned to lead, never did get off the ground.

Time after time, the manuscripts came back, or rather, time after time, notice arrived in the mailbox that a parcel was waiting for him at the nearest postal station. For a while, parcel pick-up notices and rejection slips were everywhere and, just as he had been by that first rejection, my father seemed more encouraged by them than anything else, as if, for now, it was enough that his book was making contact with the outside world, that it was playing some part in the daily lives of editors and publishers, that it was out there, in the running, making the rounds, eligible, available.

The closest he came to acceptance was what he called a "rave rejection." My father said he had been rejected so many times that, in publishing circles, an unacceptable manuscript was now being referred to as an "R.P. Henderson." It might have been those little postal notices he hated most, those non-committal and, it must have seemed to him, disingenuous cards, letting him know, without even making mention of his book, that once again it had been rejected.

There was always the chance, he admitted he couldn't help telling himself as he was on his way to the post office, that the parcel waiting for him was not his book at all, but something else, something he had forgotten having sent away for. He would go to the mailbox, hoping to find a letter from a publisher, and to the post office, hoping not to find his manuscript, but there was never a letter, and always the parcel waiting for him was his manuscript, though he admitted that, even as it was being handed to him, he clung to the hope that it was merely manuscript-shaped and not his manuscript at all.

This went on for months, the list of publishers who had not rejected him growing ever smaller. The strain of waiting and the run of disappointments began to take their toll on my father, who became so fixated on the mailbox that he would sometimes check it even after he had picked up that day's delivery. Soon, there were no jokes about his writer's C.V., no jokes about anything, in fact. About the only time I saw him was at our tutorials, for otherwise, during the day, he stayed in his room and, at night, went out alone, often not coming back until long after I had gone to bed. I would wake to hear my mother, who always waited up for him, running down the hall to the door. They would stay up, talking in the living room, my mother's voice a soothing murmur, my father's not like his at all, his tone one of panicked incredulity.

What played most on his mind was not that his book might never find a publisher, but that it might not be any good, that he might have been living a fool's dream all these years.

My mother did her best to cheer him up, sometimes assuring him his book would find a publisher, sometimes sounding him out about the possibility that it would not be the end of the world if his book was not accepted. Surely, she said, he could write other books or revise this one, or take up other kinds of writing. And writing, she reminded him, was not his whole life; it was not as if, not at all as if, he had nothing else to live for.

She said that she and I had always loved him and always would, though we had yet to read a single line of his book.

"You forgot to say that I've still got my health," my father said.

She pointed out that the first novel of a lot of good writers ended up in their bottom bureau drawer. Yes, my father said, as did the first seventeen novels of a lot of bad writers. He had been writing this book off and on for fifteen years, he said. He could neither bear to think of it not getting published nor stand to go back to it and revise it for the umpteenth time, nor, worst of all, stand to put it aside and begin another book which could likewise take fifteen years to write and likewise not get published. He was not going to write or revise another page until this book had found a home; if it didn't find a home, he was not going to write or revise another page – period.

My mother told him that he was just talking this way because he was anxious and disappointed, as she had been years back when all those scripts of hers had been rejected. He would get over it, she said, if it came to that, which in all likelihood it wouldn't.

It got to the point where my father couldn't sleep, was eating next to nothing, couldn't concentrate enough to read, and wouldn't talk about anything except his book. My mother told him that he should stop sending manuscripts out, take a break from it, see how he felt about the book six months from now. He had worked himself into such a state about it he wasn't thinking clearly, she said. Six months without having to worry about what was in the mailbox and he'd be as good as new, she said. But my father said it would just be a waste of six months during which he would worry anyway, worry that the spare time of fifteen years of his life had been wasted, that he was not really a writer but merely the sort of buffoon the tabloids made him out to be. This was his one shot at it, as far as he was concerned, he said. He was full of doubt about his talent as a writer, wondering if he had all along been fooling himself, each new rejection making matters worse. Perhaps, he said, he had dragged out the writing of the book intentionally, stringing himself and everybody else along for fifteen years, keeping alive this cherished illusion of himself as a writer rather than face up to what he really was, or invest his energy in some less grand pursuit.

And then, suddenly, unexpectedly, falling from out of the blue much the way the book itself had, there came a letter of acceptance, a reprieve, a last-minute pardon. A publisher in New York called Densmore and Densmore wrote to say they loved his book and would soon be making an offer for it. My father seemed more relieved than anything else, as did my mother, who said that she would have the letter framed and hang it just inside the door where everyone who came calling would see it.

My father, over the next few weeks, spoke to his publishers on the phone, corresponded with them, hammered out with them, without the help of an agent, what he said was a fair contract for a first novel. D and D, as he called them, seemed very accommodating, even to his stipulation that his book be published under a pseudonym, that his real name and family background not be mentioned in any promotional material, and that there be no photograph of him on the dust-jacket. He realized, he told them, that in time, what with his having to make public appearances and there being so many photographs of him in circulation, people would realize that R.P. Henderson was Peter Prendergast, but by then he'd have made what he hoped would be a lasting impression.

After the initial flurry of negotiations was completed, D and D told him it would be a few months before editing began on his book and they would get back to him when things began to roll. For my father, it seemed, it would be a few months of basking in glory. No longer did he have to worry about the fate of his book, not yet did he have to worry about how it would be received. He was a few weeks into thus enjoying himself when, as though following the book and the letter of acceptance, there fell from out of the blue the third and final intervention, an announcement, a surprise, that year's instalment of the family gift.

My mother, that Christmas, had my father open what turned out to be a contract she had signed with my father's publisher to write a book about the Prendergasts. My mother's family gifts always left my father speechless, but none did so more than this one. He undid the wrapping paper and found inside two glass-framed documents, on top his letter of acceptance from D and D, and beneath it, the front page of the contract my mother had signed with D and D to write a book of her own, to be called *The Television Prendergasts*.

My father wanted to know why she hadn't talked to him about this before she signed the contract, saying she must have known that it would be of some interest to him that his publisher had approached her about a book.

"I wanted it to be a surprise," my mother said. "I thought you might even be pleased about it. Both of us with books coming out, having the same publisher."

She must have thought that, since he had refused to cross over into her world, she would cross over into his. This was what she wanted most, it seemed to me: that their worlds would overlap, that there be some common ground between them.

My father wondered why, if she could have her pick of any publisher she wanted, she'd said yes to his publisher.

"Well, for one thing, because they're your publisher," my mother said. "I like the idea of us having the same publisher, don't you?"

My father said that in a way he did and in a way he didn't.

"For another thing," my mother said, "they're the only ones who asked."

My father said the other publishers just hadn't thought of it yet. If she approached any one of them, he said, they'd be certain to say yes.

"But D and D approached me," my mother said.

"Yes," my father said, "they did, didn't they. Maybe they figured that, because they're publishing me, you'd be more inclined to say yes."

My mother said it was more likely that meeting him simply gave them the idea of asking for a book from her, reminded them that she was out there. And yes, it might have occurred to them that, having already signed him, they might have a better chance of getting her, but so what? It was just smart business on their part. She reminded him that they hadn't even known who he was when they first made an offer for his book.

My father said he still couldn't help feeling that D and D had let him down in some way. Why, for instance, hadn't they asked him to raise the matter with her, or asked to meet with them together?

"Because," my mother said, "you made such a point of wanting to keep your book absolutely separate from what the rest of us were doing." My father moved his head from side to side, as if to say, "Yes, I suppose, but something still seems fishy."

"I just don't understand why it's so important to you," my father said. "Nobody will even know we have the same publisher."

"We'll know," my mother said. "The three of us will know. And eventually everyone will know."

"I don't know why, even in spite of my objections, you seem to be insisting on it," my father said. "What will be the good of us having something in common if it's something that one of us is against?"

My mother said she wouldn't stand for being cross-examined, especially not on Christmas morning, about what she had hoped would be a nice surprise. She added that, at any rate, she had already signed the contract with D and D, so the question was academic.

Though the matter was put aside until after Christmas, we spent the holidays in gloomy silence. No sooner was Christmas vacation over than my father began to make it clear that he would not let the matter drop. He would go back to it every few days, not so much trying to get her to change her mind and break her contract with D and D, though he assured her that this could be done, as trying to worm out of her a satisfactory explanation as to why being published with D and D was so important to her in the first place. It just didn't add up, he kept saying, what with all he had told her about wanting to make his own way in the world, that she would go ahead and do such a thing without first asking him about it, just so she could surprise him with the news that they would have the same publisher.

My mother might have brought it off if she hadn't got so flustered or hadn't been so uncharacteristically defiant and dismissive of his objections. As my father said, if, as she claimed, it was to please him that she had done this, why did his being displeased not make her change her mind?

"I didn't say I did it just for you," my mother said.

"Then for whom?" my father said. "For Henry? For yourself? It doesn't add up, Audrey."

"Well, I did it. Maybe I shouldn't have, but I did, so it must add up," my mother said.

But my father grew more and more insistent about it, as if he had already hit on some explanation and merely wanted her to say it. My mother, on the other hand, grew more and more defensive, eventually refusing to talk about it at all, walking away from him when he brought the matter up, leaving the dinner table in a huff or in tears when he mentioned it and not coming out of her room for the rest of the night, all of which further convinced my father that there was more to this than met the eye. There must be, he said, or why else would she be bursting into tears at the mere mention of his publisher?

It wasn't long before my mother was looking terrible, as though she hadn't slept or eaten in days, which in all likelihood she hadn't, though she would claim to have slept normally and to have eaten at work. Saying she had the flu, she stayed away from the studio for days, more or less confined to her bed where, when I went to see if she needed anything, I would find her curled up beneath the blankets, dabbing her nose and eyes with a tissue, clearly crying, though she denied it, saying she simply had a cold.

My father stopped hounding her, taking a kind of curtly patient, forbearing tone with her, as if to say that, now that it was obvious that something was up, he was simply going to wait for her to come out with it. Finally, when this failed to get results, he said that if she could not provide him with a satisfactory explanation of what had happened maybe D and D could. He said he planned to call them the next day and if they didn't come clean he would fly down to New York and find out exactly what was going on.

At what point in the next day she told him, whether she did it face to face or on the phone, what words she chose, what his immediate reaction was, how afterwards he spent the day, I would never know.

It was not until two days later that she told me what she told him. For two days, during which my father did not come home, during which, according to my mother, he was off attending some sort of teacher's conference, she stayed in her room, in bed. On the third day, as I was making myself breakfast, she called me in. She was in her dressing gown, sitting on the edge of the bed, her hands in her lap, her body angled towards me, her eyes closed and fluttering the way they always did when she was about to explain something she doubted I would understand. And this, at first, was the tone she took, that something I needed to know about but was not quite old enough to understand had taken place, something that, though of an inscrutably adult nature, was perfectly reasonable, a difficult but necessary thing that, in the end, would turn out for the best. She had not made much headway with this version of the story when she put her hands over her face and started crying, her shoulders shaking with sobs.

"Henry," she said, a kind of girlish grief in her voice, "Henry, I've done a terrible thing." And she told me. She said she told D and D that, if they published my father's book and breathed not a word to him about why they agreed to do so, they could have the as yet unwritten story of the television Prendergasts. "I'm so sorry," my mother said. "He'll never believe that I did it just for him. I've gone and spoiled everything, everything Henry."

I stood there, not knowing what to do, my hesitation deriving in part from the way that she was dressed, the fact that she was barely out of bed, the sheets still wrinkled and looking as though, if you touched them, they'd feel warm. Then she cried as if, far from being concerned about the impression she was making, the effect it was having on me, it had slipped her mind entirely that I was there. She swayed slightly, as though she might fall sideways on the bed.

"Mom," I said, beseechingly, fighting the urge to cry, staying put. I'm ashamed to say it was the best that I could do, to tell her, with that one word, that I was scared, that I had never seen her this way before and, far from being able to comfort her, merely wanted her to stop. It was not enough, it was not what she wanted, it was less than she deserved and, for the rest of my life, it would be there between us, this letdown, this disappointment, but it was all that I could manage. And it brought her out of it. She reacted almost instantly, dropping her hands from her face, smiling as if to say that I was not to take seriously this foolishness of hers, that it was just a passing thing, a momentary lapse.

"I'll be all right," she said, turning away from me to wipe her eyes. "Just leave me alone for a little while and I'll come out, O.K.?"

I had always assumed that it was because of her own obsession with family togetherness that my mother had, all these years, been trying to get my father involved in television, but now I could see that there might be more to it than that. I wondered if, in part at least, she had kept pestering him about it because she doubted he could be a writer, or at least not the sort of writer he wanted to be, and because she was worried that he was setting himself up for a great disappointment, for failure, and wanted to save him from it, spare him the very shame and disappointment he was feeling now because of her. In other words, she tried to keep him from writing the book for the same reason that she had bribed a publisher to take it. She must have thought that if she could get him started in television, he would forget about the book or, at the very least, have something to fall back on, a kind of consolation career, if the one he wanted most did not pan out.

At the same time as she'd been trying to get him into television, however, she'd always proudly, even boastfully told people that her husband was a writer, "a real writer, a serious writer," as she often put it, "not like me."

She had always talked as if everything about him could be attributed to his being a writer, to his plan to some day write a book – his glooms, his oddities of personality and character, what she called his scepticism and aloofness. All these, she had seemed to think, were writerly traits, and, when seen in that context, were understandable, forgivable, would one day be redeemed by the book that he would write, a book, she seemed to think, that would be nothing at all like him, a book in which what she thought of as his real self would make its appearance at last. It would be a book as she imagined books to be, urbane, mature, sombrely reflective, a classic, or in the manner of one, a vindication of her faith in him, proof to her and to the world of their basic compatibility, something she could point to, refer people to when they wondered how on earth the Prendergasts had got together.

Perhaps my father, too, had hoped, in the book, to explain himself to her, justify his ways to her, help her to understand him. It was even possible, it now seemed to me, that "the Book" had been a fiction all along, mutually sustained, that there were two books, the one my father actually wrote, and the one that, in the early days, they talked about as if they would write it together, as though, in it, all their differences would be resolved, every punctuation mark agreed upon. It was not, perhaps, that they believed that such a book would ever be written, but that it had been an ideal, a symbol of something, though I doubt that either of them could have said exactly what. When my father abandoned his book, their Book too was thrown aside.

My father came back, looking much the worse for wear, but nothing was said about the time he'd been away. Very little was said, period, about the business with the book or anything else, at least for a while. I often tried to imagine what the time he spent away from home must have been like. Perhaps he had been hiding out in some hotel, feeling not only betrayed, but surely, too, absurd, ridiculous, so much so that to be seen by anyone, even total strangers, would have been unbearable. Two days, two nights trying to sufficiently reconcile himself to what had happened to go back home and face his family.

Eventually, they had it out, though if my mother hadn't insisted on talking about it, I'm not sure they ever would have. My mother said she had just wanted to get him started. She was sure he had written a good book that, once published, would send him on his way and he would never need her help again. That's all she was trying to do, she repeated, get him started, and once the world saw what a good writer he was —

My father wondered how she could know what a good writer he was without having read his book. Or had she read it? he said. What exactly had she led D and D to believe about *that* upon first approaching them? Did she pretend to have read it and, on some further pretense, ask them for a copy so she could bone up on it before their next meeting? Or did she simply admit to not having read it, the whole thing done that blatantly, Audrey Prendergast trying to bribe them into publishing a book of her husband's that even she hadn't read, D and D agreeing to publish a book they hadn't read in order to get their hands on one not yet written?

It was marvellous, he said, absolutely marvellous. He spends fifteen years writing a book for which he cannot find a publisher, and his wife finds a publisher for a book she hasn't even written yet. He could well imagine, he said, how they pictured him at D and D. And how many publishers had she gone to before she found one that was interested, he wondered, of exactly how many of the world's publishing houses was he now the laughing stock?

My mother swore that she had approached only the one publisher and that everything was done discreetly, there being only two people at D and D itself who knew what was going on, and it wasn't as if they were going to run to other publishers and let them know about it. In all likelihood, she said, no one else would ever know. Though she refused to go into details, she admitted that she had gotten a copy of his book from D and D and read it. And reading it, she said, had made her all the more determined to get it published. It was hard enough watching him suffer through all those rejections, she said, his book coming back to him, time after time, but once she had actually read it and saw how good it was, it all seemed so unfair. She knew that, if only someone would give him a chance, he could make his own way after that. She couldn't stand the thought of him suffering unjustly, she said, becoming convinced he couldn't write when in fact he could, accepting the judgement of some publishers who, if truth be known, hadn't even read his book. Books that came in unsolicited were given half a glance, she said, if that. That's what the people at D and D had told her. They also told her, she said, and seemed to believe it in all sincerity, that he had written a good book, and they agreed with her that all he needed was someone to get him started.

"They would have told you anything," my father said, his head in his hands. "To get their hands on your book, they would have told you I was Shakespeare." He wondered, he said, if anyone at D and D had even read his book. At least the publishers who rejected it had done that much. Probably the only publisher in the world that hadn't read it was the one that planned to publish it next spring.

What had she intended to do, my father wanted to know, set up an entire make-believe career for him, go on bribing his publishers forever as he went on writing books, or had she planned to buy up copies of his books so that even his publishers would think they were selling? Could she imagine, he said, what sort of figure of amusement he must be at D and D, a man who wants a publisher so much his wife goes out and buys him one?

"I'm so ashamed," my mother said, "I've never done anything like this before in my life. I'm so sorry."

I tried to imagine my mother who, all her life, had been doing what she thought was right and showing other people what she thought was right, my hyper-moral mother, creator of Bee Good/Bee Bad, Miss Mary, the kindergarten conscience-shaping "Rumpus Room," first hatching, first conceiving such a scheme, being faced with such temptation, faced with the prospect that only by doing wrong could she save her husband, my mother who believed that nothing could happen for which society was not prepared, that there was a proper way of dealing with any situation, that there was nothing that could not be better accomplished by doing right than by doing wrong, my mother realizing that the only means she had of helping the person who meant most to her in all the world was to cheat. I tried to imagine her, worried sick about my father, attempting to reconcile herself to what she was doing, to rationalize it. She went against her basic nature, against everything she thought was right, to make him happy.

My mother who believed that, as the woman who played Miss Mary, she had to be above reproach, risking everything, not just her own reputation, not just Prendergast Productions, but everything, for to help him she had even to risk losing him, my mother going alone to see some publisher about her husband's book, somehow broaching to this total stranger, though in what words or with what expression on her face, I could not imagine, the possibility of working out some sort of deal with him, somehow seeing it through, somehow saying out loud what it was she had in mind, somehow pitching her deal, as she might have imagined it was called, my mother, knowing that her shame was showing, somehow enduring the possibility that this man would say no, that, as soon as she left, he'd be on the phone to everyone he knew.

My mother did all that? Because she loved my father? However gravely she had wronged him, however misguided she had been, she had acted out of love for him – was that it? It was not for the sake of appearances she wanted his book to be accepted, not because she wanted to bring him up to speed with the two of us and at long last have a husband who would flatter the Prendergasts by his accomplishments – I was not so sure. Not that, even if she'd acted purely out of love for him, this made everything all right, or for my father, any easier to take. In a way, I think, it made it that much harder, for it disarmed him to some extent, the apparent fact that, if nothing else, she had meant well, had had his best interests, however misguidedly, in mind. But I was not convinced that she'd done it all for him. You could, it seemed to me, do something out of love for someone and still be doing it for ultimately selfish reasons. She'd risked destroying him to make him happy, so it seemed to me that she must also have done it for herself, or for "us" as she might have put it, for the family, which could be another way of saying for herself.

I was greatly confused by it all, bewildered, for it seemed to me that there was something more to it than met the eye, though what it was I couldn't say. I was only sure that I was on my father's side, that he was clearly in the right, that she had wronged him. I didn't come right out and say so, of course, but I could see that my mother knew how I felt, for even when there was just the two of us, she never spoke about it, never asked me, as in any other situation she would have done, if I had any questions, if there was something about their "disagreement" that I would like explained.

My father told my mother that he was going to pull his book from D and D, or rather release them from their obligation to publish it, to which, he was certain, they would have no objection, but added that she should simply go ahead as planned with her book, since they would very likely object to her doing otherwise, which might result in some unwanted publicity for everyone involved, him included.

The hardest part must have been reverting back to how things were before. It wasn't even that he had gained entry to the world of real writers and then been expelled from it. He only thought he'd gained entry, only thought he'd been let in. His talent had been confirmed, he thought, his self-doubt had been laid to rest for good. The manuscript-peddling, approval-seeking, would-be writer, which he had lately been thinking of as just some old, outgrown, discarded self, a stage he had had to pass through, he would have to be again, go back to being, possibly forever. He had only been living an especially convincing, especially lifelike dream. The great test of his life, which he thought he had passed and put behind him, was still there, in front of him, yet to be passed.

His one comment about it to me was that it seemed hard to believe that a letter of acceptance from a publisher could fool him into thinking he could write, that he was someone other than the man he really was. Luckily for him, he hadn't told anyone outside the family of his "success," nor, as per his instructions, had the two of us, and so he didn't have to concoct some story about why his book would not be published after all.

It must have been hard for him, especially in the months that followed, the months in which, if not for what had happened, his book would have been released, hard not to imagine where this other life would have taken him, where in it he would be by now, what sort of launching he'd have had, how the book would have been received, what it would have been like to go to a bookstore and see it on the shelves. He had made a false start, and had had to double back, though perhaps his imagination had kept on going, for his air of preoccupation was such that he hardly seemed aware of his surroundings and might well, in his mind, have been living this other life.

My father fooled us, or perhaps we just let ourselves be fooled, into thinking he was getting over it. He told my mother, in front of me, that he knew that, however ill-advised her actions had been, she had meant well and had only been trying to help him. He said he thought that we should all try to forget about it and go on with our lives. He began to act as if he had been dealt a blow from which recovery, though certain, would take time.

Not that he ever got round to resuming his search for a publisher. For a while, the blue boxes containing his manuscripts were still in evidence throughout the house, on the sideboard, on the corner coffee table, as if he were trying to demonstrate to us that, not only was he not the least bit bothered by the sight of them, but was well on his way to getting over what had happened. Soon, the implication seemed to be, when he thought he was up to it, or when the time was right, he would start again. Then, for a while, all the boxes were piled in the middle of his desk in his study, as if sending them off would be the next order of business, as if he would have to deal with them before he started something else. Neither of us mentioned them, or moved them so much as an inch no matter where he left them, as if to assure him we had got the message, as if to show him just how serious we were about not meddling this time around, as if even the precise placement of these boxes around the house was part of some not-to-be-interfered-with, not-to-be-questioned strategy of his.

And then one day the boxes simply disappeared. Or rather, I noticed one day that they were gone and couldn't quite recall when I had last seen one. No mention was made of their disappearance, either, as if even this was just him doing things his way, as if, from now on, no matter what he did, no matter how obviously ill-advised it was, we were not to interfere, not to speak to him about it.

As frequently as she dared in the months that followed, my mother asked him if he thought he would write another book some day, if he thought he'd "go back to it," as she put it.

"Do you think you'll go back to it?" my mother would blurt out, wincing slightly as she looked at him as if to ask such questions and to risk incurring his wrath was part of her penance, as if she was obliged to try to help him, whatever reaction it might provoke being no more than she deserved. The longer he went without writing, the more she mentioned it, as if she was reconciled to whatever she might bring upon herself by doing so, as if she wanted him to know that, whatever he might say, she knew she had it coming.

It must also have been true, of course, that the longer he went without writing, the more what she'd done played upon her conscience, the magnitude of her crime growing every day he spent away from his desk, which may have been why he stayed away from it. She was not guilty of having done him some fixed amount of harm which some fixed amount of expiation or atonement would undo. She had done him harm that might never stop increasing, as if every day he spent not writing she were wounding him again.

After a while, her question, "Do you think you'll go back to it?" seemed like a plea, as if she hoped he would as much for her sake as for his, as if, no matter how often he said he'd forgiven her, nothing except his going back to work would convince her that he had.

And yet, this pleading tone of hers did not last forever. That it might be, in part at least, to punish her that he wasn't writing occurred to her, I think, for her tone, when she asked him about "going back," began to sound faintly aggrieved as if, though she knew she would not yet seem justified in saying so, she thought he was exacting more than his pound of flesh; or it was as if she were letting him know that, at some point, her responsibility, her culpability would run out and that, if by this time he was still not writing, he would have only himself to blame.

As time went on, therefore, the balance of guilt between them changed. My mother stopped asking when he thought he might go back to it, as if, as far as she was concerned, her penance was up. That there was a kind of gracelessness in declaring oneself forgiven, and that this was something he had forced upon her by withholding his forgiveness, so that she would never seem wholly in the right and the matter would be left unfinished, unresolved between them, was something she would hold against him forever.

There developed between them a kind of awkward solicitousness, as if they hadn't known each other long, as if they had yet to make up their minds about each other, were reserving judgement, waiting for some telltale characteristic to show itself. They were formally polite with one another, thanking one another for every little thing, my father now and then doing a kind of parody of gratefulness, bowing low to accept some compliment about the way he looked.

"Why, thank you, sir," my mother would say as my father helped her on with her coat, trying to sound faintly tongue-in-cheek, as if together they were doing a kind of send-up of gallantry; but that, too, never quite came off. It seemed they were doing a send-up of everything, sometimes, glazing everything with parody, proceeding as usual with the day-to-day business of life, but doing ironic asides every few seconds, accompanying the serving of a meal with a kind of strained patter, a running commentary, as if some sort of mock documentary were being filmed.

"Here is the father pouring the tea," my father would say. "Now here is the father drinking his tea."

"Here is mother handing boy a slice of bread," my mother would say.

"Here is boy eating and finding pleasant to the taste a slice of bread," my father would say. It was as though after fifteen years of ignoring them, resisting them, missing the point of them, my mother had decided to go along with what she called his "games." She took part as if she still couldn't see the point, as if she had learned this one game by rote and was simply reciting her lines. Her expression and her tone of voice were so deadpan, it was almost as if some double layer of parody was intended, as if she were mocking the mockery itself.

My father, though he kept the game going, supplying most of the lines, did so without much relish, as if the whole purpose was defeated by her taking part. It used to tickle my father to pretend that my mother was not so much humourless as a master at keeping a straight face. As soon as she was by herself, he'd tell me after saying something funny, looking at her as he spoke, she'd be cracking up, slapping her knee, holding her stomach, doubling over. My mother would look at me and smile as if to say that there was no better explanation of why she never laughed than this latest attempt of his at humour. There had been two punchlines to every one of my father's jokes, the punchline itself and the fact that my mother didn't get it, which made it that much funnier. Now here she was, the woman in the front row who all along had refused to laugh, up on stage with him as part of his routine.

I didn't quite know what to make of it. Was she doing this because she thought this was what he'd wanted all along, because after all this time, she was trying to fit in? The game was like some kind of code between them. Certainly, I was not encouraged to join in, though I kept trying to, saying things like, "Boy puts butter on bread and passes plate to mother," at which my parents, as if the line was not up to their standards, would ignore me.

It is little wonder that my mother came up with the idea of having my father write *The Television Prendergasts*. She must have been unable to resist making one last attempt to salvage things. That to broach the matter with him, to suggest that he replace the book he'd lost by writing the book she'd used to get him a publishing contract in the first place was tactless, to say the least, she seemed not to care, as if she was so convinced she had hit on the one thing that could make things right it didn't matter if, at first, it caused some unpleasantness between them. She seemed to believe that she could talk him into it, but my father resisted her at every turn.

What D and D wanted was a book about the Prendergasts from "Rumpus Room" to "The Philo Farnsworth Show," she said, so who better to write it than him? My father declined. Then better yet, she said, both of them could write it. She could give him what she called "the raw material," and have him shape it into book form, the end product to be put forward as having been jointly written, a collaboration at last.

Perhaps, my father said, what was needed was one of those double-sided books, on one side *My Life in Television*, by Audrey Prendergast, on the other side *My Life Avoiding Television Like the Plague*, by Peter Prendergast. Before she could take him up on the "plague" bit, he assured her he was joking. He simply didn't think, he said, that it would be appropriate for someone who had had nothing to do with either one of her shows to write a book about them.

They could play down his non-involvement in the shows, my mother said. They would simply say that, while he had had no direct involvement in the show, he had always been supportive to both her and me, and that she had often used ideas of his, though he would accept no credit for them. "But that's not true," my father said. "You've never used an idea of mine."

My father further rained on my mother's parade by saying that, while he wouldn't mind having a few photographs of him appear in the book, wouldn't mind being mentioned in it wherever the telling of our story made it necessary, wouldn't even mind there being in it a few biographical paragraphs about him, he had no intention of having his life story, as told by him or by anybody else, appear in print. For one thing, he said, the story of our days in television and the story of what he was doing those days were completely different stories and couldn't possibly be told in one book. For another thing, he said, his story would be of no interest to anybody, it would be so ordinary, so mundane.

My mother was especially put out by this, but though she objected, my father would not relent. It wasn't as if he was suggesting that the book be written as if he didn't exist, he said, he just couldn't see why any sort of portrait of him was necessary in a book that was really about us.

And so it was that *The Television Prendergasts* was ghost-written for my mother by an author hired by D and D and, before publication, had to be approved by my father, of whom there was little mention in it. The book was published with much fanfare, despite my mother's refusal to do more than the bare minimum amount of publicity.

It was quite a sight, bookstore windows filled to overflowing with copies of a book bearing my mother's name and a full-cover photograph of her and me. The irony of people who never read books coming out in droves for one about TV was not lost on my father. My mother and I did bookstore signings, the sidewalk lineups for which began before the stores even opened and hardly diminished throughout the day.

My father kept his distance, even skipping the launch. It must be a strange thing to walk along the city streets at night and see, in the window of every bookstore that you pass, a picture of your wife and son smiling at you exactly as they smiled at strangers, as though enticing you to buy their book, as though you know nothing about them. It was a sight my father must often have seen, for he went out walking every night and *The Television Prendergasts* was everywhere. He always left Pristine Place when the sun was setting, as though he couldn't stand to be at home when it was getting dark, preferring to be outside, preoccupied, or in some store, pretending not to notice, preferring to look up from what he was doing and discover that it was dark already than to stand at some window while it happened.

Likewise, it seemed to be just as important to him not to see the sun come up, to lie in bed with the curtains closed until the change of day had taken place.

10

We stopped watching "The Philo Farnsworth Show" together. My father simply made himself scarce when it was on, and, while my mother was watching by herself in the living room, I was in the Dark Room, in front of the Gillingham.

I liked watching it on the Gillingham because it seemed appropriate that a television show set in the 1950s look like it was made in the 1950s; that is to say, that it be in black and white. I sometimes found it hard to resist the notion that it was only after the 1950s that colour came into the world. I liked watching myself in black and white, too. Sometimes I could block out all memory of having taped the show, suspend my disbelief to the point of almost thinking I was in there, in that other-worldly black and white, Henry Prendergast moving about among the cast of "The Philo Farnsworth Show."

I'd been watching the show for about a year in this manner when the Gillingham began to go again. The picture sometimes shrunk inwards from one side, the vertical hold flipped over at intervals, the screen was snowy. These were not quite the same problems as before, which was some comfort, for it seemed to indicate that the picture tube was not to blame. I fiddled with it for days, hoping the difficulties might just clear up, but they didn't.

My father was not much help. Once, he put his hand on the Gillingham as though to take its temperature, then threw a blanket over it, saying it was best to keep it warm. He put a saucer of milk beside it and pronounced himself worried upon coming back a while later to find that it was untouched. He rolled what he said was its favourite ball in front of it and hung his head dejectedly when there was no response. "Very funny," was all I said to each of these mock ministrations.

I told my parents we had to get someone in to fix it. I figured the only TV repairman who would not go to the tabloids with the story of my upside-down TV was Mr. Gillingham himself, who presumably, if he was still in the TV repair business, would not want his mistake to become common knowledge. I was relieved, upon checking the phone book, to find that he was still in the business.

My father called him and had some difficulty convincing him to come, Mr. Gillingham saying it wasn't worth our while to spend money on the upkeep of such an old TV for which, in any case, parts would be almost impossible to find. "I haven't worked on a set like that in ten years," he said, explaining that he serviced only those sets made by the large company for which he now worked. At last he relented, however.

He came on a Saturday morning, in his own car instead of the company car and in casual clothes instead of his uniform so that it would not get back to his employers that he was working on the side. When he arrived, my father couldn't resist a joke about how long it had taken him to get back to us. "Ten years," my father said. "You weren't kidding when you told us you were busy."

Mr. Gillingham managed a smile, but that was all. My mother, for whom, I suppose, Mr. Gillingham was a kind of symbol of our early days, stayed out of sight. Mr. Gillingham had with him what looked like the same oversized suitcase-shaped repair kit as before. It was strange, seeing him again, availing of his services again. I was flooded with memories from the time we lived on St. Clair Avenue, felt, for a few seconds, the way I felt when we were there. I could see that something of that sort had happened to my father, too, for he was looking at Mr. Gillingham as fondly as if they'd been great friends. Mr. Gillingham, too, seemed to be casting back, though he looked uncomfortable, as if he thought we were measuring ourselves against him, noting how much further along we'd come in the past ten years than he had. He was looking at the floor, as if he thought it would have been an invasion of our privacy to look around.

He asked to see the Gillingham – not that he called it that. My father told me not to call it that while he was there. My father hadn't mentioned on the phone that the picture tube was upside-down, not wanting to scare him off, and so we'd been wondering if Mr. Gillingham remembered and were looking forward to his reaction when he saw the set again. I thought about asking him if he had seen the picture of it in *The Television Set* magazine a while back, but decided not to.

The three of us walked down the hall to my room. My father and I had turned the Gillingham right-side-up so that, when he switched it on, the picture would be upside-down.

We watched as he crouched down in front of the set and turned the button. All he did upon seeing the upside-down picture was rear back slightly, raising his eyebrows. He straightened up, his hands on his hips, a faintly perplexed look on his face.

"Don't you remember?" said my father, who must have thought we'd all have a good laugh about it, Mr. Gillingham especially, whom he seemed to think would be tickled at coming face to face with this blunder from his past. "Don't you remember? The last time you were at our house you put the tube in upside-down." For a while, Mr. Gillingham said nothing, just stood there, staring at the screen. It crossed my mind that he might be thinking we had called him in just to play this joke on him, just to confront him, after all these years, with his mistake.

"I was just starting out then," he said finally, "I didn't have the training then that I have now."

"No, of course," my father said, his face reddening as he shot a glance at me. "I never – I've made bigger mistakes myself, I was just –"

"Do you want me to fix it?" Mr. Gillingham said.

"Of course," my father said, "of course we do. I'll just get out of your way. Henry can tell you what the problem is."

When my father had made his hasty exit, I helped Mr. Gillingham turn the set over again, which he made a point of saying he'd have had to do anyway, no matter what was wrong with it. In no time, the floor was littered with tubes. Mr. Gillingham offered to restore the picture tube to its proper, right-side-up position, but I declined, telling him that I had gotten used to it the way it was, that the set would look odd to me now standing on its legs.

It turned out that my suspicions were right, the problem was not with the picture tube but one of the secondary vacuum tubes. Which one was another question. Finding out was a laborious process that tried the patience of Mr. Gillingham, who made it clear by his tone of voice and his expression that he thought I was some frivolous rich kid, to satisfy whose whim that the Gillingham be kept in working order, his foolish parents were sparing no expense. It was like looking for the dud in a set of Christmas-tree lights, he said, each tube having to be taken out, substituted for and then replaced until the dud was found.

"Why don't you get a nice new set?" said Mr. Gillingham, who seemed to warm up to me a little once he started working. "You could buy the best set they make nowadays; you'd never have to get it fixed." I assured him I was happy with the Gillingham. I watched as he peered into the back of the set, though I stayed on the other side, thinking vaguely that it would be bad luck for me to see what he was looking at. I was so anxious I kept asking questions. Did he have all the parts he needed? Were there any parts in it, even working parts, for which replacements no longer existed? He ignored me. He worked kneeling down, sitting back on his feet, though sometimes he lay on his back, the better to see inside the set. It occurred to me that the end result of all this might be that the Gillingham would not work at all. The floor was littered with tubes, as the floor at St. Clair Avenue had been the day he put the picture tube in upside-down. He kept on trying different tubes, asking each time he put one in if the picture had improved.

"Still the same," I had many occasions to say, but eventually he found the dud and the picture cleared up instantly.

"There it is!" I shouted, "there it is!" for fear that he'd undo whatever he'd done. I was greatly relieved when he re-attached the wooden panel on the back and put all the tubes back in his suitcase. He peered in through the grid to satisfy himself that the little red pilot light was on, then turned off the set.

"Call me if you have any more trouble with it," Mr. Gillingham said, his mood that much more improved now that the set was fixed. I followed him to the door, at which point my father reappeared.

"All done?" he said, trying a little too hard to sound offhand.

"All done," said Mr. Gillingham, a trace of his former embarrassment returning. My father reached for his wallet and I inwardly grimaced at the thought of an awkward exchange of money taking place between them, but Mr. Gillingham put up his hand.

"I'll send you the bill," he said and hurried out with his suitcase as my father held the door. A few minutes after he left, my mother came out of her room.

"Did he fix it?" she said, in a faintly disbelieving tone.

The three of us went to my room and my parents watched as I switched on the set. The picture was perfect. "The next twenty-four hours are crucial," my father said.

For days after Mr. Gillingham's visit, my father seemed especially preoccupied, even more oblivious to his surroundings than we had lately gotten used to him being. "How in the name of God did we ever end up here?" he'd say, standing at the window, or looking down from the balcony at the tennis courts below on which what seemed to be the same group of trim old men, "the Pristine Seniors," my father called them, was always darting smartly about, playing doubles. My father said he'd have been down there with them except that, to play at Pristine Place, you had to not only dress in white but have white hair.

My mother seemed to think that, if ignored, this mood of his would go away. She began to act as if I were the unhappy one, the only one of us who had a problem. Half-jokingly, it seemed to me, she asked me what I was going to do when the Gillingham was unfixable. My father said that, as depicted in the classic movie, *Ol' Black 'n' White*, it was a boy's responsibility to shoot his television set once it was past repair. He could just see it now, he said, him and my mother, in the kitchen, waiting to hear the shot that would mean the Gillingham was dead.

My mother looked at me and frowned and wondered if taking me out of Upper Country College had been such a good idea after all.

She insisted that I "join something" that would get me out of the apartment and give me some sort of social life. At first I thought I could put off doing so until she forgot about it, but she kept insisting so I ended up enrolling in a professional actor's workshop for young adults that was led by a man who said that we should call him Hamish. Most of my fellow students were television actors who wanted to "step up" to something better, acting for the stage perhaps or roles in "serious" movies. I had a good deal more acting experience than any of them, but they made it clear from the start that, as far as they were concerned, my kind of experience was worse than none at all. As someone who played the inventor

of television on TV, I was to them the very epitome of television, the medium personified. Like almost everyone else outside
my immediate family, they referred to me as Philo or sometimes as "the boy who gave the world TV." Also, because Philo
was a country boy, people, my classmates included, called TV
the "rube tube," and Philo either the "boob who gave the
world the rube tube," or "the rube who gave the world the
boob tube."

That, in spite of themselves, they envied and admired me
was not something I even considered until one day, after class,
Hamish told me so. Hamish, a short, bearded, bespectacled
fellow who said he taught actors because, in the eyes of the
world, he was not "pretty enough" to be one, took an intense
interest in me. I think he was somewhat surprised that an
actor as well known as I had turned up at his workshop and
he was obviously bent on making the most of me. He told me
there was nothing wrong with my "medium" as long as I didn't
think of it as an end in itself but merely as a training ground
for something better. He told me he thought I was "uniquely
positioned" to become a stage actor, "perhaps a major stage
actor." I had, he said, a "head start on my contemporaries,"
but warned me that I mustn't squander it.

It seems hard to believe now that there exist professors
who will tell students not yet old enough to drink that they
are "uniquely positioned" to become major actors, though it
didn't seem at all hard to believe then, nor did I have any
trouble accepting this assessment of my talents. "Uniquely
positioned to become a major actor." It seemed like a line
straight out of the show, life imitating art, or, as Hamish
would have put it, life imitating mindless entertainment.

And yet it was his line. According to him, I was the acting equivalent of Philo Farnsworth, of whom I could easily imagine someone saying that, at seventeen, he had been uniquely positioned to become a major inventor. Having played Philo for the past three years, I was all too willing to think of myself as uniquely positioned for greatness and as having a head start on my contemporaries. That I had contemporaries, that I was thought of as having them by someone who knew what they looked like, was proof enough of my unique positioning, it seemed to me.

I was surprised when the upshot of all this was that Hamish advised me not to give up my TV career. For a while I was crestfallen, thinking that this was just his standard way of letting his students down easily. Perhaps this was how he reconciled all his idealistic but, when it came right down to it, talentless students to a life of establishment-serving mediocrity, by telling them their only chance of becoming major actors was to keep their day jobs. Or perhaps he wanted so badly to discover someone that he predicted greatness for half of each class, the better to increase his odds of being right. It even occurred to me that my mother had got to him in some way, intervening secretly in my life the way she had in my father's. I couldn't raise this possibility with either Hamish or my mother, of course, so I dismissed it.

I didn't much mind the thought of staying with TV for a while. There was a long and, it seemed to me, romantic tradition of real artists doing hack work to support themselves. Doing hack work seemed to be almost a requirement for anyone who wanted to be thought of as an artist. It was one of the things artists did, part of their authenticating struggle like drinking too much or being misunderstood by critics. That highest on this list of supposedly soul-improving hardships was poverty was something I managed quite easily to overlook. That's how I would think of myself, I decided, as a real actor who for the moment was spending his days doing hack work, earning enough now to sustain him through the lean, though far more fulfilling years ahead.

It didn't take me long to go from having had greatness predicted for me to believing myself to be already in possession of it. In a book of my mother's that I read over and over, Philo Farnsworth was described as having so far been "curiously neglected by historians." I could think of no greater distinction, no greater honour than to suffer the same fate, to be subjected to such neglect as would confirm my genius, then finally, perhaps posthumously, to be discovered by someone to whom that genius was so apparent that, to them, my having been "neglected" would seem "curious," implying, it seemed to me, that something fateful was behind it. The question of how a stage actor, of whose performances little or no record could be kept, would be discovered posthumously, did not occur to me.

My father's suggestion that the hope of being posthumously appreciated might not be enough to sustain me through a life of obscurity and poverty I found ridiculous. When he assured me that obscurity was not everything it was cracked up to be, I nodded as if to say, "Yes, yes, I've heard it all before," then smiled as though I were keeping to myself some witticism that would have clinched the argument and put him in his place. My father said he couldn't help feeling, in the face of such fervent and selfless devotion to art, a little chastened at having let a paltry matter like a hundred and seventy-five rejection slips get him down.

No doubt about it, playing Philo had gone to my head, convincing me, and I didn't need much convincing, that, for me, anything was possible. "The Philo Farnsworth of actors" Hamish had called me and that was how I saw myself. I figured that, if it was possible to become a great inventor by the age of twenty, it would also be possible to be a great actor by that age. When my father asked me if it bothered me at all that, in theatre history, there was a paucity of great teenage tragedians, I shrugged as if to say that, genius being by definition unprecedented, such considerations were irrelevant.

I implied that I was at something of a loss to understand why my father found the life of an artist so taxing since it was taking no great toll on me. That I had yet to make even as much progress towards greatness as would be constituted by rehearsing the first line of my first real play didn't matter, inasmuch as the connection had yet to be established in my mind between being a great actor and acting.

I began to affect a faintly mocking, tongue-in-cheek attitude about the show, and indeed about the whole idea of Prendergast Productions, the very notion of a lifelong family enterprise. I acted as though it amused me that anybody could take anything as seriously as my mother took her television programs.

"Imagine working for your mother for the rest of your life," I'd say whenever, after she had made yet another pitch to us about Prendergast Productions, my father and I were alone. "Imagine making television shows for the rest of your life," I'd say, then give a snort of derision. I'd carry on in this manner, lampooning not just television, not just "The Philo Farnsworth

Show," but everything, as if I knew of some better world and would soon be leaving for it, as if it was only because of the hilarious ineptitude of the people who had so far been in charge of it that the world was such a mess. It seemed to me that there were an infinite number of alternatives to any course of action, and an infinite amount of time in which to pursue them.

When playing the part of Philo, I always tried to seem as though I were making no more effort, putting no more into it, than, in photographs of him, Philo looked like he had put into inventing television. The thought of rehearsing a scene on my own time would have struck me as being hilariously out of the question, tantamount to selling out to the other side, caving in, swallowing what I now dismissed as propaganda. The idea of being earnest about anything, or being so concerned about anything as to spend hours trying to get it exactly right, was one I scorned.

One night, at dinner, I let slip that I wasn't sure that I wanted to be a lifetime member of Prendergast Productions. My mother didn't take much mind of me, at first, laughing as though at some childish notion I had of growing up to be an astronaut, or as though the time when real decisions needed to be made about such things would never come, as though I were trying to engage her in some merely hypothetical debate about my future. When, in what she called an "impudent" tone, I reiterated, time after time, that I was serious, that I wanted to take up stage acting, she appealed to my father to talk some sense into me.

He replied that, though I was as yet too young to know what I really wanted to do with my life, the decision, when I was old enough to make it, would be mine.

"Well, thank you very much, Peter," my mother said, "that was a big help, I must say. Am I going to get this sort of thing from both of you, from now on, is that it? Audrey's to blame for everything. I suppose I've scarred you for life, have I, Henry, by making you a TV star? Well, pardon me, I hope you'll get over it."

She said it was my father's fault, that I was merely aping him, assuming a pose, a stance that I thought was "romantic." The "rebel," the "loner," the "conscientious objector," the ironist doing his commentary from a safe distance, the safe height of his ivory tower – to a boy my age, such a figure seemed far more attractive, far more impressive than someone like her who, instead of remaining entertainingly aloof from the world, got down into it and tried to make it better. From watching him, she said, I had gotten it into my head that television wasn't good enough for me, or that I was too good for television, or something. My father told her that he had never said anything, one way or another, to me about television.

She seemed to think that I was merely getting back at her for something, punishing her for some real or imaginary grievance. I heard them talking about me, after I had gone to bed. Perhaps, my father said, it was just some phase of rebelliousness that I was going through, and the best thing might be to ignore it, not make too much of it.

But she did not ignore it. She warned me against wasting golden opportunities and squandering the head start I had on all my competition. By the time I was twenty-five, my mother said, I'd have been in television for twenty years; there were probably no more than half a dozen people on the planet who could make that claim. While there might be some things

I thought I'd rather do, there was nothing at which success for me was guaranteed the way it was with television. And what about the money I could make and the security and peace of mind that it would bring me? It would be foolish of me, she said, not to take into consideration the practical side of things. "Remember how things were when we lived on St. Clair Avenue," my mother said. She kept trying to enlist my father's help, but he kept repeating that, while I should take seriously her advice and give it due consideration, the choice in the end would be mine alone to make.

"Has it occurred to you," my mother said, "that one thing you'll be giving up if you leave Prendergast Productions is a lifetime partnership with me? Doesn't that mean anything to you, Henry, anything at all?" I looked at my father and grinned, though he did not grin back; I averted my eyes as if to keep from laughing out loud, as if we were sharing a silent joke about her being so hilariously earnest as to place importance on such things as lifetime partnerships. My mother caught the expression on my face and, assuming my father had flashed me some sort of look or conspiratorial wink, ran crying from the table.

My father was more on her side than she realized, though, as always, he had his own way of showing it. We made our trip to New York again that summer, my mother and I, my father staying home. It was in great excitement that I wrote my first ever letter to my father. I for some reason imagined that, now that I had declared my intention to choose his path in life and be an artist, we would get on differently with one another. We were still father and son, of course, but I imagined that we were on a more equal footing, had a lot more in common now than we'd had formerly. I was writing to my father who, I congratulated myself for realizing, was more than just my father, who was out there in the world, pursuing a life of his own, a life apart from mine and from my mother's. It seemed to me we were fellow artists up against the same things, chief among them my mother, about the tribulations of living with whom I imagined we would exchange wry anecdotes. I had in mind, I suppose, the sort of correspondence between artists that, fifty years hence, would be published as *The Prendergasts: Collected Letters*. I wrote, or imagined I was writing, in the great letter manner, with an eye to what would be referred to by posterity as my "early style." I won't reproduce my letter here; from my father's answer, which follows in full, you can all too easily imagine what mine was like.

Dearest H.:

Yours of the 17th, for which much thanks, reached me while I was musing on the terrace. Your drama professor, Herr Hamish, is, I believe, quite astute in his assessment of you. I especially agree that, what with your show business background and your being inclined so much more towards serious art than mere entertainment, and your intelligence, the high quality of which your marks in Drama 101 are ample proof, you are, "uniquely positioned to become a stage actor, perhaps a major stage actor." I can see him looking at you to see if you quite understood the significance of his remark, if you realized that it was meant to be a kind of challenge to you. Drama professors who let their students call them Hamish and urge them to write in what he so trenchantly calls "the Brechtian mode" know a uniquely positioned student when they see one, let me assure you.

You ask me if I have any advice to give you. Do not became vain, remain your humble self, be kind to those whose futures are not as bright as yours. Not everyone is uniquely positioned to become a major actor. For instance, your mailman becoming a major actor, or even a run-of-the-mill actor, is so cruelly out of the question that you ought to be embarrassed for him.

And, by the way, becoming a major actor is not the only thing that you're uniquely positioned for, you know. Being seventeen, you're uniquely positioned to reach the age of twenty-four seven years from now. Also, consider: being uniquely positioned is not always a good thing, the *Titanic* being the most obvious example of this.

I share your bewilderment about the behaviour of that television crew, by the way; I have no more idea than you what they could possibly have found amusing about the fact that, at the studio, in between takes of "The Philo Farnsworth Show," you sit around reading the plays of Luigi Pirandello.

That you admire the real Philo Farnsworth, with whose precocious genius you so readily identify, but hate "Philo Farnsworth" is understandable.

You're right, your mother should take on more challenging projects, and yes, perhaps a Japanese Noh play wouldn't be a bad idea, though I must confess a preference for the Canadian No Play, throughout which the audience sits for hours, staring at an empty stage. Perhaps you could mention it to her.

How she could fail to be stirred, nay, refreshed by the sight of a seventeen-year-old thumping the table at Lindy's about the Theatre of the Absurd, the Theatre of Blood, about the need for a new kind of drama that will wake up the world and shock out of their complacency the bourgeois elements in our society is past pondering, as far as I'm concerned.

You ask me if I have any suggestions about the sort of play that you should perform in. I myself am writing one called "Waiting for Philo," in which two characters sit around on stage talking about another character named Philo whom they hope will relieve their boredom by inventing television. Have you read *The Hairy Nape*, a play by Eugene O'Neill's brother Fergus about a man who, because his barber always forgets to shave the back of his neck, is mocked and jeered at by society? Or, by the same playwright, *Morning Becomes Afternoon*, in which nothing but a clock appears on stage? If Fergus O'Neill doesn't inspire you to act, no one will.

You ask me what I'm writing at the moment. Aside from "Waiting for Philo," for the first line of which I am in fact still waiting, I'm contemplating an answer to Marcel Proust's *Remembrance of Things Past*. My book, which will be a much slimmer volume than Proust's and which I plan to start when I am eighty, will be called *Forgetfulness of Things that Happened Only Yesterday*. And thus will the "Novel of Senility" be born.

By what writers have I been influenced, you ask. I have been greatly influenced by Tolstoy, so much so that I now support myself by managing a vast estate in Russia.

As for calling me old father, old artificer, I blush, as I hope you do.

Yours, if no one else's,

Peter Prendergast

Now what, at the age of seventeen, was I supposed to make of that? I was not quite sure. I got some of the message, but not most of it, not enough to form an impression of the sort of figure I'd been cutting lately. I was surprised that he seemed to be taking my mother's side against me, or defending her at least, but I assumed that he was merely doing so out of loyalty, not wanting to seem to be criticizing her to me.

11

I found out from one of the other actors that, to get me the part of Philo, my mother had had more or less to give the network "The Philo Farnsworth Show." According to the contract she negotiated with them, she would be the show's producer and would get some small share of the profits, and I would play Philo, but beyond that, everything was to be network-owned and network-controlled. My mother had stipulated in my contract that neither she nor I would have to endorse any of the spinoff products from the show or do more than the bare minimum of Philo Farnsworth–related advertising or promotions, but that didn't exactly put a damper on such things, for the network was allowed to use photographs and likenesses of me done up as Philo any way they saw fit.

The show was in its fourth year when the Philo fad developed, and the market was suddenly flooded with "Philo Farnsworth Show" products. Suddenly, people were wearing Philo Farnsworth T-shirts with his likeness on the front, and on the back the slogan "Philo Farnsworth, the boy who gave the world TV."

There were other slogans, among them, to my mother's mortification, "Philo Farnsworth, the rube who gave the world the boob tube." There were Philo Farnsworth ankle-high black and white sneakers which had Philo's likeness on the sides, Philo Farnsworth shorts, Hallowe'en masks, lunch-boxes, bubble-gum cards. What my father called "phony Philos" began cropping up all over the place; suddenly, all those discount warehouse hucksters who went by the names of "Crazy" this and "Wacky" that were dressing up to look like Philo, standing on the sidewalks outside their stores, pitching their products, waving people in from off the street, posing with people to have their pictures taken, or appearing as Philo in television ads, as though Philo had not only invented television, but had been the first of their kind, the original everything-must-go guy, their prototype.

It must have been a nightmare for my mother, the sight of her pure-minded, idealistic, non-commercialistic Philo Farnsworth, whose memory the program was intended to honour and whose reputation she didn't want sullied in any way, this inventor of television, appearing in television ads for television sets, hawking his own invention on a dozen different channels.

Fame resulted from Philo Farnsworth, for me and for my mother, but especially for the "real" Philo Farnsworth, who became a kind of posthumous celebrity. My mother could do nothing but sit back and watch as, one after another, Philo Farnsworth products hit the market. Of course, it wasn't the real Philo Farnsworth's image that appeared on the posters or the T-shirts, it was the television Philo Farnsworth, the image of me made up to look like him, a composite of our two images, I suppose, with some of Philo's features and some of mine, bearing to each of us a kind of family resemblance. There was as much Prendergast in it as Farnsworth, which may have been what displeased my mother most. She would talk of absolute strangers going about with "Henry's picture" on their clothing, having "Henry's picture" on their walls. It was not the real Philo, or even the television Philo, but her son she saw plastered everywhere. (My father described me as "the real phony Philo," and all the rest as imitation phonies, phony phonies you might say.)

All this was nothing compared to what was soon to come, however. A group of what my father called "Philo worshippers" was formed. They called themselves the "Philosophers" and, with the co-operation and assistance of the network, they soon numbered in the tens of thousands, with chapters being formed all over North America, as well as in other parts of the world where dubbed or subtitled versions of the show were playing.

These Philosophers began to dress and wear their hair like Philo, or like other characters from the show. Soon there were Philo look-alikes all over the place, dressed in the style of the late 1950s, some people even going so far as to mimic his gestures and try to talk like Philo. It was the sort of craze usually reserved for dead cult celebrities like Marilyn Monroe or James Dean.

My father didn't quite know what to make of these Philosophers. They were probably not what Plato had in mind, he said, when he imagined an ideal state run by philosophers. Nor even what Clifton Fadiman had in mind when he imagined his Utopia in which Plato was more popular than Raymond Chandler. Nor did the TV Philo quite fit the role of Philosopher King, he said, though this didn't stop him from referring to my Dark Room as "Philo's Cave."

My father said it was too bad there wasn't a real philosophers' movement, too bad people all over weren't dressing up like real philosophers. He imagined children at Hallowe'en fighting over who had the best Machiavelli costume or whose turn it was to be Herodotus. People dressed like Francis Bacon lining up to catch a bus or board a plane – now that was a sight he'd like to see, he said. Or what about philosopher bubble-gum cards, on one side a picture of Spinoza, on the other side his lifetime stats, number of books written, lenses ground, conundrums solved, ultimate questions answered, kids trading them back and forth, "I'll give you one Nietzsche for two Schopenhauers." Imagine, he said, if the mission of the Gideon Society was to make sure that in every hotel room in the world there was a copy of Hegel's *Phenomenology of Mind*. Barbershop arguments about who was the greatest philosopher of all time, Plato or Aristotle: "All right, so Plato had more imagination, but Aristotle had the intellect." Philosophy-espousing evangelists touring the world, preaching from Sartre's *Being and Nothingness* at televised revival meetings, inviting testimonials from people who have found salvation by embracing existentialism. In bookstore windows: *Logical Positivism Reconsidered*, fifty-four weeks on the *New York Times* Bestseller List, now a major motion picture starring Professor Hyman Udelson. Imagine a world where the pragmatic, career-minded college students take philosophy, while a small minority of flakes and fringe lunatics sign up for business, a world in which a degree in philosophy guarantees you a job, while most accountants wind up driving taxi-cabs.

When he saw how unsettled I was by the sight of these Philosophers, however, he told me it was just a fashion craze. For a while, he said, the "Philo Farnsworth look" would be in and everyone would dress like him, but after that it would go the way of other fashions and be discarded and forgotten.

As it turned out, he was wrong. The Philosophers increased in number and began to take themselves even more seriously, at least according to press reports, though my father said it was just that they were having fun more elaborately than before. Philosophers read what Philo read, they said what Philo said, they said what Philo said other people said. Philo was forever quoting maxims from Horatio Alger's novels and the Philosophers were said to be forever quoting Philo quoting Horatio Alger. There was a kind of Horatio Alger revival among the more hard-core Philosophers, who read his books, they said, the better to understand Philo himself.

Not that Alger was the only writer that Philo was forever quoting. Philo was a great quoter, often citing some authority to prove a point or hammer home some moral precept. My mother had him quote everyone from Shakespeare to Martin Luther King. (That it was anachronistic to quote, on a show set in the 1950s, King and other writers who didn't even come along until the 1960s didn't bother my mother in the least.) Philo always attributed his quotes and always got them right, word for word, but the Philosophers would often either repeat famous sayings as if they were his or attribute them wrongly, sometimes misquoting into the bargain. My mother drew Philo's sayings from books of famous quotations, but among Philosophers it was assumed that she and, by extension, Philo, had read all the writers that he quoted.

According to television reports which we watched avidly, Philo was seen by Philosophers as some sort of learned moral guru, the brainchild of someone who had read virtually everything there was to read, someone who had gleaned from the body of existing knowledge everything worth knowing and had fashioned from it an original philosophy of life. There began to be talk of a Philo Farnsworth "philosophy," some world view, some grand synthesis, "profound in its very simplicity," they said, that was being set out, bit by bit on the show.

The Philosophers considered themselves to be well informed about scientific matters from watching "The Philo Farnsworth Show." Their philosophy, in fact, was supposed to be founded on scientific principles. Certainly, much was made on the show of the connection between the two. Philo was forever alluding vaguely to things like the Theory of Relativity, quantum mechanics, black holes, the Big Bang Theory. My mother, who wrote her scripts with the help of a "science consultant," said that her intention had been merely to spur interest in such things, not to give the impression that she understood them or that the program represented some sort of grand synthesis of science and philosophy, as these Philosophers seemed to think, or thought it might be fun to pretend, for she was convinced at first that the whole thing was just a gag to them.

It seemed that by "philosophy" they meant something like religion, the nondenominational, all-embracing, pan-tolerant religion that Philo himself espoused. The real Philo Farnsworth had been a devout Mormon, but on "The Philo Farnsworth Show" the character's religious denomination was never mentioned. Valensky, on the other hand, was portrayed as a sceptic, a "materialist," Philo called him, who believed only in the evidence of his senses, whereas Philo, though himself a scientist, was a dreamer, a poet, an ardent believer in the existence of some nebulous, featureless supreme being under whose guidance all things would work out for the best.

The Philosophers went so far as to try to piece their philosophy together and published something called *The Philosophy of Philo Farnsworth*, an eclectic mish-mash that included: a compendium of Philo Farnsworth quotations; an abridged version of George Everson's book, *The Story of Television: The Life of Philo T. Farnsworth*, leaving out all but the bare bones of Philo's life, the rest of it being "too technical," they said; a bibliography of books about, or even partly about, television; "commentaries" of individual episodes, line-by-line explications of my mother's scripts, with detailed footnotes at the end. (These footnotes not only attributed quotations and explained historical and scientific references, but also explained allusions to events in former episodes, such as, "Scene 3, Line 34, Philo: 'I've already shown that my picture tube is better than yours, why can't you just accept defeat?' Philo is referring to Episode 27 in which, at an international science fair, his picture tube beat out Valensky's to win first prize. See also Episode 19, in which Philo himself accepts defeat, admitting that colour TV will have to wait."); what were called "preliminary notes" towards the philosophy of Philo Farnsworth, which my father described as a kind of "free-form, dream-logic inspired" synthesis of quotations, both famous and obscure from, among others, Horatio Alger, Mahatma Gandhi, George Everson, Audrey Prendergast, Albert Einstein, Philo Farnsworth, Thomas Edison, Norman Vincent Peale, John Smith, Brigham Young, Martin Luther

King, John F. Kennedy, Jesus Christ, Winston Churchill, Eleanor Roosevelt, Marshall McLuhan, Marie Curie, Queen Elizabeth I, Joan of Arc, and Confucius.

The book also included words to the theme song:

It was clear to all that Philo
Was no ordinary fellow.
This young man from Idaho
With genius was aglow.

CHORUS:

His name was Philo, Philo Farnsworth,
The boy who gave the world TV
They called him Philo, Philo Farnsworth,
He gave his life so others could be free.

He laboured long for you and me,
He gave the world its first TV
He defeated V. Valensky
So that others could be free.

(CHORUS)

And though it surely is a shame
That all the world forgot his name
And gave him neither gold nor fame,
We praise his memory.

(CHORUS)

Not bad, my father said, especially that first verse, though far more impressive would have been finding three rhymes for "Farnsworth."

My mother, who had always said that her dual purpose was to entertain and educate, was at first quite pleased to see how closely her audience was paying attention. She said she thought it was great that people were quoting Philo and that a "Philo Farnsworth Show" fan club had been started. My mother and I received hundreds of invitations from various chapters of the Philosophers to participate in their events and, though she declined them all, my mother was always quite polite about it. It was only when she realized the nature and the extent of the Philosophers' devotion that she began to worry and, in spite of opposition from the network, publicly appealed to Philosophers to take her show less seriously and cautioned them that to try to derive from "The Philo Farnsworth Show" some sort of philosophy of life or moral creed would be a waste of time.

Her appeal had no effect, however, at least none of the kind that she'd been hoping for. What it did do was turn the Philosophers against her. They issued a press release of their own, saying that, just because Audrey Prendergast wrote and produced "The Philo Farnsworth Show," she didn't have some sort of "monopoly" on it, and her "interpretation" of it was not necessarily the only valid one. They said it was possible for other people to see in a work of art things the artist hadn't even known were there. They pointed out that Philo himself had said this very thing on the show when George Everson explained some aspect of his own invention to him. They said that, while they were sure that Audrey Prendergast meant well, they were free to interpret the show their own way, and would go on doing so no matter what further misguided statements she made about it in the future.

"You've created a monster," my father told my mother.

If anything, my mother's opposition to them spurred the Philosophers on. They announced that they were devoted, not just to "the study and celebration of Philo Farnsworth, but to the study and celebration of his invention, the television set, and television culture." They began setting up retreats, where, they said, Philosophers could go and, free from all distractions, immerse themselves in Philo Farnsworth, attend lectures given by Philo Farnsworth experts, television experts, TV historians.

There was talk in the press of "Philomania," the "Philo phenomenon." The network started putting pressure on my mother to play along with it, to make the most of it, as they put it. They said we should welcome all the attention we were getting, publicity of this magnitude being something even money couldn't buy. We were not so famous, they said, that we could afford to say, "We want to be alone." In twenty years perhaps, but not now, not yet. Publicity was a form of congratulation, a form of applause, they said, and to turn it aside might seem to some people impolite, if not downright ungrateful.

Every one of these Philosophers wished us well, the network said; they wanted to know more about us. Their curiosity about how people just like them had made it big was understandable and ought to be satisfied.

TV vans were lined up night and day outside the gatehouse, which was besieged by reporters who called themselves entertainment journalists and who had Mission Control relay to us their requests for interviews and photographs until Mission Control lost patience with denying their requests on our behalf and told my mother that, from now on, she would have to deal with them herself.

My mother worked out with Mission Control an arrangement whereby the reporters would be sent up to our apartment one by one, at half-hour intervals. When each of them arrived, sometimes with a camera crew in tow, my mother met them at the door and, instead of granting them an interview, referred them to the family handbook, as one reporter called it, *The Television Prendergasts* which, she told them, was available in an inexpensive, paperback edition at most bookstores, and which contained all the biographical information about us that anyone might wish to know, information we had released to the world voluntarily. So much, she said, for our being secretive or guarded with our private lives.

When it was apparent that merely telling them about the book was not having much effect, my mother had two large boxes of *The Television Prendergasts* delivered from her publishers, left them in the vestibule just inside the door and, whenever Mission Control sent up someone looking for an interview, she sent them away with a book; the doorbell would ring, my mother would go to answer it, taking a book from the box along the way; it was like Hallowe'en, my father said, my mother handing out books for treats.

Far from being satisfied with this, however, most of these entertainment journalists were greatly put out at being given what became known as the book brush-off. The book brush-off, in fact, soon became *the* story, the angle, every paper, magazine, and television program that was following the

Philo phenomenon having a different version of it. Accompanying one item in *The Television Set* was a photograph, taken from partly behind the door of our apartment, though appearing to have been taken from in front of it, showing nothing of my mother but her hand, holding the book, as if this was all she let them see, as if this was what they got by way of greeting, a hand, described in the story as being "presumably that of Audrey Prendergast" and later as being "hastily withdrawn."

"As you look up at the apartment in which Philo and his family live," one television reporter said, pointing at Pristine Place as the camera zoomed in on the windows of 1606, "the first thing you notice is that, despite it being broad daylight, all the drapes are drawn."

But the story that most upset my mother appeared in a respected news magazine, *Event*:

"Upon requesting an interview, you are wordlessly handed a copy of *The Television Prendergasts*, the official family story, written, or so the story goes, by Audrey Prendergast herself, a year ago, before even *she* knew how popular 'The Philo Farnsworth Show' would become. Old news, in other words, if you can call it news, for the book gives nothing away, especially where the enigmatic Peter Prendergast is concerned, husband of the producer, father of the actor, but neither producer, director, nor actor himself. Of his total non-involvement with any of the shows his wife produces, nothing is said except that 'his bent is more to books than television.' A typically cryptic remark.

"While Audrey, like some brooding mother hen, repels all would-be invaders of their privacy, one imagines safely ensconced somewhere in the apartment, so far from the front door that no sound of them is heard, are the father and the boy, recluse and celebrity. For them, as for Audrey herself, the fame dream has come true, only it's not what they expected; it never is – more like a nightmare than a dream perhaps. One wonders what life must be like now for the boy, who has been in show business, in front of the camera, since the age of six, for all of his remembered life, no doubt. The fame he enjoyed – perhaps to some extent endured – before 'The Philo Farnsworth Show' must seem now like obscurity to him, the extraordinary life he used to live ordinary by comparison with this one. One wonders how well, in the long run, he will handle fame, whether he, too, like so many others who have tried to fight it, will wind up in some fortress, some Graceland of his own design or, hiding out from the world that once adored him . . . While outside, the TV vans are waiting, the reporters and the camera crews are on the doorstep, the Prendergasts are inside, their doors locked, their drapes drawn, the phone, TV, and radio unplugged perhaps. More concerned with family than with fame, they are trying to live their lives, trying to remember where they came from, how they got here, who they are, trying to remember what it was like when the world did not come knocking at their door."

It was a very uplifting article, my father said, its writer obviously a cheerful fellow not at all given to exaggeration or making doom-laden predictions about the fate of people he had never met and about whom he knew nothing. My mother agreed that the article overstated our circumstances some-what, but wondered if the day might not soon come when it would seem like a fairly accurate assessment of how we lived.

"We wouldn't let him in," my father said, "so he had to make something up, that's all there is to it. He made the whole thing up. None of it is true." He assured her that this Philo Farnsworth thing would soon blow over and we would all go back to being the only-just-barely famous people we had always been.

"One can't help wondering about the boy." The phrase stuck in my head. The thought of this man and countless others like him, down there at all hours of the day and night, looking up at our apartment, wondering about me, having their doubts about me, shaking their heads as though I were some lost cause, already written off, kept me awake at night. "One can't help wondering about the boy." Especially if you happen to *be* the boy. I would stand at the corner of the window, peeking out through the curtains at the gatehouse, wondering how long a stakeout of this magnitude could continue. They weren't getting any interviews, any photographs, any news. The TV people just kept doing these reports with Pristine Place as the backdrop, telling their viewers that, though there was still no sign of Philo, he was known to be at home, reliable sources confirmed that he was up there, his whereabouts were known.

Sometimes the camera panned Pristine Place itself, as if a lot could be learned about me from a close examination of it, as if I'd had it custom built to suit me. "Philo's fortress," it was called, aptly perhaps, for we had almost everything we needed in the building and what we didn't have we ordered in. We hardly ventured out of Pristine Place and when we did it was merely to go for a drive, and not in our own car, which would have been followed, but in a limousine which, though likewise followed, had tinted windows, and so afforded us some privacy. We sat, all three of us, in the back, my mother giving the uniformed driver directions while my father and I looked out the windows.

"Nothing like a nice relaxing motorcade," my father would say. "Nothing like driving through the countryside on a Sunday afternoon making conversation with an armed chauffeur." Routinely, TV vans would pull up beside us and someone would hang out of the passenger window to aim a camera, bazooka-fashion, at the limousine, a shot of which would appear later on the entertainment news. Coming and going from Pristine Place itself, the car was swarmed by reporters and photographers all screaming "Philo" and extending their microphones towards the window, tapping them on the glass.

After the stakeout had been in place for several weeks, my father, against my mother's wishes, began making a daily appearance on the balcony. Folding his arms up high on his chest and, with a smug expression on his face, he would look about in all directions, nodding pompously like Mussolini. Other times, he would gesture with his hands, as if in acknowledgement of adulation the way the Pope did from the terrace above St. Peter's Square.

The first day, all the cameras started rolling the instant he appeared, so many television lights coming on all at once that there occurred, though it was a sunny day, a kind of super-illumination of the ground around Pristine Place. All the reporters down below started waving and shouting at my father, telling him to send me out.

"They want the boy to come out," my father told my mother. "Perhaps if we give them the boy, they'll leave us alone." At this my mother sat with her back to the balcony.

"They are asking for the boy; they want to see the boy," my father said again, this time motioning for me to join him, but a look from my mother kept me in my place.

"Send Philo out, Peter," I heard one reporter say, and then all the reporters started calling him by name, first shouting, "Peter," to get his attention, then making some request. "Peter, Peter, look over here, Peter.... Peter send Philo out, let Philo come out, hey, Peter.... What's he doing, can Philo come out?" My mother said she wished they wouldn't refer to me as Philo as if Henry Prendergast had ceased to be.

"Peter, come in from there," my mother said. "You're just making things worse for us, that's all you're doing. Don't encourage them. If you encourage them, they'll never go away."

That evening, we watched what was in fact my father's television debut. They showed some of his Mussolini/Pope routine though, what with his beard and his coat, he looked more like Fidel Castro receiving applause from a crowd of fervent revolutionaries. Sometimes the camera panned the reporters as, looking up at my father, they vied for his attention, jumping up and down, waving their hands and their notebooks, shouting "Say something, Peter, say something," all of them grinning as if this was just the sort of stunt they'd been hoping he would pull, as if they'd known all along that, behind the supposedly publicity-shy, reclusive Peter Prendergast, there lurked this sort of character who, far from being happy to toil at his art in obscurity, envied his family the limelight and was at long last making some sort of hilarious bid for notoriety. Here, at last, was Peter Prendergast, their expressions seemed to say, long kept under wraps by the autocratic Audrey, long rumoured to be some sort of "character."

Here was their angle on the Prendergasts, on Philo. At everything he did, they laughed as if it was they who were having
him on, and not vice versa, as he seemed to think.

Once a day, every day, at 3:00 in the afternoon, my father
made his appearance on the balcony, each time doing something different. Once, he read, roared in fact, a selection of
poems from an anthology called *Modern Poetry*. The reporters
thought he was reading from his own work and asked him to
throw them down a copy. The reading, or some of it at least,
was aired on TV as well, presented as evidence of Philo's father's
oddball personality, the camera panning from directly below
the balcony so that only my father's bearded face, like that of
some terrorist's, was visible as, in a quavering, almost liturgical
tone, he loudly declaimed his favourite poems while the
reporters grinned and shook their heads and shouted at him to
stop reading and bring out Philo and Miss Mary.

On another occasion, he spent the first part of the afternoon making up a supply of paper planes which, at 3:00, he
began launching off the balcony, the reporters below, thinking there might be something written on them, thinking this
might be my father's highly eccentric method of issuing a press
release, chasing after them as the wind blew them every which
way, grabbing at them, avidly unfolding them, and, upon finding that they were blank, crumpling them and throwing them
down so that, soon, the ground was littered with balls of paper.

Even after television coverage of these balcony appearances of his was discontinued, my father went on making
them, though my mother asked him not to, the matter
becoming such a point of contention between them that they
hardly spoke. Eventually, the reporters turned on him and,

the moment he appeared, began to boo and shake their fists at him, shouting that they had no interest in him so he should stop hogging the balcony and let Philo come out for a while.

At night, when most of the reporters had gone back to their hotels, I would open the drapes and stand at the window. Opposite, so close that people on facing balconies could have played a game of catch, was Tower Two, an exact replica of Tower One, looking so much like a reflection of it, in fact, that the first few times I stood at the window, I fancied I could see myself across the way. Most of the people in Tower Two left their drapes wide open until bedtime, some of them watching TV with all the lights turned off.

Sometimes, my father and I, after my mother had gone to bed, would stand at the ceiling-to-floor window in the living room, watching people watching television. We couldn't quite see what was on each screen, but we knew that any set that flickered when ours did was tuned in to the same channel. Sometimes, we'd be watching "The Philo Farnsworth Show," but keeping one eye on Tower Two to see who else was watching it. Simultaneously with ours, a great many sets across the way would dim or brighten, or seem to go off altogether, only to flare up again. It got so that I didn't have to look but could see peripherally this sympathetic, synchronous flicker from across the way, a corresponding wink of light from top to bottom of Tower Two. I would see, out of the corner of my eye, the same pattern of light each time and became so attuned to it, was able to isolate it so completely, that I stopped noticing what my father called the competition, the flickering of sets tuned in to other shows, seeing only the "Philo Farnsworth" sets, going on and off in time with ours as though they were linked lights in some great console, my audience, as my father said, flashing me a signal, the sudden burst of blue a kind of visual applause. I was watching people watching me, my father said. "Your public," he'd say, indicating Tower Two with a wave of his hand.

One day, when my father came in from the balcony, my mother told him that someone from *The Television Set* had started asking about "the book," by which she meant, not *The Television Prendergasts*, of course, but my father's book, which they had somehow found out about.

"It's my fault again," my mother said. "I should have known, handing out those books the way I did, that somebody would start snooping around." She said she wasn't sure how much this reporter knew, only that he had called her network, asking to be put in touch with Audrey Prendergast so he could talk to her about her husband's book.

He was bluffing, my father said. That a book by Peter Prendergast had at one time been slated for publication and then withdrawn for what had been described as editorial reasons was probably fairly common knowledge among people in the publishing industry, but only two or three people at D and D knew the whole story and must be just as anxious as we were to keep it under wraps. This reporter, he said, had probably heard about the book and thinking that, by some long shot, there might be more to the story than met the eye, was just snooping around, asking questions in the hope that someone might let slip something they thought he already knew.

My mother, after making up some story to satisfy the curiosity of the people at the network, who themselves were unaware that my father had written a book, phoned D and D, who assured her that, while some reporter had indeed called them about the book, they had told him nothing. My mother wondered if she shouldn't agree to meet with this reporter. She thought it was Larry, though she wasn't sure. She wasn't too crazy about Larry relaying to her through the network some question like, "Did you make a deal with D and D about your husband's book?", which might well be what he was leading up to.

Perhaps if she met with him, she said, she could convince him that he was on the wrong track before he started spreading rumours. My father said that that was exactly what this man was hoping for; once she agreed to meet with him, he would know that she was hiding something and would not give up until he found out what it was. And if he already knew, nothing she said would convince him not to make it public.

Maybe he'd agree to keep quiet about it in exchange for something else, my mother said, at which my father lost his temper, saying that nothing would please this man more, nothing would round off his story more nicely, than to have Audrey Prendergast offer him a bribe. This was the worst possible thing she could do, he said, for everyone concerned, and extracted from her a promise that she would not, as he put it, go behind his back again. At this, my mother started crying and he put his arms around her. He knew, he said, that she was only trying to do what was best for all of us, but the important thing was not to panic. Soon, my mother was saying he was right and that it was an indication of how much this thing was wearing her down that she had suggested bribing someone.

"At least I hope it is," she said, bursting into tears again and wondering if she was really the sort of person who did such things, if she was really all that much different from this reporter who was hounding us.

"Of course you're not," my father said. "Your ruthlessness knows no bounds. It's a wonder you didn't suggest putting out a contract on the man."

"It's all right for you to make jokes," my mother said, "you don't have a guilty conscience. You're not the one he's after."

My father told her not to worry. There was no way of proving, short of extracting a confession from someone, that the two books had been a package deal. It wasn't something that anyone involved on the publishing side of it would ever own up to. At worst, it would just look very fishy, with people being left to draw their own conclusions. Or at the very worst, it would look like a simple case of nepotism, a famous woman's publisher doing her a favour by taking on her husband's book, the way of the world, the sort of thing that, although you might not hear about it, was understood to go on all the time. At best, it would be seen as a woman simply doing everything she could to help her husband. There was after all, my father said, nothing illegal about it.

"Maybe not illegal," my mother said, "but unethical." She said it was not proof she was talking about, but faith, the faith people had in her and which, by doing what she'd done, she had betrayed.

"If it wasn't for how it would affect you and Henry," my mother said, "I'd tell the whole story. I would." She said that, in her heart of hearts, she hadn't felt the same about her programs or about anything since the business with the book. She didn't care, she said, about the effect any of this would have on her reputation or her career, or the money she'd lose if her shows were cancelled, at which my father assured her that, if anything, a little notoriety would be a boon to her career. Most people, he said, would know that she and I were not the saints our programs made us out to be, so it was not as if they would be so disillusioned upon finding out that she was human after all that they would stop watching. He did remind her, however, that, among the unpleasantness that might arise from this course of action would be a lawsuit from D and D.

I wondered, hating myself for it, if the "fix" was on, so to speak, if my mother had some way of fixing things, of making even this problem go away, that neither my father nor I would ever know about. I wondered how many other such secret interventions there had been, if anything I thought I had earned or assumed I had lucked into had come my way because of her. I tried to think of things that had come too easily, or in which a suspicious amount of coincidence had been involved. I scrutinized the events of the past to see if they had strings attached. I had this fleeting notion of my mother fixing everything, staging my entire life without my knowing it. I knew, in that instant, how absurd, how ridiculous, my father must have felt upon finding out what she'd done.

The Television Set kept after the network, saying that, unless they were granted an interview with all three of the Prendergasts within two days, they were going to run a story about Peter Prendergast's book.

"I'm not sure what I dread more," my mother said, "being found out, or not being found out."

My father assured her he knew which one *he* dreaded more. It was not so much that she had intervened to get him published, but that she had done so, and had felt she had to do so, without his knowledge, allowing him to think his book had made its own way in the world and that his talent as a writer had been confirmed; that he, upon finding out, had pulled the book and, so far as anyone could tell, had never tried again to get it or any other book published, laid them both bare. It was their telltale secret, a sorrow distinctively theirs, the event to which their life together seemed to lead.

It was inevitable that my mother would try, as she saw it, to save my father, and my father, because he would not accept help, could not be saved unless she went behind his back, so it was inevitable, too, that she betray him. It was having this made known to the world that my parents feared most, I think. People would see that here they were, still together, still, presumably, with this thing between them, surely not forgotten, not forgiven, but still there, part of their nature now, part of who they were together.

He might as well have been there, this reporter who, as my mother put it, was stalking us. My parents talked as if he was, as if for the record, as if some extended interview was taking place night after night, the story of the Prendergasts, told from their conflicting points of view. The two of them tried to justify themselves, in front of me, to some man whom, if they had their way, they would never meet, tried to make themselves look good to the world in the story that we hoped would never see the light of day.

They went back over everything, it seemed, for there was not much else to do, holed up in Pristine Place as we were. One night, after I had gone to bed, my father lost his temper and told her that she was to blame for his not having become a writer, not because of that business with the publishers, as he called it, but because she had so changed his life, so changed the circumstances of his life, that whatever it was in him that had made him want to be a writer had disappeared. He could no longer even remember, he said, what the kind of life he had planned to write about was like. Even the income he derived from teaching had been rendered meaningless, he said, by the amount of money the two of us were making. Even to call that income pin-money would have been ridiculous, he said. My mother did not argue with him, or not, at least, in a voice loud enough for me to hear. It was only him I heard, letting loose as though he'd been planning what to say for months.

I sometimes wonder if, at first, he was certain he would write again and it was only to punish her that he stayed away from it, intending later to pick up where he'd left off, to revise his book or start a new one once his pound of guilt had been exacted – except that his spite had gotten the better of him and, when he finally did make up his mind to start again, he found he couldn't. Or perhaps, from the very beginning, the whole thing had been his alibi, his excuse for not doing what he no longer had the urge to do. Perhaps it was only when he could fool himself no longer, when he was forced to admit to himself that he would never be a writer, that what she'd done seemed unforgivable. As long as he'd been able to convince himself that one day he'd go back to it, he'd been able to keep himself from blaming her.

For that, in the days that followed, was what she accused him of, though he denied it. Why had he waited so long to tell her how he felt, to let loose, harbouring this grudge he had against her, brooding, sulking, nursing his grievance until now, magnified tenfold, festered to the point where the whole family had become infected by it, now he owns up to it, admits to having been hurt, gets round to telling her that she's to blame, as though this business with his book had happened yesterday, as though it didn't matter that, by now, the whole thing could have been far behind them, didn't matter that the time they could have spent getting over it had in fact been spent making matters worse?

They would start out arguing about the book and end up arguing about their marriage, about their lives together, as if all things bad had been made so by the book. They blamed each other for falling short of youthful expectations, for being unable to make themselves over, for persisting as themselves from year to year, for presenting a merely finite range of possibilities, for having already revealed, halfway through their lives, everything about themselves. Such, they both seemed to be saying, is the mere mortal to whom I gave my youth, with whom I threw in my lot and to whose fate, unless I change things now, my own will be forever tied.

As we had perhaps all along known it would, the story finally broke in *The Television Set*. It was, ironically, what with all the joking he had done about it, my father they were after, though they hadn't even known it themselves, hadn't been able to make out which one of us they were chasing until they caught him, until they brought him down and turned him over. It was the most they could have hoped for, in a way, that my father be what *The Set*, in a phrase that quickly caught on, be the "missing piece in the Prendergast puzzle."

Suddenly, it was as though there had always been a Prendergast puzzle, as though the public had been receiving updates about it for as far back as they could remember and, with this latest revelation about my father's book, it was solved at last. It had all along been obvious to everyone that we'd been hiding something, *The Set* implied, or else there had always been the nagging sense that there was something not quite right about us and that this something, in all likelihood, had to do with Peter Prendergast, the family mystery man.

The magazine took certain liberties with the time scheme, so that it seemed as though the business with my father's book had happened just after "Rumpus Room" became a hit; the implication was that it was out of bitterness and humiliation that he had stayed away from television, to get back at his wife for what she'd done to him. There appeared in all the stories this image of my father as a man apart, a loner even within his own household, nursing a lifelong grievance, a kind of wounded failure whose own wife had inadvertently taken the good out of him and whose own son was ashamed of him.

Soon, other tabloids picked up the story. My father was referred to as "Philo's father" in most of the headlines, the name Peter Prendergast appearing only in the stories themselves. "Philo's Father Fakes Book," the headlines read. "The Shocking Story of Philo's Phony Parents." "Philo's Meddling Mother." "Miss Mary Bribes Publisher for Philo's Father." "Philo's Father's Shameful Secret."

Finally, they had something on us; there was, after all, at the heart of all the pure fantasy, embellishment, and speculation a

kernel of scandal. The mainstream newspapers and maga-
zines were more restrained, if not more accurate. "The Perfect
Prendergasts Not So Perfect After All," read the headline
in *Event*.

My father, at long last, was considered famous enough to
warrant their using an actual, if somewhat touched up, picture of him. It was the photo from *The Television Prendergasts*
that appeared in most of the tabloids, though no two repro-
ductions of it looked the same. Sometimes, there was just the
head, those strands of hair across his scalp, his bushy beard.
His eyes looked faintly lit up the way eyes do in negatives or
old photographs. They had managed to make him look half-
crazed, fever-driven, forced to a life of dark eccentricities and
reclusiveness by the meddlesome Miss Mary. A full body shot
appeared on the front of *The Television Set* like some paper cut-
out pasted on the page, the accompanying story shaped around
the outline of his body, sentences broken up by his head, his
arms, his legs, leaving off on one side of him and picking up on
the other, my father embedded in sentences, in text, enclosed in
words. He was wearing his Castro coat, his hands on his stomach, which as always made it look as though he had reared back
in surprise or disbelief, though his expression was composed, or
brazenly unrepentant, as though, caught off guard by the
photographer, he was staring down his accusers.

It was reported in one paper that my mother hadn't just
found him a publisher, but had actually written the book for
him. It was elsewhere reported that he had written *The Television
Prendergasts* for her and that it was because she felt so guilty
about putting her name to it that she secretly arranged to have
his book published.

The upshot of all this was that many of the publishers who had years ago rejected it when it was submitted to them under a pseudonym suddenly showed great interest in this long-abandoned book of my father's. A book by Audrey Prendergast's husband – I imagined the front cover reading exactly that, *A Book, by Audrey Prendergast's husband* – a book with the history this one had, already so well publicized, would be a guaranteed bestseller, the publishers told him.

"Everyone is curious about it," one publisher wrote. "What's it like, this book that Audrey Prendergast secretly arranged to have published? That's what everybody wants to know. Is this book, that Peter Prendergast pulled from publication, really all that bad?" (It was his fondest dream, my father wrote back, to have people buy a book of his to see how bad it was.) "What if it's a masterpiece? Wouldn't it be ironic if Peter Prendergast could really write?" ("Wouldn't it just be a scream?" my father said.)

He could write a foreword to it, another publisher said, a foreword that set the record straight, perhaps paying some sort of tribute to his wife who, it might be appropriate to point out, had been acting with the best of intentions. He could defend the circumstances of its belated publication in whatever way he pleased, perhaps making reference to the fact that a great many good books had been published for what some people might consider to be the wrong reasons. My father told this publisher that if he would change a "great many good books" to "a good many great books," he had himself a deal. It took him quite a while to convince him he was joking.

Still another publisher told him that "in this less-than-perfect world," a writer who believed in his book was obliged to get it published and promoted any way he could. Some of the publishers told him – and assured him he could say so in his foreword – that his book had been rejected by some junior editor who was no longer with their firm. There had, it seemed, been a purging of junior editors not long after my father's book had made the rounds. Others told him they remembered his book, remembered agonizing over whether or not to publish it, in the end deciding not to for what they "readily" admitted were financial reasons.

In the end, he turned aside all offers, trying to sound as though he were doing so reluctantly, "admitting" to more than one publisher that he was tempted, which placated them to some extent, though he couldn't help deriving a certain satisfaction, at first at least, from rejecting his rejectors, though this soon wore off, what with some of them persisting no matter what he said.

He told the most persistent of them that he had long ago reconciled himself to the fact that his first and last book did not merit publication. (The one thing he would regret, he said, was not having a chance to win the Best First and Last Novel Award, which, he said, was given annually to what was secretly judged to be the worst first novel and, as he understood it, was taken away from the winner if they published a second novel, the purpose of the award being to cut down on the number of bad books in the world.) When this did not work, he told them he had long ago destroyed the book, burnt it, there no longer was a book, which turned most of them aside, though one publisher told him that, even if what he said was true, which he doubted, it was not a problem, since a book could easily be written for him.

12

My father's discontent became more and more apparent. My mother had always been the one to wake him from his early evening naps, but now she started sending me to do it. He would wake up like a man having what might be his last sleep, a man who had gone to bed knowing he had to face surgery or combat in the morning. He would give a great start, rising quite smartly to a sitting position, his feet on the floor, his hands on the edge of the bed, as if to impress upon whoever had come for him that he was reconciled to what must happen and prepared to face it. Then, upon realizing that it was the usual world that he had wakened to, he would lie back down again, his eyes open, shifting about as if it was slowly coming back to him who and where he was. "What time is it, Henry?" he'd say, running his hand over his face. When I told him 7:30, he would nod and close his eyes.

Some friends of my mother's offered us the use of their cottage north of the city. It was a place where we could go to get away from all these pestering reporters, my mother said. My father, who at first said he was not interested in going, went along reluctantly. It may have been the strange surroundings that set him off. We were sitting in the kitchen one evening when it was getting dark, eating a meal my mother had prepared, no one talking, when suddenly my father rose, pushing back his chair, which screeched loudly on the floor. He couldn't cross the kitchen because, the urge to cry having come over him so quickly, he didn't think he could compose himself even that long. He had to make the quickest exit available to him, which was out the back way. The porch door was just behind him and he had no choice but to turn that way, clearing his throat as if by way of explanation, as if going out to the porch in the middle of dinner was something people did at cottages, as if the porch was there for just that purpose. He closed the door behind him and, for a while, we heard him jingling the change in his pockets, which meant, in all likelihood, that he was standing at the storm-door window, staring out at the cottage across the road, for I had often come out to the kitchen in the last few days to find him there, his back to me, hands in his pockets. My father, on the other side of the door, was trying to break down in the way that would least upset his wife and son.

Then we heard him leave the cottage, the storm door opening then neither slamming nor being eased shut, but closing normally, as if he had said he was going for a walk. Seconds later, we heard him come in the front door in the same, unhurried, offhand way. I have often since tried to picture him, walking around the cottage, no doubt hoping that, from a distance, it didn't look like anything was wrong, taking the outdoor route from the kitchen to the bedroom so his family wouldn't see him crying. I often see him, in my mind, as someone watching from across the road would have seen him, coming around the corner of the house, taking the front steps as jauntily as always, his body still composed.

Sometimes it's the sound of his footsteps as I heard them from the kitchen that I remember, my father crossing the hall to the bedroom and closing the last of four doors behind him. My father doing his circuit of the cottage in stages, closing doors like bulkheads behind him, as if each door closed sealed off the world a little more.

A few days later, back home, my father, for the first time ever, convened a family meeting, actually going so far as to call it that.

"We're having a family meeting," he said when he poked his head inside my room. "There's something you and your mother need to know."

We sat at the dining-room table as usual, my father and I opposite each other in the middle, my mother at the end. He and I sat hunched forwards, our arms on the table, as if something was about to be placed in front of us that we wanted to get a good look at. But my mother did not even draw her chair in, but instead sat back, formally erect, her hands in her lap. I could not decide whether this posture was meant to convey that she knew she had it coming, whatever "it" might be, and would not defend herself, or that, having done everything she reasonably could to atone for her mistake, she would do no more — if he was still unsatisfied or bent on taking some sort of petulant revenge, then so be it.

He told us he was planning to go away for a while. I looked at my mother, waiting for her to say something, but still she sat there, eyes downcast, as though she were looking at her hands. When, after a few seconds, nothing more was forthcoming from my father, she raised her hands, then let them fall flat on her lap as if to say, "Right then, if you've nothing more to say, I'm sure we've all got things to do."

"I don't want you to think – to get the wrong idea," my father said, looking at me. "I'm just going away for a while, that's all, to get things straightened out." At this, my mother raised her eyebrows, stood up, and, as she turned to go, looked back at me.

"I'll leave you to get the details," she said, though the remark, of course, was directed at my father, her tone implying that his going away for a while was not the momentous event he seemed to think it was, nor could this course of action have been more predictable or his motives more transparent. It had its intended deflationary effect on my father, who had clearly been expecting, even hoping for, something else, some sort of scene perhaps. He turned to me as if to see if I was taken properly aback by his announcement. I was.

"How long will you be gone?" I said.

"I'm not sure," my father said, but added that he was certain he was coming back, so I needn't worry myself on that account. He said he thought that if he could go back to being Peter Prendergast for a while, just Peter Prendergast, not Audrey Prendergast's husband, not the father of Philo Farnsworth or Henry Prendergast, but just himself, he could get over what had happened.

When, unsatisfied with this explanation, I asked my father what was really going on, he simply told me not to worry. True, he said, there was going to be a larger gap than usual between his bed and my mother's, a matter of miles instead of feet, but separate beds were only that, separate beds, no matter how far apart they were.

It only then occurred to me to wonder if he was going away with someone. He must have seen it in my face, for he assured me that he and all of womankind would be sleeping in separate beds for a while.

I decided that what he had in mind was a walkout of the sort my mother used to stage, a temporary, short-lived walkout done more for shock effect than anything else. What bothered me was that he had no word for it, wasn't calling it anything, not even by way of explaining it to me. Divorce was never mentioned, nor separation, nor even trial separation. What it was, this move of my father's, what its purpose might be, what, if anything, it might be leading to, preparing us for, easing us into, how long it might last, he didn't say. A kind of family sabbatical of indeterminate length and purpose had been declared.

I kept expecting my mother to explain how, somewhere in the operating manual of life, the exact course of action my father was taking was recommended as a way of dealing with exactly the sort of problem we were having. Provision had been made in the manual for just this set of circumstances, I was sure. But though I waited for my mother to explain it patiently to me, she never did, never mentioned it, in fact.

He tried to talk to me about my mother, telling me the story of how they'd supposedly met. In fact, he told me several versions of the story.

An ad in the personals. It was always he who placed the ad and my mother who answered it, he said, though I was more easily able to imagine it happening the other way around, my mother screening a host of applications, administering every known personality test before conducting interviews, grilling the applicants as NASA did prospective astronauts. (My father being spun about in some G-force chamber, every so often giving the thumbs up to my mother, who, watching from outside, controlled the lever, keeping a dispassionate, critical eye on my father, waiting for the first signs that he was passing out.) How my father would have got through this rigorous process was much harder to imagine.

He said they had met through the "Opposites Attract Computer Dating Service," which, after doing a roaring trade for ten years, had switched to divorce counselling.

He said he was sitting among the merchandise at his parents' garage sale when my mother came along and asked how much they wanted for him.

They saw from the start that they were very different people, my father said, but it never occurred to them, at their age, that different might mean incompatible — just the opposite, in fact, for they believed that they were not really different. They each seemed to have had the notion that what the other said and did had nothing to do with who they really were, or more to the point, who they might be in the future. Each of them thought of the other as immature, not fully formed, undecided about who they should be, trying on beliefs and opinions just to see how they fit. The fact, therefore, that their opinions clashed didn't worry them, for they believed that their basic natures were the same, each of them thinking that, with time, the other's true self would come to the surface. As it turned out, they were wrong, he said, but it hadn't seemed to matter until recently.

He must have been planning it for weeks, for he left the next day. He packed enough boxes and suitcases to make it look as if he was never coming back.

"Where are you going?" I asked.

He shrugged. All he knew for sure, he said, was that wherever he was going he was driving there. He told me not to worry about him, that he could take care of himself. He would write with his return address as soon as he had one, as soon as he found a "suitable" place, a place, he said, where people would have no idea who he was. It was even possible that he would go from place to place, two weeks here, two weeks there.

It occurred to me that he wasn't leaving to punish my mother or to free himself from her so he could be with someone else, or to get away from prying reporters. It wasn't obscurity or anonymity he wanted, or to get back to being Peter Prendergast, but rather to get away from being Peter Prendergast, perhaps for good.

Mission Control told him to park at the back and load the car there, using the service elevator on which we were booked for half an hour, so there was no one else around while we worked. We first put everything into the elevator on the sixteenth floor, then rode down to the basement and, jamming the elevator door, began taking things to the car.

There was nothing so heavy that lifting it required both of us and, although we started our first trip from the elevator to the car more or less together, we were soon at a staggered pace, meeting each other in between, feigning preoccupation with whatever we were carrying, rushing past each other, eyes averted, the only words that passed between us having to do with how much progress we were making, and wasn't it amazing how much one elevator car could hold.

Finally, when I came out with the last armful of boxes, I found my father waiting at the back of the car. I hurriedly put the boxes in the trunk and, just as I saw him out of the corner of my eye make a move towards me, I said, "I think there's still something left," and, turning away from him, went back inside.

We both knew full well that there was nothing left in the elevator. Even though he couldn't see me from where he was, I went through the motions of looking in the elevator. Then I stood there, just outside the elevator, just out of sight of my father.

"Henry," he shouted, a kind of laugh in his voice, trying to sound as if he found my awkwardness amusing, as if he felt none himself and was trying to cajole me out of mine, or at least into joking our way through some sort of goodbye, if that was how I wanted it.

"What?" I said, matter-of-factly, as if I had no idea what he wanted.

For a while, neither of us spoke. "All right then," he said finally, as if to say that, if I wasn't up to it, he wouldn't push it, wouldn't insist on doing anything that might embarrass me. I stepped out where he could see me.

"I knew you'd go," I said. "I didn't think you'd go so soon, but I knew you'd go."

He glanced around at the bare green walls as if to say, "It isn't much to be taking a last look at together, is it?" Or it was as though he were saying, "You're staying here. When I'm gone, you'll still be here," as though he had already jumped forward in his mind to a time when he was gone.

"I wanted to write a good book," he said.

"I know," I said.

He smiled. "Be a good boy," he said, his voice breaking. He got in the car and rolled down the window, "I'll probably be back by Thanksgiving," he said.

"Oh, you will?" I said, as if to say that, in that case, he wasn't really leaving and there was no need to say goodbye.

I was eighteen and it seemed to me that, because time was infinite, everything good would eventually happen and everything bad would either be undone or be forgotten.

"Well, I've already said goodbye to your mother," he said, "so I guess I'll see ya later."

"See ya later," I said, more loudly than was necessary, for I didn't trust my voice at anything less than a shout.

He sat there in the car, waiting, I eventually realized, for me to go, not wanting me to see him begin this new stage of his life, not wanting me to see him alone in his car, starting out. I wondered what sort of goodbye they'd had, what was said. She had remained out of sight while we were loading the car. I guessed she'd been in the second-floor spare room, one floor higher than he'd have had to go to get anything he needed. I could imagine him going up to the room to tell her he was leaving, standing in the doorway as, facing away from him, she lay on the bed. But I couldn't imagine what might have happened after that.

I turned away, got on the elevator and rode back up to our apartment, where there was still no sign of my mother.

It occurred to me again that he might just be bluffing. I went to the window, hoping to see his car, hoping to spot it in the stream of traffic heading up the ramp toward the freeway, but I didn't. Perhaps the bluff would go no further than his driving once around the neighbourhood and coming back to sheepishly unload the car. That would be something. Over the years, my mother had staged perhaps a dozen walkouts and, though she had never gone so far as to load the car with her belongings, I couldn't help thinking that this was just my father at long last taking his turn, that, later that night, when we were both in bed, we would hear him come in and that would be the end of it. He would put his things back where they belonged, go to bed and, in the morning, we would all pretend it hadn't happened, just as we had always done.

But he did not come back, though I kept watch from the balcony for hours, staying out there until after dark, when it seemed to me that every pair of headlights that turned in at Pristine Place might be him. Once, a station wagon just like his pulled up to the gatehouse, but only to turn around.

It was nearly eleven o'clock when I went inside. Perhaps it was the sound of the balcony doors closing that brought my mother down from the spare room. She wasn't crying, nor could I say for certain that she had been, though her face was flushed, the skirt she wore wrinkled on the front, suggesting that she'd been lying on her stomach for quite a while.

"He's coming back," I said, "I'm sure he's coming back," but when she tried to put her arm around me I moved away, raising one hand and shaking my head as if to say that, right now, for her to hug me would only make things worse, or perhaps even to say, "Not now, not yet, let's wait and see," that she should save the hug for a time when I might need it more.

People fall from grace with one another. Something, brought on by both of them, takes place, a lapse of love, something that, afterwards, is always there between them, always, a flicker of the eyes when they look at one another, though they may never speak of it again. I have had many such falls from grace, but none that I regret more.

My father had promised me a letter within a couple of weeks, but no letter came. Two weeks, three weeks, a month went by and still we hadn't heard from him. My mother, saying that she was sure that nothing was wrong but that you could never be too sure, phoned the police and had them do a North America–wide computer search of hospitals, which turned up nothing. The police said that, given that he had made no secret of leaving and had told us he would be away for quite some time, they couldn't consider him a missing person. Still, my mother convinced them to do a second computer search, this one of the jails of North America. She assured me that you could easily wind up in a jail without having done something wrong. This, too, turned up nothing, though, probably as a result of it, rumours began flying about that Peter Prendergast was missing.

The press resumed their stakeout of Pristine Place, and my mother declared the balcony out of bounds until they left. As always, not being able to interview or photograph us did not stop reporters from doing stories about us. "Where is Peter Prendergast?" read the headline on the front page of *The Television Set*. It was accompanied by a story that claimed that, without a word to either me or my mother, my father had simply disappeared, that he was now an official missing person, that we had a team of private detectives scouring the country for him.

TV reports, the video portions of which consisted of still more balcony-and-drawn-drapes footage, all ended with the announcer doing a solemn, deadpan recap of the failure and humiliation Peter Prendergast had recently endured, and the testimony of "family friends" who said my father had been showing signs of strain before his disappearance.

The tabloids, which I read as avidly as ever but kept hidden from my mother, had their usual field day with it. My father – I took special pains to make sure my mother didn't see this one – was said to have committed suicide, unable any longer to be "the family nobody," "the family failure." Another tabloid said "witnesses" reported seeing a man who looked like Peter Prendergast being forced into a car in a restaurant parking lot in southern Michigan by a group of "mangy-looking" men. He had walked out on us, yet another claimed, run off with another woman, an average ordinary woman who, unlike my mother, didn't think that "fame was the measure of the man." Some said my mother had sent him packing, thrown him out because she could no longer stand to have a failure underfoot, or that she had done so on my instructions – "'It's him or me,' Philo tells mother, in final showdown with Dad."

One report said that he was so humiliated by what had happened that he was having major plastic surgery and, when the bandages came off – and they wouldn't, for at least a year – he would have a whole new face. This must have been "a year" in tabloid time, for soon, pictures purportedly showing the new, completely overhauled Peter Prendergast began appearing. This plastic surgery angle gave the tabloids licence to identify virtually anyone as the "former Peter Prendergast." Suddenly, my father was everyman, or every fat man anyway, for scores of fat men who otherwise looked nothing like him were identified as him. He had a new "new" name every week, depending on which tabloid you were reading. I wondered what my father made of it all, whether he was still scanning the tabloids or if that was not consistent with taking a break from being Peter Prendergast.

Where, indeed, was Peter Prendergast? It was hard to resist the notion that, in some of these tabloid stories, there might be a grain of truth. Maybe he wasn't coming back, maybe he really did plan to start all over again somewhere else. People did it all the time. And as for disguising himself, my father didn't need plastic surgery or any other kind of disguise. He had only to get rid of the disguise that he'd been wearing all his life – namely his beard. I doubted that I would recognize my father without his beard. I imagined him driving along some country road, clean-shaven for the first time in thirty years, hardly able to recognize himself in the rearview mirror, a new man, looking not much more like Peter Prendergast than did the men in most of the tabloid photographs.

My father was as prime a candidate as you could get for this sort of thing. I had no trouble at all picturing him as one of those runaways who turns up from out of nowhere in some town and sets about acquiring a new life, his past unknown to anyone but him, the village stranger who in time wins every-body's trust – my father an actor, an impersonator at last, with a full-time, lifelong role to play, a character of his own creation, my father making this new self up as he went along, inventing a past for himself, revealing it bit by bit, no trouble at all for a man who in his previous life had been a novelist. There was a certain symmetry about it, the whole family tricked out with alter egos now, my mother had Miss Mary, I had Philo Farnsworth, and my father, his previous attempt to acquire an alter ego having failed, R.P. Henderson having been prematurely laid to rest, had God knows who.

Or could it be that there really was another woman? It didn't seem out of the question. And as for suicide, you could never tell, could you? Families and friends of suicides almost always said it happened out of the blue, no warning signs, nothing. Should we have let him just go off like that, when there was no telling how well he might have been disguising his real state of mind? Perhaps that was what this odyssey of his was all about, a prelude to a more complete escape. He could be out there, driving aimlessly for days on end, mulling it over, considering the possibilities, weighing his alternatives. And who could tell, in a strange place, a thousand miles from home, all alone in some hotel room, what even a man like my father might do?

Foul play at the hands of someone else was not out of the question either, especially not if he'd been recognized. He had cashed no cheques and used no credit cards since he had left, which worried my mother at first until, upon checking at the bank, she had found that he'd made a large withdrawal just before leaving. He understandably had not wanted to sign his name to anything, but a (kind of) public figure, travelling alone, with that much money? Or robbery might have nothing to do with it. There were people who would get a kick out of doing in some celebrity if they got the chance. Images of my father being worked over by a group of mangy-looking men who said they couldn't stand a man who let a woman run his life and his family earn his keep kept running through my mind.

"What do you think, Henry?" my mother said. "What do you think your father's up to?"

I told her I didn't know, but that, probably, it was just as he had said: he was lying low somewhere, getting things straightened out.

"But you'd think he'd call or write to us or something," my mother said. "At least let us know that he's alive." I said that maybe this was all part of getting things straightened out, needing to be away from us completely for a while. My mother shook her head as if to say it didn't quite add up. Even if he had simply run off to make a new beginning somewhere else, she said, her voice breaking, it was very inconsiderate of him not to let us know that he was safe. He could easily have done that without revealing where he was. "I hope nothing's happened to him," she said. She alternated between seeking reassurance that he was all right and declaring that, if she never saw him again, it would be too soon. One minute, it was "just come back and all will be forgiven," the next it was "it's too late; things could never be the same between us, so don't bother coming back."

I kept telling her I was sure that he was all right, that he hadn't run off, that he was coming back.

"You haven't heard from him or anything, have you?" my mother said, looking at me as if my expression might give me away. "You'd tell me if you had, wouldn't you?"

I assured her I would.

"Maybe he's just doing it to punish me," my mother said. "He might stay away forever just to punish me," and she started crying, putting her face in her hands, her shoulders shaking. "I'll never forgive him for putting us through this," she said.

When a month went by and we hadn't heard from him, my mother convinced the police to list him as a missing person, though she said that, as they seemed to have their minds made up about what had happened to him, they probably weren't going to try very hard to find him. She considered hiring a private investigator, but decided against it, saying that if some stranger sent by her were to seek him out and barge in on this self-analysis, or whatever it was, of his, it might provoke him into thinking that she was just too meddlesome to live with and he would never come back. My mother went through a time, about a month, when she was more or less incapacitated by worry and uncertainty. She began having migraine headaches, which she hadn't had since she was a child, she said. I would often find her lying on the chesterfield, a cold compress on her forehead, her hands over her face. At night, unable to sleep, she would watch TV, often staying up until it was time to get ready for work.

She would go through whole days with hardly a word to me, the two of us eating in silence at the dinner table, it being never more impossible to ignore than at meal times that one of us was missing. The strain of it all began to show on her face; even when she appeared on TV as Miss Mary, she had a haggard, weary look about her.

About a month after my father went missing, the reporters staking out Pristine Place were joined by a contingent of Philosophers who began staging a kind of vigil in support of "Philo and his mother." Now this vigil became the story, an indication, according to people said to be experts in such things, that the Philosophers were well on their way to becoming a full-fledged cult, albeit a leaderless cult, for it was apparent that their putative leader, Henry Prendergast, wanted nothing to do with them, but a cult none the less. Large numbers of

Philosophers were said to be on their way to Pristine Place from all over North America, though at any one time there were only twenty or thirty of them gathered below, some Philosophers leaving to go back home when "replacements" arrived. By day, cameras filmed the Philosophers as they staged their silent demonstration, holding aloft or wearing signs that read, "We love you, Philo Farnsworth," "Peter Prendergast Come Home," "We forgive you, Miss Mary," though whether they were forgiving her for earlier speaking out against them or the business with the book was not made clear.

Their intention, they said, was to keep vigil below our windows until the fate of Peter Prendergast was known. Most of them were dressed and made up like Philo, wearing fedoras, pin-striped suits, two-tone Florsheims. But there were Philosophers dressed like other cast members too – Victor Valensky, George Everson, Teacher Tolman, Sarah (Philo's fiancée), and Mrs. Farnsworth. In observance of the fact that my father was missing, no Philosophers dressed like Mr. Farnsworth. It was a strange sight, the cast of the show cloned many times over, walking up and down the sidewalk outside Pristine Place, one that Mission Control told us had better soon disappear or we would be evicted, for tenants in both towers had started to complain.

At 3:00 each afternoon, when my father would normally have made his appearance on the balcony, the Philosophers would observe a moment of silence, lowering their signs, removing their hats, bowing their heads. A clip of them thus engaged appeared once on the evening news, the announcer describing them as "fanatic devotees" of "The Philo Farnsworth Show." At 8:00 on Tuesday nights, they would gather around their portable television set and watch the show, all of them huddled together, sometimes, if it was raining, under umbrellas, arms around each other.

My mother said that either they were crazy or the whole thing was just a joke, an elaborate gag that the media was playing out of all proportion. They seemed, when interviewed, to be in earnest, but this was just an act, just playing to the cameras, she assured me.

I had my doubts about this explanation. When the show was over, they would light candles and walk around in a circle, softly singing the theme song, "Philo, Philo Farnsworth, the boy who gave the world TV, Philo, Philo Farnsworth, the boy who gave the world TV...," looking up at our windows and waving when one of us peered out through the drapes.

Slowly, the Philosophers holding vigil at Pristine Place grew in number, until there must have been a couple of hundred of them and police began showing up to watch the goings-on and to make sure they dispersed at 11:00, as they were required to do by law. Where they went at night, we had no idea, but they were always back by 6:00 in the morning, no matter what the weather.

"This is getting altogether out of hand," my mother said, but, when she called them, the police assured her that, because the Philosophers were on public property and were not disturbing the peace or harassing us in any way, there was nothing anyone could do. They told her that perhaps if one or both of us spoke to them and thanked them for their concern about Mr. Prendergast they might go away, but my mother was sure that this would only make matters worse, they would take it as encouragement and would never go away.

I wasn't so sure, however, and the next day I darted out through the balcony doors before my mother could stop me, ran to the edge of the balcony and waved, at which a great cheer and shouts of "Philo, Philo" went up from below. I was there little more than a second, was just on the verge of shouting "Thank you" and telling them that, though we appreciated their concern and their support of the show, we'd rather they not stand vigil anymore, when I felt my mother's hands on my shoulders, turning me around and leading me inside.

A clip showing just that was aired on TV that night. Shot from below, it showed me peering out over the edge of the balcony and waving, and then my mother intervening between me and the camera, putting an end to what the host of the program called my "obviously unauthorized" gesture of appreciation. This was how the rumours began of a falling-out between my mother and me over the Philosophers and how I should conduct myself as Philo Farnsworth.

My mother scolded me, asking me what on earth I imagined I was doing, telling me that I was just like my father, egging them on for no reason. Now that they had seen me, she said, they would never leave. I told her that if she'd let me say everything I'd wanted to say, they'd be gone by now, or at least there'd be no misunderstanding about what I'd been trying to do. As it was, I began to be portrayed in the media as being sympathetic to the Philosophers, as being a Philosopher, in fact, and wanting to take a more active role in leading them, though what leading them might entail, to where or to what I would be leading them, no one, not even the Philosophers themselves, ever said.

13

My mother stayed home from the studio most days to keep me company, saying she wasn't too crazy about the idea of my being alone with all those Philosophers hanging about outside. We hired a tutor to fill in until my father came back, but he was usually gone by noon and my mother and I would spend the rest of the day trying not to notice what the Philosophers were doing.

One day, my mother said she thought that, as Miss Mary, she was no longer projecting the image of a nursery school teacher. The difference between her age and that of her target audience was just too great, she said. These days, Miss Mary looked out of place among the preschoolers on "Rumpus Room." She looked like some maiden aunt, she said, having her nieces and nephews over for the day. Perhaps it was time for someone else to play the part, someone the age she'd been when she was starting out.

I said it was just the strain of my father's disappearance that was making her talk this way, but she assured me it was not. She had been thinking about it since before my father left, she said, and now her mind was made up. In fact, the search was already on for someone to replace her as Miss Mary. She almost brought if off, almost had me convinced, but no sooner had she told me that the date of the last episode in which she would play Miss Mary had been set than she started crying and, sitting at the kitchen table with her face in her hands, told me the rest of it — that the network was forcing her out, that they were able to do so because, years ago, in order to get me the part, she had had to sign over to them, not only the rights to "The Philo Farnsworth Show" but the rights to "Rumpus Room" as well.

I couldn't help wondering how many more such revelations might be coming, how many more such secret deals she had made over the years. Not that this one had been entirely secret, for I had known at the time that she had intervened on my behalf and had put aside any qualms I had about being given the part over someone more deserving of it or, indeed, about whatever she'd had to do to get it for me. But though I felt sorry for her, I felt more guilty than grateful that she had sacrificed so much for me.

I said it was no wonder my father had left; the wonder was he hadn't done it sooner.

"He left me with you," I said, "but who am I supposed to leave you with?"

My mother, though she kept her face hidden in her hands, stopped crying, inhaled once like someone who'd been stabbed, then froze, looking as though she wouldn't so much as draw another breath, let alone move, until she was sure I'd left the room.

I had more to say but couldn't bring myself to say it. I went to the Dark Room and, slumping in my chair, turned on the Gillingham, turned it up loud, for I didn't want to hear her crying, or her to hear me. I had a notion that, although I had not gone with him, I had joined sides with my father against my mother, that he and I were in this thing together, confederates, kindred spirits. He had done what I, when I was old enough, would do. From now on, when she spoke against him, I would defend him, take up for him in his absence. He had left to make a point, on a matter of principle, because it was the right thing to do.

I wondered if she had told me the truth or if stepping down as Miss Mary might be just another ruse of hers, a way of sending him a message. Perhaps she hoped it would make him realize how profoundly his disappearance was affecting her, bring him to his senses, bring him back. Or perhaps she was sending him a different kind of message, letting him know that his had been received, loud and clear, that she was reconciled to having lost him, that as far as she was concerned, it was over and it was time for her, too, to start again and make her own break with the past. She would only be bluffing, of course, but that didn't mean it wouldn't work. I told myself that, whatever her reasons for quitting, I hoped he didn't fall for it, I hoped that, just to punish her, he stayed away forever.

The network announced that, after November 17, "Rumpus Room" would continue with a new Miss Mary, hand-picked by my mother, to whom thousands of young women from around the world had been sending taped auditions. Likewise, they said, my mother would oversee the transition to "the new 'Rumpus Room,'" making sure that everything went smoothly. In fact, my mother had nothing whatsoever to do with choosing her successor, nor any say in what the new for-mat of the show would be. She was, however, allowed to write and produce the final Miss Mary episode and so dictate how Miss Mary's departure should be handled.

My mother decided that, even in this, her last program, she would not step outside her character to address the audience as Audrey Prendergast, but would simply say goodbye as Miss Mary. She wondered if she should say where exactly Miss Mary was going. It would surely seem strange to children, her just going off like that and never coming back, she said. She regretted not having foreseen this problem, not having given Miss Mary some sort of family who, from time to time through the years, could have come to visit. She thought about saying that Miss Mary was going to live with her sister, but was worried that the sudden, last minute introduction of some never-before-mentioned sister might make the children suspect that something was wrong. In interviews she gave in the days leading up to the airing of the final show, my mother recommended that parents explain to their children in advance that Miss Mary was "retiring," that way they'd have time to get used to the idea before the last show was aired and wouldn't form any misconceptions about why Miss Mary was not coming back or where she was going.

Despite all the forewarning, however, it was said that, for days afterwards, a good many of the children who watched the last episode were inconsolable. Not that it was only children that watched it. A lot of people who had long since grown too old for "Rumpus Room," teenagers, even adults whose children had outgrown it, tuned in to see Miss Mary say goodbye.

My mother, who had taped the show a week before, did. I did. She watched it in the living room, I watched it on the Gillingham.

My mother had decided that, for the last episode, there would be no studio audience, and that the boys and girls who were "visiting" that day, instead of staying until the end, as was the custom, would be led offstage halfway through. On the episode itself, not much was made of this being Miss Mary's last show until near the end, when it was time for her to look through her Looking Glass. There, when the spiralling pattern disappeared, was my mother, her face framed by the glassless mirror, filling, in fact, the entire screen.

"Boys and girls," she said, "this is the last chance I'll have to speak to you, because after today I won't be coming back to 'Rumpus Room.' I'll miss you very much. Will you miss me?" My mother paused, as if to give the home viewing audience a chance to answer, but there was such an eerie, awkward silence in the studio that she quickly resumed speaking, for the first time looking flustered, as though she were trying not to cry.

"Remember everything I told you," Miss Mary said. "Keep watching 'Rumpus Room' and do what Bee Good says. Try to be good, try very, very hard. The Looking Glass is especially powerful today, I can see all of you, all my boys and girls, too many to name. But I'll make you a promise. If you'll remember me, I'll remember you. Promise? All right then." Miss Mary smiled. "Goodbye, boys and girls, goodbye," she said, her image starting to fade as the swirling pattern reappeared. For a while, the red and white spiral filled the screen, then disappeared again to show Miss Mary gone, the mirror now framing the empty set of Rumpus Room, on which the lights went down.

I felt terrible, sitting in the Dark Room, in front of the Gillingham, knowing that, out in the living room, my mother was watching what I was watching, watching the character she'd created and had played for thirteen years say goodbye. I had no doubt that, sitting there by herself, she was crying, but I told myself that to go out and keep her company would just be giving in, which I was determined not to do.

But then, a scene that, for improbability and sentimentality, outdid anything my mother had ever come up with for her television shows, began playing itself out over and over in my mind. I imagined my father, far from home, alone in some apartment, looking out the window, happening to hear on the TV that Miss Mary would soon be leaving "Rumpus Room." Suddenly realizing that by leaving home he made a terrible mistake, that he loves my mother after all, he jumps up, races to the studio, arriving just in time to reconcile with my mother and to appear as John in the final episode, thereby not only making my mother happy, but saving Miss Mary from having to go off into neverneverland alone. I imagined him, bounding out from backstage, from off screen, surprising her, my father joining my mother, John to her Miss Mary, the two of them together forever in the black and white world of the Gillingham.

It just wouldn't let go, this daydream. A week after the final episode had aired, I was still having it, still imagining my father, in bow-tie and suspenders, appearing on "Rumpus Room" as John just in time to leave with Miss Mary, to escort her into the wings, the two of them strolling arm in arm. I would go into the Dark Room and turn on the Gillingham but, instead of paying attention to what was on the screen, I would superimpose this daydream on it, my parents strolling arm in arm across the screen.

It seemed to have taken over my mind, my waking mind at least, for I woke almost every morning from a different sort of dream, one in which my parents were still together, in which it was I and not my father who had left. I woke, sometimes, in the dark, convinced, for the first few seconds, that I was alone in some strange house, that I had done something, betrayed them in some way that could never be forgiven, so that no apology, no appeal could change things. I was often halfway out of bed before I recognized my room. I would lie back, wondering if, in the first few seconds after waking up these days, my father knew where he was, or if he thought he was still at home.

I would go to the window and peek out through the drapes to see if the Philosophers were still there. Often, they would see me or notice the drapes moving and shout, "Good morning, Philo," all of them laughing, obviously taking the whole thing less seriously at that hour than they seemed to do at night. I wondered who they were, from how far away they'd come.

My mother and I had tacitly agreed to pretend we hadn't had a falling-out. We were civil with each other, staying out of each other's way as much as possible. Now and then she would talk about my father as though she were talking to herself. She became more and more convinced that nothing had happened to him, that, for reasons of his own that would never seem acceptable to her, he was staying away. The more certain she became that no harm had come to him, the more certain she became that he had left her for good. She began to despair of ever seeing him again, I think, though, to spare me, she didn't come right out and say so. For my part, the longer my father stayed away, the more resentful I became of her, though I was sure that he was coming back. So many of his things were still in evidence throughout the house, exactly as he'd left them. Ties of his still hung on doorknobs, his toiletries were in the bathroom, his study was crammed to overflowing with his books. We moved among these things as if they belonged to some previous tenant who, until he returned for them, would want them left exactly where they were.

In the tabloids, my father was no longer front-page or even front-section news. Most of the stories about him, poked away at the bottom of the back pages, were of the recap/update variety: "The Search for Philo's Father Continues," "Still No Sign of Philo's Father," "Hope Fading for Philo's Father," "Philo's Father Feared Dead."

One evening, as we were having dinner in awkward silence, my mother told me that, after this year, she was having nothing more to do with "The Philo Farnsworth Show." It had gotten out of hand, she said, this fad, this cult, whatever it was. People seemed to have developed some sort of obsession with the show that, as far as she could see, had little or nothing to do with the show itself. People weren't getting from the show what she'd hoped they would, she said. She asked me if I knew that people all over the world were dressing up like characters from "The Philo Farnsworth Show," then going out to bars and even sports stadiums, not just to watch the show, but to play along with the actors on the screen, saying their lines with them, mimicking their gestures.

"It's called a say-along," I said. "Like a sing-along. And yes, I'm aware of it. The whole world's aware of it."

It was crazy, she said, people almost worshipping a TV program. It wasn't what she had in mind when she first conceived the show. Because she didn't have exclusive rights to it, she couldn't stop the network from going on without her, but she was washing her hands of it.

"They can have it," my mother said. "As far as I'm concerned, they can have it. From now on, I'll be more careful. It's a shame losing the show, but there's apparently nothing I can do about it. And even though I'm not playing Miss Mary anymore, I'm still producing 'Rumpus Room.'"

She looked at me. "Of course, you're old enough to make up your own mind about what you want to do," she said. She paused as though waiting for me to say something. "I'm sure they'd like you to stay on as Philo, if that is what you want to do," she said. When I said nothing, she said she hoped I would think seriously about it before making up my mind.

I wondered if, just to spite her, I should come right out and tell her that I was staying on as Philo Farnsworth. I thought better of it, however, when I saw that she was on the verge of tears. No doubt she'd been hoping that I would dismiss out of hand the very thought of staying on without her. Clearly, it hurt her deeply that I even had to think about it. "It's a very important decision," she said, her voice quavering, "and I wouldn't want you to act rashly."

I told myself that I had no intention of betraying her, that it was only to punish her that I was pretending I had to think about it and to make a point about having a mind of my own. I would leave her in suspense for a while and then, acting as if it could have gone one way or the other, I would tell her I was quitting.

Soon afterwards, however, I got a phone call from a producer with the network, a "Mr. Mack," who wondered if we
could "meet somewhere to talk about some things." I told
him that my mother and I had an agreement that I was not to
talk television with anyone unless she was with me.

"I guess it doesn't work the other way around," Mr. Mack
said. I considered hanging up, apparently pausing long
enough to make him realize he'd overdone it, for he made a
flustered apology, assured me he'd been joking. He told me
that he had been talking with my mother just the other day
about how best to handle the "Philo phenomenon" and she
had told him she was leaving the show.

I said nothing. He said I could probably make a good living indefinitely from playing Philo Farnsworth. He said he
was going to be frank with me. He had broached with her the
possibility of my staying on as Philo and she had flatly turned
him down.

"I asked her to raise the matter with you to see what you'd
say, but she didn't think that was such a good idea. She said
you weren't old enough to make that sort of decision."

"She did raise it with me," I said.

"But she told us she was quitting for both of you," said
Mr. Mack. I didn't know what to say, though it seemed entirely
possible to me that my mother had taken it for granted that I
would go along with her decision.

"The question is, Henry," said Mr. Mack, "do *you* think
you're old enough to make up your own mind? We think you
are. Your mother can opt out, of course, that's her right, but
the show, as the saying goes, will still go on." He asked me
again if we could meet somewhere and I told him I didn't

think it would be a good idea.

"Would it be O.K. if we just hashed the whole thing out on the phone then? Would that be O.K.? That would be O.K., wouldn't it? She hasn't got you that much under wraps, has she?" Mr. Mack said, laughing as if to assure me that, once again, he was joking. "I'd like to talk to you as a mature, independent grownup," Mr. Mack said, "someone old enough and smart enough to make his own decisions. Do you think we could have that kind of conversation, Henry?"

I said I thought we could.

"Have you thought about what the future holds for you, Henry?" he said. When I said nothing, he said he didn't think I had. He wondered if I realized that this could be my one chance to make it on my own, to gain some independence.

"I know what it's been like for you, Henry," he said. "Everybody knows what it's been like for you." He told me that he had been put in charge of what was now known at the network as Philomania.

"You've heard of Tutmania, Beatlemania. Well, this is Philomania." He outlined to me how the network hoped to exploit Philomania in the years to come. When the television show had run its course, or perhaps even before then, they would start making Philo Farnsworth movies, a series of sequels, one every couple of years, all featuring the original cast of the television show.

But there was more to it than just movies, he assured me. He asked me if I was aware that membership in the Philosophers now numbered, world-wide, in the tens of thousands. The network was organizing what they hoped would be an annual Philosophers' Convention, a coming together of

Philosophers from around the world; some of my fellow cast members on "The Philo Farnsworth Show" had already agreed to appear at next month's founding convention at Maple Leaf Gardens in Toronto. But, of course, the person the Philosophers would most want to see there was me, the star attraction, the man himself. No Philo Farnsworth convention would be complete without Philo himself. My mother and the network could agree to disagree and no harm would be done, Mr. Mack said. Producers, whose every right it was to pull out of projects they didn't feel were right for them could be replaced – it would not be easy to find a replacement for my mother, they'd hate to have to do it, but it could be done. Not so actors, however, especially not one as closely identified with my role as I was. Philo was the whole show and, as far as the public was concerned, Henry Prendergast was Philo. I'd been playing Philo for four years now, I had defined the role – I was uniquely, distinctively, irreplaceably Philo: the public would accept no substitutes.

"I'll be frank with you, Henry," Mr. Mack said. "We need you. Without you, there's a good chance that none of this would work. A Philo Farnsworth movie with someone other than Henry Prendergast as Philo? Out of the question, as far as we're concerned. A phony Philo addressing the annual Philosophers' Convention? It would never work. It just wouldn't be the same. And you need us, Henry. You need us. You're so closely identified with this role that you might never get another part. That's a fact you've got to face. This could mean financial independence for you. And this time, we'd be paying you directly, don't forget. This could mean your freedom, Henry."

When I told him of my plans to become a stage actor, he gave a kind of rueful laugh and asked me if I had ever heard of something called "role identification." It was, he said, the most extreme form of typecasting. The chances of someone as closely identified with a famous television character as I was ever getting a part in a serious play or even a serious movie were astronomically low, he said.

"'The Philo Farnsworth Show' is not great art," said Mr. Mack, "we both know that. It's great entertainment, but it's not great art. It's pretty campy, hokey stuff when you come right down to it. Everybody thinks of Henry Prendergast as Philo, and they'll never stop thinking of you as Philo. And let's not forget you started out playing the Bees on 'Rumpus Room.' The kind of acting you have in mind is just not in the cards, Henry. I've seen this kind of thing a thousand times." He said that what I ought to do, instead of ending up like so many other typecast, role-identified actors, child actors especially, who were has-beens by the age of twenty, was make the most of my situation, exploit it, turn it to my advantage.

He said I didn't have to agree to what he called "the big picture" right away. We could do things one at a time. He named an impressive sum of money that I'd receive were I to agree to be the guest speaker at next month's founding Philosophers' Convention in Toronto.

"This is going to be big, Henry," Mr. Mack said. "This is not just a meeting of some local chapter of the Philosophers. Thousands of people from all over the world will be there. There'll be newspaper and television coverage, Philo Farnsworth merchandise on sale." All I would have to do was make some sort of speech, appear on the podium as Philo

Farnsworth, address the Philosophers. There would be simultaneous translations, into however many languages were necessary, of every word I said. It would be the United Nations of Television with me as the secretary-general, so to speak. Then I would do some one-on-one publicity: circulate, meet people, make myself available for interviews, pose for photographs with fellow Philosophers, sign autographs, that sort of thing. One weekend of my time was all it would take. One weekend.

The network saw the show as their flagship, said Mr. Mack, and Philo Farnsworth himself as a kind of symbol of their medium, the very essence, the very epitome of television, at once its inventor and soon to be its most famous character. What better person on whom to base the most famous television character of all time than the inventor of television? It was perfect. It was pure television. Of course, Philo Farnsworth was not yet the most famous television character of all time, but that was what they were shooting for, that's what they intended to make him and would make him, with my help.

"Think of what it would mean for you, Henry," Mr. Mack said. "Compared to how rich you'll be, you're poor now. Compared to how famous you'll be, you're a nobody now. Compared to how happy you'll be, you're miserable now."

I told Mr. Mack that I wasn't sure it was something that I would feel comfortable doing. I asked him if I could think about it for a while. "Sure, sure you can," he said. "But not too long. This is Thursday, Henry, and we'd like you to address the convention two weeks from Saturday night. Give me a call this time next week, O.K.?" I said I would.

He closed by saying that only I knew what was best for me, urging me to think about it, about what my alternatives were, about what I could realistically expect my life to be like if I turned him down.

Not long after my mother made known to the network her intention to resign from the show, the story hit the press. We were swamped with calls and requests for interviews, relayed to us by the men of Mission Control. The network in New York was likewise swamped, the two big questions on everybody's mind being whether or not I would stay on as Philo and, if not, would that mean the end of the show? In her one printed news release, my mother said that she had come to her decision after much soul-searching and that she had no idea what I would do or what the network planned to do with "The Philo Farnsworth Show."

The network's official response was that, until Henry Prendergast made his decision, the future fate of the show was uncertain. Soon, there were rumours that the Prendergasts were getting out of television altogether, that the strain of my father's disappearance was taking its toll. My mother had quit as Miss Mary and resigned from "The Philo Farnsworth Show," and I would soon follow suit. There were rumours, too, however, of a rift between my mother and me, rumours that, in spite of her attempts to make me quit against my will, I would defy her and stay on as Philo Farnsworth.

The scrum of reporters staked out across the street was about triple the usual size. Every time a car came or went, any car, but especially if it was a limousine or had tinted windows, the doors of all the media vans and station wagons would come flying open, and a mob of reporters and photographers would run towards Pristine Place like some surprise invasion force, only to be repulsed by the men of Mission Control. The building's management told my mother once again that there was a limit to their patience and that, if this kept up, we would have to leave. We lived under siege, my mother leaving the building only to go to work, me not at all.

Public opinion polls were taken as to what Henry Prendergast should do, quit or stay on as Philo Farnsworth. Opinion was overwhelmingly in favour of my doing the latter. The newly elected president of the Philosophers wrote me and, on behalf of his entire membership, urged me to defy my mother. She'd been running my life long enough, he said. It was time I ran it myself, time I cut the apron strings. He also asked me to keep in mind the millions of people who were counting on me to DO THE RIGHT THING!

Feeling ran high against my mother who, for the first time in her TV career, began receiving hate mail, addressed, not only to Audrey Prendergast, but also to Miss Mary, which she found especially upsetting. There were letters full of obscenities and threats. One of the more moderate, more literate correspondents said she was a "pushy, bossy, bitchy, overbearing, smothering, exploitative, uppity, selfish, incestuous, brainwashing, child-molesting prostitute" who, if she knew what was good for her, would let Philo live his own life.

Another, in a jagged, barely legible scrawl, said simply, "We'll get you for what you did to Philo, you stupid slut."

Another: "If 'Philo Farnsworth' is cancelled because of you, you'll pay. Anyone who knows me will tell you I'm not kidding. You've been warned."

Yet another: "Miss Mary. Little Miss Know-it-all is more like it. She thinks the Philosophers don't understand her show, we're not smart enough I guess. It's not enough she makes 'The Philo Farnsworth Show,' she tells us how to watch it, too. We'll watch it anyway we please, Miss Smarty-pants. The Philosophers won't just go away because she wants them to."

In almost all of the letters addressed to my mother or to me, I was referred to as Philo. We'd always assumed that the many adulatory letters that came in were addressed to Philo just for fun, as a kind of tribute to the vividness and likeability of the character that we'd created, or because people didn't know offhand what my real name was. But now we were not so sure. Letters addressed to Miss Mary in which I was referred to as Philo were particularly unnerving. Even if they couldn't distinguish between TV and real life, which seemed hard enough to believe, it seemed inconceivable that the writers of these letters could think that some sort of interaction was taking place between Miss Mary and Philo, fictional characters from two different television programs.

My mother was, to say the least, taken aback by how seriously some people took their television. She couldn't believe that all the goodwill she'd built up over the years could be undone in a matter of weeks. It was as if she had announced her plan to assassinate some beloved public figure. She hadn't known, she said, that there was so much bitterness, so much anger in the world, let alone that the mere possibility of the cancellation of a television program could bring it out. That it was directed at her by these so-called philosophers, by people who claimed to admire and be followers of Philo Farnsworth, a character whom she'd created and in whom there was not a trace of bitterness and anger, was incomprehensible, she said.

The mail addressed to me was of a different sort. People, having heard that I was wavering in my decision, agonizing over what I should do, tried everything to make me stay on as Philo.

"If you quit, I'll kill myself," one correspondent said. "The Philosophers have changed my life. They are everything to me. If you quit, I just don't know. I'll start drinking again maybe or something worse. I won't be able to help myself, I swear."

"If you quit, I'll kill you," said another. "Why are you afraid of her, Philo? Sure she's your mother, but she's just a woman, you're a man. Or are you? That is the question that everyone is asking. Are you a man? Be a man, Philo. Someone with your money, you're famous, you don't know what it's like. You owe it to us, we made you rich and famous. Who are you to say 'I quit,' when millions of Philosophers say no? Most people would give anything to stand for just one second in those shoes of yours."

The Philosophers discontinued their vigil, or rather, they transformed it into what was at once a protest against my mother and a kind of pep rally for Philo. It was hard to resist the notion that they had simply turned their signs around, that on the back of the placards proclaiming sympathy for my father there had all along been these slogans that criticized my mother, slogans like "Down with Mary Queen of Tots," and "You Drove Peter Away, Don't Do the Same with Philo." As for me, I felt like some politician whose supporters were exhorting him to stand for re-election. Down below, at peak times of the day, there was a sea of signs of the sort one sees at party conventions, signs bearing blown-up photographs of Philo and Philo's name in large block letters.

"I swear to God they've all gone mad," my mother said. "There's no other explanation except that they've all gone stark raving mad."

I had never stopped before to wonder what might be the implications of the success of "The Philo Farnsworth Show" for my future in acting. I wondered if I would be the first actor to have a lifelong shadow role, Philo Farnsworth and me aging at exactly the same rate until death do us part. It seemed to me that my mother should have foreseen this role-identification thing. She was in the same situation herself, known to all the world as Miss Mary, but for her it wasn't a problem, because she'd never wanted to play any other roles and having been Miss Mary was no barrier to getting backing for and producing the kind of programs that she favoured. She could not have known from the start, of course, how big a hit "The Philo Farnsworth Show" would be, could not have predicted the Philo fad, but once the thing was underway, she should have considered what its long-term effects would be on me, especially when I told her of my intention to take up acting for the stage.

Looking down at that throng of Philosophers, now numbering over a thousand, according to the press, I realized that Mr. Mack was right. I would never live down the role of Philo Farnsworth, in art or in life. I couldn't even quit acting and take up something else for, whatever I did, I'd be doing it as Philo, the thought of which, of never being taken seriously no matter what I did, seemed intolerable.

It seemed to me that my mother was to blame for everything, right from the start, that my father was right, that, by getting us involved in "Rumpus Room," she had ruined any chance we had for happiness, diverted us from our true course. I decided I would do what my father had done: I would leave her, get away from her for good, gain my independence, start to live my own life. I would go on being Philo until I had made enough money to spend the rest of my life doing as I pleased. If need be, I would build myself some sort of estate, some secure and private place where I would not be bothered. I assumed that I would have some sort of family, that I would have companionship of some kind in this cloistered life of mine, but I didn't give it too much thought, telling myself that such things would have to wait until the practicalities were taken care of. I might never see my father again, but I would be following his example, doing what he had inspired me to do, acting in solidarity and consort with him. He'd shown me what I had to do and I would do it.

No sooner had I thus resolved, however, than once again I imagined my father, showing up unannounced on the set of "Rumpus Room," my prodigal father come back to play the part of John to my mother's Miss Mary just as the lights were going down. Then I imagined him sending for me, contacting me in secret, having me meet him somewhere, coming to Pristine Place while my mother was out and asking me if I would rather live with him than with her and off we'd go, just the two of us, in the station wagon, off to a new life in which I would neither be Philo nor Henry Prendergast but someone else.

Several nights in a row, I sat for hours in the Dark Room, not even bothering to switch on the Gillingham, recalling my conversation with Mr. Mack. Though I had no illusions about what was motivating Mr. Mack, it seemed to me that he was right: that, of the three alternatives available to me – staying with my mother, trying to make a whole new start on my own, or continuing on as Philo Farnsworth – the third was by far the best, the best of a bad lot, perhaps, but still the best.

I might not have to be Philo forever, it seemed to me, at least not in front of the camera. There was at least a slim chance this way that I could end up doing something worthwhile. People might always think of me as Philo but the money I would make from, say, ten or fifteen years of "The Philo Farnsworth Show" might be enough that I could get started on some projects of my own. Even if nothing more came of it than getting rich, I could eventually give up playing Philo and live on the money I'd made for the rest of my life.

I phoned Mr. Mack at our appointed time and told him I would address the Philosophers' Convention; that is to say, that I would appear in front of it and read the speech they had written for me, but that was all. The rest of it – the schmoozing with the Philosophers, the picture-taking, the autograph-signing, the concourse walk-about, judging the look-alike contests – I wasn't ready for, I said.

He sounded as relieved, as delighted as if I had agreed to the whole multi-year, multi-movie package deal. "I knew you'd make the right decision, Henry," Mr. Mack said, "I knew you would."

I told him we had to work out some plan to get me to Maple Leaf Gardens without my mother finding out. It wasn't that she would prevent me from going, I said, it was just that I didn't want her to find out about it any sooner than she had to. Mr. Mack wondered if I couldn't just tell her I was going out with friends. I told him I didn't really have any friends, which did not seem to register with Mr. Mack except as a problem of logistics.

He told me he'd get back to me about it but, as it turned out, the problem was soon solved, for, on Thursday, two days before I was due to address the convention, my mother accepted an invitation from those friends of hers for us to spend the weekend with them at their cottage. My mother said she thought it was a good idea for us to get out of town for the weekend. What with the Philosophers' Convention, at which, it was said, the network was going to reveal its plans for the show, and what with all the rumours about my being the Saturday night mystery guest, Pristine Place would be under siege all weekend long, she said. She looked at me as she spoke as if to say, "Well, this is it, you'll have to tell me now, one way or another, what you intend to do."

I felt bad about agreeing to this plan of hers, for it was tantamount to saying that I was quitting the show, and would therefore have no need to stay in town. I did agree to it, however.

"Oh I'm so glad you're coming, Henry," she said. "I'm so glad, sweetheart." She made as though to hug me, but hung back when she saw, by the expression on my face, that I didn't want her to.

It was better that we spend the weekend in privacy in the country, she said, among family friends, than stay at home under what amounted to house arrest. There was no telling, what with so many of them coming to town, how many more Philosophers would congregate at Pristine Place or what sort of antics they would get up to.

I told her I'd already agreed to go away for the weekend, so she didn't have to go on pitching the idea to me.

"Sorry, sorry," she said, as if she wanted me to know that she realized that it wasn't just to please her that I was going.

The plan, which my mother called "real cloak-and-dagger stuff," and seemed to get a great kick out of devising, was for me to leave the building, undetected, we hoped, in the superintendent's van on Friday afternoon and go to her friends' house where she, after some such covert departure from the studio, would meet me.

I went to the Dark Room and peeked out through the blackout drapes. Down below, a small band of Philosophers who, despite the cold, were still in costume, were standing around, talking, leaning on their signs, a few, with their backs to the wind, trying to keep candles lit. Because of the weather, they were a skeleton crew and would soon be heading off to wherever it was they went when they left Pristine Place. It was late November now and I wondered if they would try to maintain their vigil/protest/pep rally through the winter. Surely not, though in the four months since my father left, they hadn't missed a single day or night. I imagined them dogging me for the rest of my days, no matter where I went, standing as though on guard outside my home, like some self-appointed security force.

And if I stepped down as Philo? "If you quit, I'll kill you." How's that for devotion? The thought of them still stalking me – but for different reasons – crossed my mind, but I dismissed it, assuring myself that they were harmless, really, just loners, cellar dwellers who had become Philosophers for want of anything else to do.

I switched on the Gillingham and found a rerun of the show. I thought that perhaps my decision would not cause the kind of rift between my mother and me that I'd all along been assuming that it would, that I might not be giving her enough credit. It could be that what I was contemplating was not the great betrayal that it seemed to be. Perhaps we could have it out, clear the air, agree to disagree, and remain close despite the fact that, professionally, she would go her way and I would go mine. I wished it were so. But I knew that, justifiably or not, she would surely feel betrayed and that, after everything else that had happened, to be betrayed by me would break her heart. This knowledge did not convince me that I should spare her that heartbreak, only that I should spare myself the sight of it.

It was not my fault that she had set herself up to be betrayed, by me, by my father, even by the network. I knew that my mother was not the manipulating, conniving woman the press had for years been making her out to be; just the opposite, in fact. She was guileless, morally ingenuous, naive. She was exactly what she seemed to be and assumed that other people were, too. Hidden motives, reserved judgements, insincerity, irony, dissemblance of almost any kind – most of the time, you wouldn't know by her that such things existed. For her to have done, however ill-advisedly, what she had done for my father, was something of a miracle, made possible only by that other aspect of her unstinting nature, her capacity, her compulsion to love unreservedly, and to do, even against their wishes, in some cases even without their knowledge, what she thought was best for those she loved. Had she really told Mr. Mack that she had quit for both of us, that the decision about whether or not I would stay on as Philo Farnsworth was really hers to make? I wasn't sure. She was something of a saint and saints either renounce the world or try to save it. My mother was of the latter kind, the kind whose destiny it is to be betrayed, for they keep foisting their kindness on people who wind up betraying them in self-defence. That's what I was engaging in, I told myself, an act of self-defence.

I was still watching TV when my mother, as I'd known she would, came in to say goodnight. I was slumped in my arm-chair, in front of the Gillingham, which provided the only light, a flickering blue light that, at its dimmest, left the room completely dark.

"I'll see you tomorrow then, Henry," she said, standing in the doorway. "Don't stay up too late, O.K.?"

I was sure my voice would fail me, give me away, so all I did was raise my hand in a kind of half-wave, then let it drop as if I was barely awake. My mother gave a little laugh and closed the door.

Looking at the set, I remembered the day Mr. Gillingham first came to fix it. It seemed to me like a memory from another life, the life in vain search of which my father had set out four months ago.

I found yet another episode of the show, the "Eureka" episode in which Philo makes his big breakthrough. "I've done it," I watched myself saying on the screen, Philo running into the Farnsworth house where his mother and father were sitting in front of a television-sized radio, "I've done it, it works, it works." Philo's parents jumped up and, linking arms, the three of us danced around in a circle, celebrating my invention.

The image on the television screen consisted of swarms of interchangeably identical electrons, my father had once told me. In the same way that it was true that no two snowflakes were alike, it was true that no two electrons were different. "If you've seen one electron, you've seen 'em all," my father said. "There is absolutely no way of telling them apart." It was only the number and arrangement of electrons that differed from object to object and person to person. Though my father assured me that electrons were too small to see, I had been unable to resist the notion that what I saw when I put my face close up to the screen were indeed electrons, swarming, undifferentiated, clones without a prototype. I peeked out through the blackout drapes just in time to see the Philosophers heading away from Pristine Place in single file, their signs on their shoulders.

I turned on the light and tried to read George Everson's book about Philo, hoping to rekindle some of the admiration and affection I had felt for the real Philo Farnsworth when I had first read about him. I had lost all ability to concentrate, however, to put one word in front of another, to follow through, to its conclusion, even the most simple sentence. Each word seemed like a discrete entity, cut off from the words around it, each sentence like some randomly arranged sequence of words. I did not read, but remembered, the passage where Philo calls Everson in to the dark room to see the first television image. It reminded me of seeing myself on TV for the first time, sitting in front of the Gillingham, watching as, out of some nebulous past into television land Bee Good came running, waving, his antennae bobbing up and down, to stand beside Miss Mary, who put her arm around him and introduced him to the audience.

On Friday morning, I called my mother at the studio and told her that I'd changed my mind, that, as I didn't know her friends very well, I thought I'd just stay home but that she should go ahead as planned. I was prepared for her response. When she said she wouldn't think of leaving me alone on such a weekend, I told her I was looking forward to having the place to myself for a change and implied that, if she were to insist on keeping me company, I would feel put out at what I would consider to be an all-too-typical example of the sort of behaviour that had driven my father away. At any suggestion that she was repeating with me the mistakes she'd made with my father, she would back off and did so in this case, though she recited quite an extensive list of things I should do or refrain from doing to avoid the Philosophers and the press. I assured her that Mission Control would be as vigilant as always and that she had nothing to worry about.

"All right, sweetheart," she said, "I'll see you Sunday night. Love you. Bye."

"Bye," I said. If there had been the slightest doubt in her mind about my reasons for staying home, it hadn't registered in her voice. My sweet, saintly, trusting mother, how ashamed she made me feel.

14

One of the reasons that I hadn't wanted my mother to know beforehand what I was doing was that I didn't plan on coming back. I was not planning to disappear like my father, without a trace. It would have been all but impossible for me to do so. But I was planning, after the Philosophers' Convention, to begin the best of the bad lot of lives available to me, the only one that, in the state that I was in, seemed tolerable.

Mr. Mack, whom I would never actually meet, rose to the logistical challenge of getting me out of Pristine Place and to Maple Leaf Gardens without the press finding out. He was not so much worried about the press spoiling his surprise as he was about my mother hearing something on the radio or on TV that would bring her back in time to talk me out of going on or otherwise cause trouble.

We settled on a plan like the one my mother had devised. Mr. Mack said that, to fool the press, it would be best if I left for the Gardens long before I was due to address the convention at 8:00 in the evening. Also, he said, it would be a good idea for me to arrive at the Gardens before the convention crowd was up and around in any great numbers. I was smuggled out around noon in a dry-cleaning van which, upon leaving, was followed for a while by two cars that turned back when we stopped at the address written on the van to pick up a load of dry-cleaning.

We met up with Mr. Mack's limo at the appointed place. Though I was assured that, because of the tinted glass, no one could see inside the limo, I shifted down in the seat to below window level anyway as we made our way towards the Gardens, too ridden with guilt to stand to have even people who couldn't see me look in my direction. That I was riding in style to my place of betrayal somehow made it that much worse, as though it was in exchange for such things as limousines that I had chosen to sell my mother out.

At the Gardens, the limo went round to the back where I was hustled into a service elevator and then to a private box enclosed by one-way glass from which I would be able to watch the convention unseen. I had told Mr. Mack that, until it was time for me to go on, I wanted to be left alone, which he agreed to, though he cautioned me not to leave the box.

Judging from the convention kit that had been mailed out to all those planning to attend, and a copy of which had been left for me in the box, the whole thing was very well organized. Philosophers were to enter the Gardens according to which character they chose to play – Philos entered at the East Gate, Victor Valenskys and Teacher Tolmans at the West Gate, and so on. Once inside, look-alikes were to sit in the same sections as well, birds of a feather flocking together, though you could wander about the concourse at your leisure, taking in the exhibits and meeting other Philosophers until some scheduled event was about to start. The floor, where extra chairs had been set up, was reserved for the Philo faction, the gold seats for the Valenskys, the reds for the Teacher Tolmans, and so on.

The Gardens normally seated about sixteen thousand, but with even the playing surface laid with chairs, the crowd by the time I went on would number more like twenty thousand, all of them dressed up like characters from "The Philo Farnsworth Show." I stood for hours staring out at the crowd that was gathering below. At the south end of the Gardens, opposite where I was sitting, there was a giant screen, referred to in the convention kits as the "Magni-vision set, the world's largest TV." "Little did Philo Farnsworth know when he first conceived of his invention that one day there would be a television set that measured 33 feet high by 115 feet wide, or whose screen would be lit by 420,000 light bulbs." Immediately below the screen was an elevated stage, from which, later, I would speak.

Reading in the convention kit that there would be television coverage of the event, I reached up and turned on the overhead set and stretched out in my chair and watched. A mobile camera was making its way slowly around the concourse, which resembled an especially busy sidewalk. Some Philosophers, as they parted to make way for the camera, shoved their faces up close to it, stuck out their tongues, put their hands in front of it, screamed, but most people affected the kind of faintly ironic nonchalance celebrities do when photographed in public.

Philosophers did impersonations of their "Philo Farnsworth Show" characters; one Teacher Tolman looked at the camera and, without a trace of self-consciousness, as if he'd been playing this part for years, as if he'd defined the role, rattled off, verbatim, a speech from a recent episode. Others confined themselves to speaking some of their character's better-known lines, signature sayings like Mrs. Farnsworth's "Philo, you're home," or Philo's (always to George Everson) "by George, I think you're right."

Now and then, the unseen cameraman would stop to interview someone, ask them who they were, where they were from. Some people answered as themselves, but most did so in character, saying, "Hi, I'm George Everson from Los Angeles." Others did a kind of fashion-show routine, modelling their "Philo Farnsworth Show" costumes, twirling about, showing the linings of their jackets.

Most of the Philos would not have done very well in a look-alike contest, though a few bore an eerie resemblance to him and to me. There were Philos of all shapes and sizes, variant, idiosyncratic Philos, fat, short, young, old Philos whose zeal to look like Philo had not extended to shaving off their beards and moustaches. There was a child Philo, walking about the concourse with parents dressed like Mrs. Farnsworth and Teacher Tolman. There were cross-dressing Philosophers, unmistakably female Philos, most of them in their teens or early twenties, strolling about with their hair hanging down behind their hats, their hands in their pockets.

There was a clear plurality of Philos, who outnumbered any other character by about three to one. There were Philos fraternizing with Valenskys who were going about in their black, pin-striped suits, their hands in their pockets, their vests and pocket-watches showing. There were a good many George Eversons, dressed in tweed from head to ankle, sporting a pair of Florsheims like Philo's, and, in a manner faintly reminiscent of Charlie Chaplin, twirling canes. There was a surprising number of Teacher Tolmans, that character's popularity perhaps owing to the simplicity and inexpensiveness of his costume – white shirt, polka-dot bow-tie, brown slacks kept up by tartan suspenders that crisscrossed at the back. Almost all the women were dressed as Mrs. Farnsworth, though a few had opted to be Philo's rarely glimpsed childhood sweetheart and fiancée, Sarah, who, no matter what the weather, no matter if a scene in which she appeared were indoors or out, always wore a white lace-fringed bonnet tied beneath her chin.

The camera lingered at the stall where the actors who played Victor Valensky and George Everson were signing autographs. "George Everson" was signing copies of the new edition of George Everson's book. It seemed to be selling well. There was hardly a person walking about who didn't have a copy in their hands.

Along the concourse, opposite the concessions where the hockey souvenir stands were usually located were the various exhibits. The theme of those exhibits not devoted specifically to "The Philo Farnsworth Show" was television: television nostalgia, television's early days, featuring a life-size photograph of the Nipkow disk, the first mechanical TV and the first of any kind, invented in the 1880s; a walk down television's memory lane, a gallery of posters depicting a sampling of television shows from TV's inception to the present day: "Ozzie and Harriet," "Your Show of Shows," "I Love Lucy," "The Virginian," "Cheyenne," "Bonanza."

A few hours before I was due to go on, two makeup women dressed like, I suppose disguised as, Mrs. Farnsworth came to the box and began, with hardly even a word to one another, to transform me into Philo. They made me up exactly as they did for the show, for while I was at the podium speaking, Philosophers would look, not at me, but at my image on the Magni-vision screen. It was strange to think that there was no way that I could look like Philo in real life; the makeup, the purpose of which was to make me look "natural" on the screen, to counteract the effect of the television lights and the distortion of the camera, looked like a kind of mask; I looked as though some quack mortician had done a rush job on my face, my skin a powdery, ghastly white except for a blotch of orange here and there. After dyeing it, then slicking it with some sort of holding gel, they combed my hair straight back, then got me into my Philo outfit, everything except my hat, which they would probably have put on my head if I hadn't picked it up first. When I asked them why it was necessary to get me ready hours ahead of time, they shrugged and, collecting their things, left without a word.

For fear of rumpling my costume or smudging my makeup, I sat upright in a chair, staring at myself in a mirror. I looked like Philo come back from the dead, Philo's ghost as he might have been portrayed on the show.

I ran through my address, which read like some sort of campaign speech or charge to the troops. I was to start by holding out my arms and saying "My fellow Philosophers," a phrase which recurred throughout the speech, each time signalling that a new topic was about to be addressed.

"My fellow Philosophers, you haven't seen the last of Philo Farnsworth. We'll go on making new episodes of 'The

Philo Farnsworth Show' as long as you want us to. Next year, the show will be better than ever. Philo Farnsworth movies are in the works. Philomania is not some passing fad; it won't just go away. Philomania is here to stay. My fellow Philosophers, we owe a great debt to Philo Farnsworth, whose name and whose invention we honour here tonight. The name Philo Farnsworth is synonymous with television. Philo Farnsworth is television…"

I fell asleep and was awakened by a mass chanting that I thought at first was coming from the overhead TV, though in fact, as I soon saw upon standing up, it was coming from outside the box.

I had slept through most of the afternoon events and now the say-along was underway. The Gardens was all but dark. An episode from the show was playing on the Magni-vision screen, perhaps the best-known episode, the one most often shown in reruns, the official say-along episode that all Philosophers were said to know by heart. It was Episode 17, in which Valensky steals the blueprints for Philo's picture tube. Philo recovers the blueprints but, as the theft cannot be proven, Valensky goes unpunished, Philo having to be content with a moral victory and with a lengthy chastisement of the villain.

As much as possible, the Philosophers aped their on-screen prototypes. The Victors adjusted their ties when Victor adjusted his, wrung their hands when he wrung his. When Philo removed his hat, the Philos in the Gardens, in one mass movement, removed theirs. When he replaced it, they did likewise. Each Philosopher carried several props to be used throughout the say-along. When, on screen, Philo crumpled up and threw in the air a piece of paper, the Philos on the floor did the same, thousands of balls of paper going up in unison. When Philo lit a Bunsen burner, the Philos flicked their lighters and held them aloft. Each time Philo spoke, his voice was drowned out by the Philo faction speaking his lines with him, as were the other characters' voices drowned out by their factions. The effect of this mass chanting of my mother's dialogue was to make even lines like "Here's Philo now" sound deeply significant, profound. Episode 17 came across like some sort of mass drama in which each character was played by a chorus of thousands.

I was still watching when several men from Gardens security arrived at the door to the box to escort me to the podium. I put my hat on and went with them, once again using the service elevator which took us down to ground level.

There was a specially constructed covered walkway leading to the stage, so my presence was kept secret until the last moment when, emerging from the makeshift tunnel, I climbed the stairs onto the stage, at which there suddenly went up a frightening roar that I didn't realize at first was meant for me.

Along the front of the stage, facing the crowd, their backs to me, was an arm-linked line of policemen who, because they were all dressed alike, might themselves have been a faction of Philosophers. Beyond them, so brightly was the stage lit, I could make out only vague shapes. A podium that I was glad I'd be able to hold on to and, to some extent at least, hide behind, stood in the centre of the stage which otherwise was bare, though there were streamers and banners of some sort overhead.

I looked over my shoulder for an instant and was startled to see a live image of myself on the Magni-vision screen, my face in profile, my expression like that of a child surprised in some shameful act. I had never seen myself on a cinema screen before, let alone one this big. My every facial feature was magnified to the point of parody, the Prendergast chin ridiculously large, as if the image on the screen was mocking me, flouting my self-consciousness. It was not Philo Farnsworth but Henry Prendergast I saw up there, my essential self writ so large, laid so bare I had to look away.

As my eyes grew more accustomed to the light, I saw that I was looking out upon a sea of Philo Farnsworths, a crowd of look-alikes dressed exactly as I was dressed, an army wearing the uniform that I'd made famous. They were jumping up and down, applauding with their hands above their heads. I could see the Valenskys, too, a dark band of them in the seats above the Philos.

These people knew that I was here against my mother's wishes, possibly even without her knowledge, that my presence here meant that I was defying her, defecting from the family. I was their revenge on her. And revenge, I now realized, was my motive as well, revenge on my mother for driving my father away. I could think of no future without him that was likely to be tolerable, let alone make me happy.

"We love you, Philo Farnsworth," someone in the crowd shouted. "Philo, Philo," the Philosophers began to chant.

I had fooled myself into thinking that a kind of power play was taking place within the family. I'd thought my father and I were on the same side, taking my mother to task, teaching her a lesson, and not just because of what had happened recently. I thought that it was as much for me as for himself that he had left, that things had merely come to a head with this business of the book, that it was to protest her long-standing habit of meddling in both our lives that he had staged this temporary walkout. And so I'd supported him, even assisted him in what I thought was his gesture of protest. In his absence, I had been his delegate, his representative. Whenever my mother and I had arrived home together, I had taken the elevator, leaving her to climb the stairs alone.

It never occurred to me that he might have walked out on both of us and that it was because of both of us that he would not be coming back, that he might have considered me to be just as much of an impediment to his happiness as he did my mother. "I wanted to write a good book," he had said. I had nodded as if I understood and perhaps he had thought I did. How could I have missed his real meaning? "It's because I want to write a good book that I'm never coming back."

Perhaps he thought I knew that he was never coming back and that, even so, I preferred to keep my distance from him when we said goodbye. But surely, if I'd known he was not coming back, I would have hugged him, would have done or said something. Or perhaps I had known, perhaps it was true that, not even to say a last goodbye to him could I over-come this squeamish self-consciousness of mine, that, not even to avail myself of what might be my last chance could I forget myself long enough to tell my father that I loved him.

I remembered him telling me that, for a few weeks after I was born, he couldn't pull himself away from my crib, couldn't stop looking at me, for he had a notion that a crea-ture so rudimentary, so devoid of self-consciousness, had to be kept constantly in mind or would simply cease to exist.

My mother, my lonely, misfit mother. She had known when she looked in on me before going to bed what I'd made up my mind to do. She had known when I called her at the office. Probably, she'd cooked up the idea of a weekend in the country just to make it easier for me to leave, though it might have meant never seeing me again. I was not supposed to know this, any more than my father was supposed to know, ever, that she'd arranged to have his book published, that she'd risked everything for him.

She was capable, as it seemed neither of us were, of utter selflessness. My mother was willing to love and not be loved back, and to do so in secret, without acknowledgement of any kind. She always had been, although, unable to imagine that anyone could be that way, I'd been blind to it. It was hard for me to resist the notion that to love this way was fool-ish, reckless, or that it wasn't really love at all, but gullibility or something like it. I wondered, not so much if I deserved it but if I inspired it, if something particular to me, some part of my essential nature of which I was not even aware, brought it out of her, or if she would have loved any son of hers this way.

"I'm sorry," I said, out loud, into the microphone, and the Philosophers, perhaps thinking I was apologizing for having paused so long, roared back, "We love you, Philo."

I started to cry. Whatever it was that all my life had pre-vented me from loving her without reserve was gone, not gone for good, though I was young enough to think so, but gone for now. It filled me with shame to think that what I felt for her in the few minutes that it lasted was what she always felt for me. Audrey Prendergast was someone I had never met, could never know.

I wondered if it was possible that the business with the book had been partly my father's fault, that something in him had driven her to do it, that he might have let himself go to pieces over the book with the intention of forcing her to intervene, to do it secretly on his behalf, as he must have known she could, what with all the offers of help she had made. She had seen in him signs of giving way, signs that this failure, at this point in his life, would destroy him. Was it possible that he had left his fate in her hands while at the same time making a great show of not wanting any help? Could she have picked up from him some signal that, for all his protestations, he wanted her to meddle, to interfere? When he "found out" what she'd done, he blamed her for having spoiled his bid to find a publisher and then, as if for reasons that had nothing to do with its literary merit, gave up on the book. Humiliation is a strange way of saving face, but if you looked at the matter one way, that's what it was for him: a face-saving way of getting out, of relinquishing his dream, unloading his failure onto her, of seeming, in fact, more like a victim than a failure. He might even have been able to convince himself that she'd done him out of something, that, if not for her, he might have made it.

This, all of this, I realized, might be going too far, but something about my father's manner made me wonder if I wasn't at least partly right. Mixed in with all the outrage, all the humiliation, crushed hopes and disappointment had been a hint of something else – relief, perhaps, deliverance. So was it going too far, as well, to indulge in one last bit of speculation, which was that my mother knew all along what he wanted and what would happen, that her real sacrifice had been to take upon herself his failure, let him blame her instead of himself, be a kind of scapegoat for him? Was it possible that, all along, from the moment D and D accepted his book, they both knew that it would end this way, that they had been acting in a kind of consort, tacitly conspiring?

Everywhere I looked, I saw Philo, saw myself, writ large on the screen behind me, endlessly multiplied in front of me. A wave of self-loathing, self-disgust washed over me. My legs went weak, I staggered backwards slightly and had to grab the podium to keep from falling. We had lost each other, the three of us, my father, my mother, me. With this halving of the family fragment, this sundering of what my father left behind, we were finished. We would, it seemed to me, spend the rest of our lives travelling away from one another, moving further and further apart until even memory would fail us and we would no longer even be able to remember what it felt like to be together.

"My fellow Philosophers," I said, my voice breaking. When I held out my arms as I was bade to do in the script, a roar more deafening than the one that had greeted my entrance went up from the crowd. The stage shook so violently I thought it was collapsing.

I was barely able to resist another glance behind at the screen, though I could see that all eyes were looking past me at it. The camera that was trained on me and that I was supposed to look at whenever a closeup was called for was far away, at the opposite end of the arena. All I could see of it, in fact, was the little red light on the top. I remembered looking through the back of our first TV, the Gillingham, and seeing the little red pilot light inside. I remembered the smell of the dust that had collected on the tubes that were also faintly lit, though with yellow light, the perforated wooden panel warm against my cheek as I tried to see into the farthest corner of the set, looking for some clue as to where the picture came from, how I came to be there on the screen. "Most people watch it from the other side," my father said, when he saw me kneeling down behind it. When he assured me I wasn't in there, I scornfully denied ever having entertained the notion.

I wondered if my father would some day see the footage of me that was being shot tonight. I knew that, by looking at the camera, I could create for him the illusion that I could see him, that I was speaking directly to him. I imagined myself making some sort of dramatic appeal to the camera, talking to it as though it were my father, millions watching while I begged him to come home. I recalled having seen other people do just that, parents facing the camera, looking straight at you and, as if you were their runaway child, beseeching you to come back home, calling you by their loved one's name, saying all is forgiven, no questions asked, we love you. For a few vicarious, voyeuristic seconds, everybody watching would be my father, would think they knew what it felt like to have your son plead with you to let him know that you were still alive. As a way of making contact with someone whose whereabouts were unknown, it had no equal. It was a use to which TV had been put a thousand times, so why not once more? In all likelihood, the network wouldn't mind me springing such a surprise on them, but rather would rise to the occasion, the camera zooming in for a closeup while, for a few moments, I departed from the script, stepped out of my role as Philo Farnsworth to address the viewing audience as Henry Prendergast, a hushed silence in the Gardens as I removed my hat and spoke directly to my father what would afterwards be described as a "heartfelt" appeal. But I knew that my father would think the whole thing had been rehearsed, that I'd been put up to it, talked into it.

I looked at the black armbands the Philosophers were wearing, in memory of my father as though he were not just missing but dead, which, for all I knew, he might well be. I imagined him, disguised as one of the Philos, coming forward from the crowd to rescue me, to stop me from doing what it seemed I could not stop myself from doing.

I continued on with my speech, pausing after each line to let a new ovation run its course. I read monotonously, expressionlessly, though no one seemed to notice. At this point in the script, I was directed to walk around to the other side of the lectern and face the Magni-vision screen, which I did, turning the microphone about to face me.

This seemed to incite the Philosophers who, before I had even completed the manoeuvre, started jumping and waving their hands, surging forward so that the line of police was pushed back against the stage. I saw that it was no longer me, no longer Philo Farnsworth on the screen, or rather, that it was no longer just one Philo but many, a writhing frieze of Philos, for a camera behind and to the right of me had been switched on. It was upon seeing themselves on the screen that the Philos had surged forward in a frenzy, advancing with outstretched arms towards what might have been their reflection.

My audience was on TV and I was watching them. They smiled and waved, at me, it seemed, though they were looking at the camera which panned back to take in more of them, the Philo look-alikes replicating, getting smaller. Soon, the entire floor of Philos was on the screen; then, gradually, as the camera continued to pan back, the picture included the Valenskys, the Eversons, the Teacher Tolmans, the Mrs. Farnsworths, and the Sarahs, until the whole Philosopher-filled arena was on the screen. I raised my arms, hailing the video multitude who responded in kind, while behind me, from their real-life counterparts, a great roar went up. I tried to imagine myself as they saw me, a lone figure facing the screen with arms upraised, hailing it, appealing to it, hopelessly outnumbered by the horde on the screen, dwarfed by the screen itself.

"You haven't seen the last of Philo Farnsworth," I said, to yet another ovation. The Philosophers once again started chanting "Philo, Philo," urging me to turn around, to acknowledge their adulation, but the show was not quite over. The unseen director of the event switched to the other camera and a picture of me standing back to the crowd filled the screen.

The return to the screen of Philo, even photographed from behind this way, brought forth a roar of approval and renewed requests for me to turn around, but still I faced the screen. I looked up at the hatted, suited, stoop-shouldered figure, gargantuan, as motionless, as lifeless as a figure on a billboard; my hands withdrawn into the baggy sleeves of the suit, my wide-brimmed hat tipped back, no part of me was visible, which was exactly what they had in mind when they planned the shot, a kind of study in fabric of Philo Farnsworth, the signature shape, the outline of his clothing, the character with the actor removed.

I was glad I couldn't see my face, glad they couldn't see it, for I was crying now, and it was the worst sort of crying, done with no effect in mind, in no way willed or controllable.

The camera pulled back to show on the screen the screen itself, so that an image of seemingly infinite regression was created, screens within screens within screens, a line of ever-shrinking, ever-diminishing Philos stretching off into the centre as though into some limitless future. It was an often-used trick of the camera, but the crowd screamed its appreciation.

I was supposed to conclude by leading them in singing the theme song from the show, staying put until the screen went dark, then turning around and, saying one last time, "You haven't seen the last of Philo Farnsworth," leaving the stage.

I wondered what the Philosophers made of my crying. They probably put it down to my being overcome by the sheer momentousness of the occasion and by all the affection and adulation they were showing me, and to the emotions I was feeling at having, at long last, declared my independence from my mother.

Again I felt dizzy, pitching forward dramatically; in the same instant, I saw a corresponding movement on the screen, all the Philos appearing to bow deeply, simultaneously, the whole line about to topple, it seemed, until, after a moment in which they appeared to hang suspended, they recovered, rearing backwards. I had barely been able, by grabbing onto the podium with one hand, to keep from falling; I more than righted myself, however, rocking back on my heels, again using the podium for balance but this time tipping it so that it slid away from me. I saw the line of Philos flailing their arms in unison as though trying, on the edge of some abyss, to keep from going in. I thought, when the image of the falling Philos disappeared, that I was losing consciousness, but it was just the screen going dark, my own blackout not coming until a fraction of a second later, when I hit the floor.

Upon keeling over backwards onto the stage, I had given myself what the doctors at the hospital later described as a mild concussion, a contradiction in terms if ever there was one. The first night, they woke me at hourly intervals, a standard precaution for concussion victims, I was later told. How much time was passing between wakings I had no idea. Each time I opened my eyes, my mother was there, beside the bed, an epic feat of devotion, it seemed to me. Despite the headache, perhaps because of it, I had no trouble falling asleep, though I fancied that I was seriously hurt, that I was drifting in and out of consciousness. Once, in what must have been the middle of the night, I told my mother I was sorry. I would have said more but she made it clear she didn't want me to by putting her hand on my forehead and smiling at me, as if to indicate that it went without saying that I was sorry.

I was released the next day, going home with her in a limousine that, all the way there, was at the centre of a media motorcade, surrounded by television vans and station wagons from the open windows of which cameras were aimed at us from every angle, cameras which we could see but which could not see us. Sometimes, reporters ran alongside the limo, tapping the windows with their microphones, trying to see inside. There was a great deal of footage of what was described as "Philo's limo" on the news that night, and footage of the motorcade itself, the cameramen filming each other.

At Pristine Place, the limousine was let into the underground parking lot where we disembarked. My mother decided that, instead of taking the stairs, she would ride with me in the elevator.

We stood at the rear of the lift, a few feet apart, facing forward to avoid looking, not only at each other and the security camera, but at our reflections, for we were surrounded by mirrors in which our images were infinitely multiplied, hemmed in by replicas, so that there was a heightened sense of expectation, as if all these Henrys and Audreys, eyes averted, were listening, tactfully waiting for one of us to speak. We stood, hands gripping the rail, watching the progress of the light through the sequence of numbers above the door, counting off the time alone we still had left. I thought of remarking at how surprised the men of Mission Control must be to see her on the elevator monitor again. Then I realized that they would be even more interested in me, Philo coming home from his fiasco at Maple Leaf Gardens. I imagined them crowding the monitor, peering closely, searching for evidence of this mild concussion they would have heard about by now, or some indication of how my mother and I were getting along after what I'd done.

At last we reached our floor. "Those were the artists," I couldn't help thinking as we were getting off.

I wanted wiped out the guilt I felt, the added awkwardness it put between us, though I didn't think I could accomplish that by saying once again that I was sorry. I wanted to assure her that no more such things would come between us in the future, but I knew that only by never seeing each other again would we avoid them.

We agreed to pretend that I hadn't really betrayed her or even considered doing so, that either I'd been in such a state that I hadn't known what I was doing, or that I had only gone to that convention in the hope that my father might be watching, in the hope of making some sort of contact with him.

Perhaps it was partly for selfish reasons that my mother held to this version of events, to keep intact some cherished view of herself as a woman who enjoyed the unreserved, unfaltering love of an ideal family. But it was also to spare me, to assure me that I had *her* unreserved, unfaltering love, no matter what I did, that, though she knew I loved her less than she loved me, she didn't care, didn't resent me for it.

I suddenly saw that this was so one day while we were sitting around the apartment. All morning, I had been stealing glances at her, thinking she was unaware of it, looking away when she turned towards me. But once she caught me and smiled as if to say so, and as if to say, as well, "It's true, Henry, what you're thinking. We don't ever have to talk about it, you don't have to be ashamed about it, but it's true."

We agreed to pretend a lot that week we spent together. My mother stayed home with me and we agreed to pretend that the Philosophers were not still gathered down below. It was like a week of Sunday afternoons of the sort we'd spent together years ago, so idle, so aimless were we. We were on a kind of sabbatical from life. Once again, the point of living was to pass the time as pleasantly as possible. That time was passing, that the world outside persisted and we would have to return to it some day, we were almost able to forget.

We pretended that I was still recovering from my concussion, that it was because of my concussion that I was sitting around the apartment all day long, doing nothing, spending long stretches of time in the Dark Room alone, watching the Gillingham, or staring out through the balcony doors.

It must often have been apparent to her, when I emerged from the Dark Room, that I'd been crying, but she never mentioned it, never asked me what was wrong. Nor was my father mentioned, though it was not resentment of him or bitterness that accounted for this fact, but simple sorrow, for we could not bear to mention him.

Sometimes, my mother would sit beside me on the sofa. "How's the head?" she'd say, or "How's the noggin?" and she would make a fist and lightly bop me on the head as if to gauge its soundness. "Nearly done," she'd say, pursing her lips, nodding and looking sagely satisfied.

The press, the TV, and the tabloids took all possible angles on the convention, some of them running stories that made it sound like the peak event of a harmless fad side by side with stories that quoted cult experts on the sinister implications of these "television worshippers."

I was likened to an evangelist who, at the climax of his revival, had fallen into, or faked, some sort of rapturous swoon and had had to be carried from the stage.

I announced in a written press release that, in spite of what I'd said at the Philosophers' Convention, I would not be staying on as Philo Farnsworth. The network conducted a viewer referendum (not a poll, mind you, but a full-scale referendum) as to whether or not a new Philo should be found. The Philosophers opposed the idea, in fact campaigned against it, taking out ads in newspapers and on TV, urging people to vote no and saying that, even if hired, the new Philo would not be "recognized" by them, for there was and would only ever be one true Philo. Any new episodes not featuring Henry Prendergast as Philo would be considered "apocryphal" and would be ignored by the movement.

After handily winning the referendum, the Philosophers assured people that it was not necessary to the continued success of their movement that new episodes be made. They seemed to take more and more to the idea that "The Philo Farnsworth Show" was now complete, that the body of work by which their movement was inspired had achieved its final form, that there was a fixed, predestined number of episodes, 130 to be exact, the definitive exegesis of which could now begin.

If anything, the cancellation of the show seemed to consolidate the Philosophers, as if the program was now wholly in their hands, theirs to do whatever they felt like doing with it. Membership increased five-fold in the space of a year. The network could not keep up with the demand for *The Complete Philo Farnsworth*, a collection of novelizations that, according to TV ads, no Philosopher could be without. And as far as the Philosophers were concerned, I was still their leader; in fact, as with every other apparent setback to the Philosophers, my stepping down as Philo Farnsworth seemed only to add to the movement's mystique, at least in the eyes of its membership, who claimed to believe that my eventual return to the role was foretold in Episode 130, in which I first uttered the phrase, "You haven't seen the last of Philo Farnsworth."

Maybe it was all of this that brought my father back. He did come back. He came back. Perhaps to sacrifice his happiness for ours. Perhaps in the hope of finding happiness. He came back.

Christmas had come and gone and snow was on the ground. Where he'd been, where he was returning from, how he'd spent the last six months, we would never know. About this barely begun and then abandoned life of his, he never spoke a word. Perhaps you're thinking that surely he must have said something about all the time he'd been away. In fact, he did. He said that the hardest part of it was learning how to self-administer the Heimlich manoeuvre.

I don't think he spent the six months trying to make up his mind. I think he decided he was never coming back and had already begun his new life when something changed his mind. Perhaps, as my mother contended, it was me, seeing me on TV at that Philosophers' Convention, defecting from the family, or seeing the photos of me in the paper – the most often-used photograph, taken from the front row, showed me as little more than a speck in the extreme foreground, flat on my back on the stage, arms and legs stretched out, the world's largest television screen looming over me, making me look as though I'd been included in the photograph for scale.

I was peeking out through the drapes, sizing up that day's contingent of Philosophers, when I saw him. As though he'd all along been hiding out just down the street, he arrived at Pristine Place on foot, unencumbered, having divested himself of the station wagon and everything we loaded into it the day he left, for what reason, or in what manner, we would likewise never know. He was standing opposite the gatehouse, ignoring the men of Mission Control, who were openly staring at him, looking across the way at the Philosophers, most of whom were doing jumping jacks to keep warm and took no notice of him.

My first sight of him in half a year was from a height of six-teen stories, so distorting a perspective that, for a fraction of a second, I thought his absence had somehow profoundly changed his appearance. He was standing with his hands in the pockets of his Castro coat, his thumbs poked out, looking around as if to say, "It was here, all the while I was away. It was here."

Perhaps it never occurred to him that one of us might be watching, or perhaps it had slipped his mind that, from our apartment, you could see the gatehouse. At any rate, he did not look up. As he started walking towards the building, towards me, I felt as though I ought not to be watching, or as though I should open the balcony doors and shout something, though I could think of nothing that seemed appropriate, and at any rate didn't want to alert the Philosophers to the fact that, hardly a hundred feet away from them, returning home after six months' absence, was Philo's father.

It was the last part of his solitary journey home that I was witnessing, which did not seem right. As he neared the front door, I was better able to see his face, which was expression-less. As far as he knew, we were not yet aware that he was on his way. He was almost home, but not quite there, still sepa-rate from us, the possibility still existing that he would change his mind, that, unknown to us, he would come to within a few feet of home and turn away. It was my father as he existed independently from us, a man on the brink of re-enlisting in a life we thought he'd left for good. He passed directly below me and disappeared from view.

I went back in and sat beside my mother on the sofa, the two of us about a foot apart. She was reading a magazine, thumbing through it. I waited. I wondered if it showed on my face that I was waiting. I heard the elevator stopping on our floor, the doors opening and closing, footsteps in the hall-way, growing louder, louder, and then — no knock. I waited several minutes more, but there was still no knock. I looked at my mother.

"I think there's someone at the door," I said.

ACKNOWLEDGMENTS

Writers of books seem to have got their revenge on the inventors of television by ignoring them. My main source of information about Philo Farnsworth, the teenage co-inventor of electronic television, was George Everson's *The Story of Television: The Life of Philo T. Farnsworth* (1949; repr. ed., New York: Arno Press, 1974), a slim, sketchy volume that is more of an homage than a biography, and, so far as I know, the only book solely concerned with telling Philo's story that exists. The best treatment of the rivalry between Farnsworth and the RCA engineer Dr. Vladimir K. Zworykin is in Joseph H. Udelson's *The Great Television Race: A History of the American Television Industry 1925-1941* (Alabama: University of Alabama Press, 1982). Erik Barnouw's *Tube of Plenty: The Evolution of American Television* (rev. ed., New York: Oxford University Press, 1982) is one of the few books that traces the story of television from its beginnings at the turn of the century right up to the modern television era. Though the book takes a largely anecdotal approach, I found the first few chapters on the development of the earliest mechanical spinning disk television sets quite helpful and informative. There was, in the Smithsonian Institution at the time of the writing of this book, a life-size photograph of Philo Farnsworth posing with his just-invented picture tube. Photos of both Philo Farnsworth and Vladimir Zworykin appear in Udelson's book, but are otherwise hard to come by.

I would like to thank Ellen Seligman and Doug Gibson for their help and for their encouragement and patience during the time I was writing *Human Amusements*.

Wayne Johnston is the author of *The Story of Bobby O'Malley,*
The Time of Their Lives, The Divine Ryans. Human Amuseements,
The Colony of Unrequited Dreams — all novels — and of *Baltmore's*
Mansion, a memoir. He lives in Toronto.